Infinite Jests

Infinite Jests

•

The Lighter Side of Science Fiction

•

edited by

ROBERT SILVERBERG

•

CHILTON BOOK COMPANY
Radnor, Pennsylvania

•

Library of Congress Cataloging in Publication Data

Silverberg, Robert, comp.
    Infinite jests; the lighter side of science fiction.

    CONTENTS: Tenn, W. Venus and the seven sexes.—
Knight, D. Babel II.—Russ, J. Useful phrases for
the tourist ₁etc.₁
    1. Science fiction, American.   I. Title.
PZ1.S587Ik   ₁PS648.S3₁   813'.0876   74-2106
ISBN 0-8019-5931-4

ACKNOWLEDGMENTS

Venus and the Seven Sexes by William Tenn, copyright © 1949 by Avon Publishing Co., Inc. Reprinted by permission of the author and Henry Morrison Inc. his agents.

Babel II by Damon Knight, copyright © 1953 by Galaxy Publishing Corporation. Reprinted by permission of the author and his agent, Robert P. Mills, Ltd.

Useful Phrases for the Tourist by Joanna Russ, copyright © 1972 by Terry Carr. Reprinted by permission of the author.

Conversational Mode by Grahame Leman, copyright © 1972 by John Carnell. Reprinted by permission of the author and his agent, E. J. Carnell Literary Agency.

Heresies of the Huge God by Brian Aldiss, copyright © 1966 by Galaxy Publishing Corporation. Reprinted by permission of the author and his agent, A. P. Watt & Son.

(Now + n), (Now − n) by Robert Silverberg, copyright © 1972 by Harry Harrison. Reprinted by permission of the author and his agents, Scott Meredith Literary Agency, Inc.

Slow Tuesday Night by R. A. Lafferty, copyright © 1965 by Galaxy Publishing Corporation. Reprinted by permission of the author and his agent, Virginia Kidd.

Help! I Am Dr. Morris Goldpepper by Avram Davidson, copyright © 1957 by Galaxy Publishing Corporation. Reprinted by permission of the author.

Oh, To Be a Blobel! by Philip K. Dick, copyright © 1964 by Galaxy Publishing Corporation. Reprinted by permission of the author and his agents, Scott Meredith Literary Agency, Inc.

Hobson's Choice by Alfred Bester, copyright © 1952 by Mercury Press, Inc. Reprinted by permission of the author.

I Plinglot, Who You? by Frederik Pohl, copyright © 1958 by Galaxy Publishing Corporation. Reprinted by permission of the author.

Contents

Introduction

People who never read science fiction have an unhappy tendency to think of it as sober, joyless stuff—as a literature of stories opaque with technological gibberish and populated by blank-eyed astronauts speaking in clipped phrases, or else as a grim, somber literature depicting bleak totalitarian societies of the future. Like all uninformed beliefs, this one has a certain truth to it; but it is not the whole truth.

There is, of course, plenty of science fiction that takes itself terribly seriously. There has always been a certain didactic strain in science fiction. Some of the more technically oriented writers happily devote many pages, even whole chapters, to abstruse discussions of the niceties of celestial mechanics or the best kind of rivets to use in assembling robots, while those writers with highly developed social consciences sometimes use their stories as pretexts for delivering interminable passionate harangues against the oppression of minorities or the rape of the environment. I would not care to dismiss all such stories as ponderous or dreary or heavy-handed. There are masters of technological and sociological science fiction whose work, no matter how didactic it may get, still carries the reader along on an irresistible tide of narrative gusto and fertile invention. But there is another side to science fiction, and this book displays it.

That is the humorous side, the lighter side, the playful side: the science-fictionist as jester, the visionary as comic. Science fiction, because it is capable of achieving a degree of distance from mankind's follies, is ideally suited to be a vehicle for satire, jape, and jollity. Looking at our world through the eyes of a man from another planet or a visitor from the remote future, one gains a perspective that can hardly be attained through more conventional fiction. *Gulliver's Travels,* with its giants and midgets, its dreamy-eyed Laputan scientists, its delicious and stinging distortions of contemporary European mores, is pure science fiction of the comic sort. So is Huxley's *Brave New World;* so is Kafka's "Metamorphosis." It might be argued that these are all rather cheerless comedies, that the predicament of Kafka's huge bug is not so funny, nor Huxley's world of bottle-bred proletarians anything to chuckle about. I would not disagree; for me the best comedy tends toward ferocity rather than toward gaiety and farce. That is, one who has a true sense of the comic recognizes that the lighter side and the darker side are aspects of the same Moebius strip. In fact, one of the stories in this volume has previously been collected in an anthology of disturbing and unhappy science-fiction visions.

Here, at any rate, are eleven stories by eleven latter-day successors to Swift, Huxley, and Kafka. Some of them are genial and playful; some are dark and savage; all are, to me, stories comic on some essential level. You may not think so. The authors of some of the stories don't think so. In choosing them, though, I applied the simplest of all tests for comedy: these are stories that made me laugh. If the laughter had, more often than not, a grim edge to it, so be it. As every great humorist has known since at least the time of Aristophanes, that which is funny is often not really funny at all, and the realm of laughter lies not very far from the realm of tears. Here are eleven science-fiction stories that demonstrate the pitfalls and uncertainties of our very complex universe. Their manner is lighthearted and sparkling; their matter is generally serious. These are stories that amused me. I hope they will amuse you.

Robert Silverberg

William Tenn

•

Venus and the Seven Sexes

•

IT IS WRITTEN IN THE BOOK OF SEVENS:
When Plookh meets Plookh, they discuss sex. A convention is held, a coordinator selected, and, amid cheers and rejoicing, they enter the wholesome state of matrimony. The square of seven is forty-nine.

This my dear children—my own meager, variable brood—was the notation I extracted after receiving word from the nzred nzredd that the first humans to encounter us on Venus had at last remembered their promise to our ancestors and sent a cultural emissary to guide us on the difficult path to civilization.

Let the remaining barbarians among us cavil at the choice of this quotation; let them say it represents the Golden Age of Plookhdom; let them sneer that it shows how far we are fallen since the introducion of The Old Switcheroo by the gifted Hogan Shlestertrap of Hollywood California USA Earth.

The memory of Hogan Shlestertrap lives on while they disappear. Unfortunately—ah, well.

Please recall, when you go forth into the world to coordinate your own families, that at this point I had no idea of the kind of help the Earthman wanted. I suspected I had been honored because of my interest in literary numerals and because it was my ancestor—and yours, my dear children, your ancestor, too!—the nzred fanobrel, to whom those first Earthmen on Venus had made the wonderful promise of cultural aid.

A tkan it was, a tkan of my own family, who flew to bring me the message of the nzred nzredd. I was in hiding at the time—this was the Season of Wind-Driven Rains and the great spotted snakes had come south for their annual Plookh feed; only a swift-flying tkan could have found me in the high grasses of the marsh where we nzredd hide at this season.

The tkan gave me the message in a few moments. It was possible to do this, because we had not yet been civilized and were still using our ancestral language instead of the cultivated English.

"Last night, a flame ship landed on the tenth highest mountain," the tkan told me. "It contained the long-promised emissary from Earth: a Hogan of the Shlestertrap."

"Hogan Shlestertrap," I corrected. "Their names are not like ours; these are civilized creatures beyond our fumbling comprehension. The equivalent of what you called him would be 'a man of the Shlestertraps.' "

"Let that be," the tkan replied. "I am no erudite nzred to hide lowly in the marshes and apply numbers categorically; I am a tkan who has flown far and been useful in the *chain* of many families. This Hogan Shlestertrap, then, emerged from his ship and had a dwelling prepared for him by his—what *did* the nzred nzredd call them?"

"Women?" I suggested, remembering my Book of Twos.

"No, not women—*robots*. Strange creatures these robots: they participate in no chain, as I understand it, and yet are reproduced. After the dwelling was completed, the nzred nzredd called upon this—this Hogan Earthman and was informed that the Hogan, who feeds and hatches in a place called Hollywood California USA Earth, had been assigned to Venus on our behalf. It seems that Hollywood California USA Earth is considered the greatest source of civilizing influence in the universe by the Terran Government. They civilize by means of something called stereo-movies."

"They send us their best," I murmured, "their very best. How correctly did my ancestor describe them when he said their unselfish greatness made dismal mockery of comparison! We are such inconsequential creatures, we Plookhh: small of size, bereft of most useful knowledge, desired prey of all the monsters of our planet who consider us transcendentally delicious morsels—and these soaring adventurers send us a cultural missionary from no less than Hollywood California USA Earth!"

"Will the Hogan Shlestertrap teach us to build flame ships and dwellings upon mountains in which we may be secure?"

"More, much more. We will learn to use the very soil of our planet for fuel; we will learn how to build ships to carry us through emptiness to the planet Earth so that we can express our gratitude; instead of merely twelve books of numbers we shall have thousands, and the numbers themselves will be made to work for us in Terran pursuits like electricity and politics. Of course, we will learn slowly in the beginning. But your message?"

The tkan flapped his wings experimentally. He was a good tkan: he had three fully developed wings and four rudimentary ones—a very high variable-potential. "That is all. The Earthman wants help from one of us whose knowledge is great and whose books are full. This one will act as what is known as 'technical adviser' to him in the process of civilizing the Plookhh. Now the nzred nzredd's small tentacle is stiff with age and badly adjusted for the speaking of English; he has therefore decided that it is you who must advise this Hogan technically."

"I leave immediately," I promised. "Any more?"

"Nothing that is important. But we will need a new nzred nzredd. As he was giving me the last of the message outside the dwelling of the Earthman, he was noticed by a herd of tricephalops and devoured. He was old and crusty; I do not think they found him very good to eat."

"A nzred is always tasty," I told the winged Plookh proudly. "He alone among the Plookhh possesses tentacles, and the spice of our tentacles, it would seem, is beyond compare. Now the nzred tinoslep will become nzred nzredd —he has grown feeble lately and done much faulty co-ordination."

Flapping his wings, the tkan rose rapidly. "Beware of the tricephalops," he cried. "The herd still grazes outside the Hogan's dwelling, and you are a plump and easily swallowed tidbit. This will be difficult time for the family to find another nzred."

A lizard-bird, attracted by his voice, plummeted down suddenly. The tkan turned sharply and attempted to gain altitude. Too late! The long neck of the lizard-bird extended, the fearful beak opened and—

The lizard-bird flew on, gurgling pleasurably to itself.

Truly it is written in the Book of Ones:

Pride goeth before a gobble.

He was a good tkan, as I said, and had a high variable-potential. Fortunately, a cycle had just completed—he was carrying no eggs. And tkann were plentiful that season.

This conversation lasted a much shorter period than it seems to have in my repetition. At the time, only a few nzredd had learned the English that the first human explorers had taught my ancestor, nzred fanobrel; and the rest of the Plookhh used the picturesque language of our uncivilized ancestors. This language had certain small advantages, it is true. For one thing, less of us were eaten while conversing with each other, since the ancient Plookh dialect transmitted the maximum information in the minimum time. Then again, I was not reduced to describing Plookhh in terms of "he," "she" or "it"; this English, while admittedly the magnificent speech of civilized beings, is woefully deficient in pronouns.

I uncoiled my tentacles from the grasses about me and prepared to roll. The mlenb, over whose burrow I was resting, felt the decreased pressure as my body ceased to push upon the mud above him. He churned to the surface, his flippers soggy and quivering.

"Can it be," the foolish fellow whispered, "that the Season of Wind-Driven Rains is over and the great spotted snakes have departed? The nzred is about to leave the marsh."

"Go back," I told him. "I have an errand to perform. The spotted snakes are ravenous as ever, and now there are lizard-birds come into the marsh."

"Oh!" He turned and began to dig himself back into the mud. I know it is ungracious to mock mlenbb, but the wet little creatures are so frantic and slow-moving at the same time that it is all I can do to keep a straight tentacle in their presence.

"Any news?" he asked, all but one third of him into the mud.

"Our tkan was just eaten, so keep your flippers alert for an unattached tkan of good variation. It is not pressing; a new cycle will not begin for our family until the end of this season. Oh—and the nzred nzredd has been eaten, too—but that does not concern you, little muddy mlenb."

"That does not, but have you heard the mlenb mlenbb also is gone? He was caught on the surface last night by a spotted snake. Never was there such a Season of Wind-Driven Rains: the great of the Plookhh fall on all sides."

"To a mlenb all seasons are 'never was there such a season,' " I mocked. "Wait until the Season of Early Floods, and then tell me which you like better. Many mlenbb will go with the coming of the early floods, and our family may have to find a new mlenb as well."

He shivered, spattering me with mud, and disappeared completely underground.

Ah, but those were the carefree times, the happy childhood days of our race! Little indeed there was to trouble us then.

I ate a few grasses and began rolling up and out of the marsh. In a little while, my churning tentacles had attained such speed that I had no reason to fear any but the largest of the great spotted snakes.

Once, a tremendous reptile leaped at me and it seemed that the shafalon family would require a new nzred as well as a new tkan, but I have a helical nineteenth tentacle and this stood me in good stead. I uncoiled it vigorously and with an enormous bound sored over the slavering mouth of the spotted snake and on to solid ground.

This helical tentacle—I regret deeply that none of you dear little nzredd have inherited it from me. My consolation is that it will reappear in your descendants though in modified form; it unfortunately does not seem to be a dominant trait. But you all—all of this cycle, at any rate—have the extremely active small tentacle which I acquired from the nzred fanobrel.

Yes, I said your descendants. Please do not interrupt with the callow thoughts of the recently hatched. I tell you a tale of the great early days and how we came to this present state. The solution is for you to discover—there must be a solution; I am old and ripe for the gullet.

Once on solid ground, I had to move much faster, of course: here the great spotted snakes were larger and more plentiful. They were also hungrier.

Time and again I was forced to use the power latent in my helical tentacle. Several times as I leaped into the air, a lizard-bird or a swarm of gridniks swooped down at me; now and again, as I streaked for the ground, I was barely able to avoid the lolling tongue of a giant toad.

Shortly, however, I reached the top of the tenth highest mountain, having experienced no real adventure. There, for the first time, I beheld a human habitation.

It was a dome, transparent, yet colored with the bodies of many creatures who crawled on its surface in an attempt to reach the living meat within.

Do you know what a dome is? Think of half the body of a newly hatched nzred, divorced of its tentacles, expanded to a thousand times its size. Think of this as transparent instead of darkly colorful, and imagine the cutaway portion resting on its base while the still rounded part becomes the top. Of course, this dome had none of the knobs and hollows we use for various organic purposes. It was really quite bald.

Near it the flame ship stood upright. I cannot possibly describe the flame ship to you, except to say that it looked partly like a mlenb without the flippers and partly like a vineless guur.

The tricephalops discovered me and trampled each other in an attempt to get to me first. I was rather busy for a while evading the three-headed monsters, even growing slightly impatient with our savior, Hogan Shlestertrap, for keeping me outside his dwelling so long. I have always felt that, of all the innumerable ways for a Plookh to depart from life, the most unpleasant is to be torn into three unequal pieces and masticated slowly by a tricephalops. But, then, I have always been considered something of a wistful aesthete: most Plookhh dislike the gridnik more.

Fortunately, before I could be caught, the herd came upon a small patch of guurr who had taken root in the neighborhood and fell to grazing upon them. I made certain that none of the guurr were of our family and concentrated once more upon attracting the attention of Shlestertrap.

At long last, a section of the dome opened outward, a force seemed to pluck at my tentacles and I was carried swiftly through the air and into the dome. The section closed behind me, leaving me in a small compartment near the outside, my visible presence naturally exciting the beasts around me to scrabble frenziedly upon the transparent stuff of the dwelling.

A robot entered—answering perfectly to the description of such things by nzred fanobrel—and, with the aid of a small tubular weapon, quickly destroyed the myriad creatures and fragments of creatures who had been sucked in with my humble person.

Then—my variegated descendants—then, I was conducted into the presence of Hogan Shlestertrap himself!

How shall I describe this illustrious scion of a far-flung race? From what I could see of him, he had two pairs of major tentacles (call them flippers, vines, wings, fins, claws, talons or what you will), classified respectively as arms and legs. There was a fifth visible tentacle referred to as the head—at the top of the edifice, profusely knobbed and hollowed for sensory purposes. The entire animal, except for extremities of the tentacles, was covered with a blue and yellow-striped substance which, I have since learned, is not secreted by it at all but supplied it by other humans in a complicated chain I do not fully understand. Each of the four major tentacles was further divided into five small tentacles somewhat in the manner of a blap's talons; fingers, they are known as. The body proper of this Hogan Shlestertrap was flat in the rear and exhibited a pleasing domelike protuberance in the front, much like a nzred about to lay eggs.

Conceive, if you can, that this human differed in no respect from those described by my ancestor nzred fanobrel over six generations ago! One of the great boons of civilization is that continual variation is not necessary in offspring; these creatures may preserve the same general appearance for as many as ten or even twelve generations!

Of course, with every boon there is a price to be paid. That is what the dissidents among us fail to understand. . . .

Hogan Shlestertrap was occupying a chair when I entered. A chair is like—well, possibly I shall discuss that another time. In his hand (that part of the arm where the fingers originate) he held a bottle (shaped like a srob without fins) of whiskey. Every once in a while, he and the bottle of whiskey performed what nzred fanobrel called an act of conjugation. I, who have seen the act, assure you that there is no other way to describe the process. Only I fail to see just what benefit the bottle of whiskey derives from the act.

"Will you have a chair?" Shlestertrap requested, dismissing the robot with a finger undulation.

I rolled up into the chair, only too happy to observe human protocol, but found some difficulty in retaining my position as there were no graspable extremities anywhere in the object. I finally settled into a somewhat strained posture by keeping all my tentacles stiff against the sides and bottom.

"You look like some spiders I've seen after an all-night binge," Shlestertrap remarked graciously.

Since much of human thought is beyond our puny minds, I have been careful to record all remarks made by the Great Civilizer, whether or no I found them comprehensible at the time. Thus—"spider"? "all-night binge"?

"You are Hogan Shlestertrap of Hollywood California USA Earth, come to bring us out of the dark maw of ignorance, into the bright hatchery of knowledge. I am nzred shafalon, descended from nzred fanobrel who met your ancestors when they first landed on this planet, appointed by the late nzred nzredd to be your technical adviser."

He sat perfectly still, the little opening in his head—mouth, they call it—showing every moment a wider and wider orifice.

Feeling flattered and encouraged by his evident interest, I continued into my most valuable piece of information. How valuable it was, I did not then suspect:

"It is written in the Book of Sevens:

When Plookh meets Plookh, they discuss sex. A convention is held, a coordinator selected, and amid cheers and rejoicing, they enter the wholesome state of matrimony. The square of seven is forty-nine."

Silence. Hogan Shlestertrap conjugated rapidly with his bottle.

"Pensioned off," he muttered after a while. "The great Hogan Shlestertrap, the producer and director of 'Lunar Love Song,' 'Fissions of 2109,' 'We Took to the Asteroids,' pensioned off in a nutty fruitcake of a world! Doomed to spend his remaining years among gabby mathematical spiders and hungry watchamacallits."

He rose and began pacing, an act accomplished with the lower tentacles. "I gave them saga after saga, the greatest stereos that Hollywood ever saw or felt, and just because my remake of 'Quest to Mars' came out merely as an epic, they say I'm through. Did they have the decency—those people I picked out of the gutter and made into household names—did they have the decency to get me a job with the distribution end on a place like Titan or Ganymede? No! If they had to send me to Venus, did they even try to salve their consciences by sending me to the Polar Continent where a guy can find a bar or two and have a little human conversation? Oho, they wouldn't dare—I might make a comeback if I had half a chance. That Sonny Galenhooper—my *friend*, he called himself!—gets me a crummy job with the Interplanetary Cultural Mission, and I find myself plopped down in the steaming Macro Continent with a mess of equipment to make stereos for an animal that half the biologists of the system claim is impossible. *Big deal!* But Shlestertrap Productions will be back yet, bigger and better than ever!"

These were his memorable words: I report them faithfully. Possibly in times to come, when civilization among us shall have advanced to a higher level—always assuming that the present problem will be solved—these words will be fully understood and appreciated by a generation of as yet unborn but much more intellectualized Plookhh. To them, therefore, I dedicate this speech of the Great Civilizer.

"Now," he said, turning to me. "You know what stereos are?"

"No, not quite. You see only one of us has ever conversed with humans before this, and we know little of their glorious ways. Our Book of Twos is almost bare of useful information, being devoted chiefly to a description of your first six explorers, their ship and robots, by the nzred fanobrel. I *deduce,* however, that stereos are an essential concomitant of an industrial civilization."

He waved the bottle. "Exactly. At the base of everything. Take your literature, your music, your painting—"

"Pardon me," I interposed. "But we have been able to build none of these things as yet. We are chased by so many—"

"I was just spitballing," he roared. "Don't interrupt my train of thought. I'm building! Now, where was I? Oh, yes—take your literature, music and painting and you know what you can do with them. The stereos comprise everything in art; they present to the masses, in one colossal little package, the whole stirring history of human endeavor. They are not a substitute for art in the twenty-second century—they *are* the art of the twenty-second century. And without art, where are you?"

"Where?" I asked, for I will admit the question intrigued me.

"Nowhere. Nowhere at all. Oh, you might be able to get by in the sticks, but class will tell eventually. You've got to romp home with an Oscar now and then to show the reviewers that you're interested in fine things as well as money-making potboilers."

I concentrated on memorizing, deciding to reserve interpretation for later. Perhaps this was my mistake, perhaps I should have asked more questions. But it was all so bewildering, so stimulating. . . .

"The stereos have gone a long way since the pioneering sound movies of medieval times," he continued. "Solid images that appeal to all five senses in gorgeous panoramas of perception."

Hogan Shlestertrap paused and went on with even more passion. "And wasn't it said that Shlestertrap Productions had their special niche, their special technique among the senses? Yes, sir! No greater accolade could be accorded a stereo than to say it had the authentic Shlestertrap Odor. The Shlestertrap smell—how I used to slave to get that in just right! And I almost always succeeded. Oh, well, they say you're just as good as your last stereo."

I took advantage of the brooding silence that followed to clack my small tentacle hesitantly.

The emissary looked up. "Sorry, fella. What we've got to do here is turn out a stereo based on your life, your hopes and spiritual aspirations. Something that will make 'em sit up and take notice way out in Peoria. Something that will give you guys a *culture*."

"We need one badly. Particularly a culture to defend us against—"

"All right. Let me carry the ball. Understand I'm only talking off the top of my mind right now; I never make a decision until I've slept on it and let the good old subconscious take a couple of whacks at the idea. Now that you understand the technical side of stereo-making, we can start working on a story. Now, religion and politics are dandy weenies, but for a good successful piece of art I always say give me the old-fashioned love story. What's the lowdown on your love-life?"

"That question is a trifle difficult to answer," I replied slowly. "We had the gravest communicative difficulties with the first explorers of your race over this question. They seemed to find it complicated."

"A-ah," he waved a contemptuous hand. "Those scientific bunnies are always looking for trouble. Takes a businessman, who's also an artist, mind you—first and last an artist—to get to the roots of a problem. Let me put it this way, what do you call your two sexes?"

"That is the difficulty. We don't have two sexes."

"Oh. One of those a-something animals. Not too much conflict possible in that situation, I guess. No-o-o. Not in one sex."

I was unhappy: he had evidently misunderstood me. "I meant we have more than two sexes."

"More than two sexes? Like the bees, you mean? Workers, drones and queens? But that's really only two. The workers are—"

"We Plookhh have seven sexes."

"Seven sexes. Well, that makes it a little more complicated. We'll have to work our story from a—SEVEN SEXES?" he shrieked.

He dropped back into the chair where he sat very loosely, regarding me with optical organs that seemed to quiver like tentacles.

"They are, to use the order stated in the Book of Sevens, srob, mlenb, tkan, guur—"

"Hold it, hold it," he commanded. He conjugated with his bottle and called to a robot to bring him another. He sighed finally and said: "Why in the name of all the options that were ever dropped do you need *seven* sexes?"

"Well, at one time, we thought that all creatures required seven sexes as a minimum. After your explorers arrived, however, we investigated and found that this was not true even of the animals here on our planet. My ancestor, nzred fanobrel, had many profitable talks with the biologists of the expedition who provided him with theoretical knowledge to explain that which we had only known in practice. For example, the biologists decided that we had evolved into a seven-sexed form in order to stimulate variation."

"Variation? You mean so your children would be different?"

"Exactly. You see, there is only one thing that all the ravening life-forms of Venus would rather eat than each other; and that one thing is a Plookh. From the other continent, from all the islands and seas of Venus they come at

different times for their Plookh feed. When a Plookh is
discovered, a normally herbivorous animal will battle a
mighty carnivore to the death and disregard the carcass of
its defeated opponent—to enjoy the Plookh."

Our civilizer considered me with a good deal of interest.
"Why—what have you got that no one else has got?"

"We don't know—exactly. It may be that our bodies
possess a flavor that is uniformly exciting to all Venusian
palates; it may be, as one of the biologists suggested to
nzred fanobrel, that our tissue contains an element—a
vitamin—essential to the diet of all the life-forms of our
planet. But we are small and helpless creatures who must
reproduce in quantity if we are to survive. And a large
part of that quantity must differ from the parent who
himself has survived into the reproductive stage. Thus,
with seven parents who have lived long enough to reproduce, the offspring inherits the maximum qualities of survival as well as enough variation from any given parent to
insure a constantly and *rapidly* improving race of
Plookhh."

An affirmative grunt. "That would be it. In the one-sex
stage—*asexual* is what the bio professors call it—it's almost impossible to have varied offspring. In the bisexual
stage, you get a good deal of variation. And with *seven*
sexes, the sky must be the limit. But don't you ever get a
Plookh who isn't good to eat, or who can maybe fight his
way out of a jam?"

"No. It would seem that whatever makes us delicious is
essential to our own physical structure. And, according to
the biologists of the expedition again, our evolutionary
accent has always been on evasiveness—whether by nim-
bleness, protective coloration or ability to hide—so that
we have never developed a belligerent Plookh. We have
never been able to: it is not as if we had one or two enemies.
All who are not Plookhh will eat Plookhh. Except humans—
and may I take this occasion to express our deep
gratitude?

"From time to time, our Books of Numbers tell us, Plookhh have formed communities and attempted to resist extermination by united effort. In vain; they merely disappeared in groups instead of individually. We never had the *time* to perfect a workable system of defense, to devise such splendid things as weapons—which we understand humans have. That is why we rejoiced so at your coming. At last—"

"Save the pats on the back. I'm here to do a job, to make a stereo that will be at least an epic, even if I don't have the raw material of a saga. Give me a line on how all this works."

"May I say that whether it is an epic or a saga, we will still be grateful and sing the greatness of your name forever? Just so we are set on the path of civilization; just so we learn to construct impregnable dwellings and—"

"Sure. Sure. Wait till I get me a fresh bottle. Now—what are your seven sexes and how do you go about making families?"

I reflected carefully. I knew full well what a responsibility was mine at that moment; how important it was that I give our benefactor completely accurate information to aid him in the making of stereos, the first step we must take toward civilization.

"Please understand that much of this is beyond our ken. We know what seems to happen, but for an explanation we use the theories of the first flame ship's biologists. Unfortunately, their theories were multiple and couched in human terms which even they admitted were somewhat elementary when applied to the process of Plookhh reproduction. We sacrificed a whole generation of the fanobrel family for microscopic experimentation and only a broad outline was worked out. Our seven sexes are—"

"I heard it was complicated," Shlestertrap interrupted. "The biologists left five miles of figures in the Venusian Section of the Interplanetary Cultural Mission after they returned from this expedition. You see, there was an election right after that: a new party came in and fired them. I wasn't going to wade through all that scientific junk, no sir! One of them—Gogarty, I think—pulled every wire there was to take this job away from me and come here in my place. Some people just can't stand being out after they've been politically in for so long. Me, I'm here to make stereos—good ones. I'm here to do just what the prospectus of the Venusian Section called for—'bring culture to the Plookhh as per request.' "

"Thank you. We did wonder why the Gogarty—pardon —why Gogarty didn't return; he expressed such an enormous interest in our ways and welfare. But no doubt the operation of firing him by the new party after the election was far more productive in the human scheme of things. We have not yet advanced to the state of parties and elections or any such tools. To us one human is as omniscient and magnificent as the other. Of course, you understand all relevant data on human genetics?"

"Sure. You mean chromosomes and stuff?"

I flapped my small tentacle eagerly. "Yes, chromosomes and stuff. Especially stuff. I think it is the part about 'stuff' that has made the whole subject somewhat difficult for us. Gogarty never mentioned it. All he discussed were chromosomes and genes."

"No wonder I got such a crash bio briefing! Let's see. Chromosomes are collections of genes which in turn control characteristics. When an animal is ready to reproduce, its germ cells—or reproductive cells—each divide into two daughter cells called gametes, each daughter cell possessing one-half the chromosomes of the parent cell, every chromosome in each gamete corresponding to an opposite number chromosome in the other. Process is called meiosis. Correct me if I'm wrong anywhere."

"And how can a human be wrong?" I asked devoutly.

His face wrinkled. "In the case of humans, the female germ cell has twenty-four pairs of chromosomes, one pair being known as the X chromosome and determining sex.

It splits into two female gametes of twenty-four corresponding chromosomes, one X chromosome in each gamete. Since the male germ cell—if I remember rightly—has only twenty-three identical pairs of chromosomes and an additional *unmatched* pair called the X-Y chromosome, it divides into two male gametes of twenty-four chromosomes each, of which only twenty-three have a twin in each gamete; the twenty-fourth being the X chromosome in one male gamete and the Y chromosome in the other. If a male gamete—or sperm cell—containing an X chromosome unites with a female gamete—ovum, or egg cell, the briefing guy called it—carrying an X chromosome, the resultant zygote will be female; but if the Y chromosome gamete fertilizes the ovum, you have a *male* zygote. They really jammed that stuff in be before they let me leave Earth. Lectures, sleep-sessions, the whole bit."

"Exactly," I said enthusiastically. "Now in *our* case—"

"I recall something else, come to think of it. The Y is supposed to be a slightly undeveloped or retarded chromosome and it makes the gamete containing it a little weaker or something. That explains why there's a small preponderance of girls over boys in a given bunch of births—the sperm cell with the X chromosome is faster and stronger and has a better chance of fertilizing the ovum. It also shows why women can take it better than men and live longer. Simple. How's it work with you?"

The extended conversation was making me giddy, and the atmosphere of the dome—with its small vapor content—dried my faculties. However, this was a historic occasion: no personal weakness must be allowed to interfere. I stiffened my tentacles and began.

"After the matrimonial convention, when the chain is established, each sex's germ cells are stimulated into meiosis. The germ cell divides into seven gametes, six of them with cilia and the seventh secreted either inside or outside the Plookh, depending on the sex."

"What's this chain?"

"The chain of reproduction. The usually stated order is srob (aquatic form), mlenb (amphibian), tkan (winged), guur (plantlike), flin (a burrower), blap (tree-dweller). And, of course, the chain proceeds in a circle as: srob, mlenb, tkan, guur, flin, blap, srob, mlenb, tkan, guur, flin, blap, srob—"

Hogan Shlestertrap had grasped his head with his hands and was rocking it slowly back and forth. "Starts with srobs and ends with blaps," he said, almost inaudibly. "And I'm a—"

"Srobb," I corrected him timidly. "And blapp. And it doesn't necessarily start with one and end with another. A birth may be initiated anywhere along the chain of a family, just so it passes through all sexes—thus acquiring the necessary chromosomes for a fertilized zygote."

"All right! Please get back to chromosomes and sanity. You just had a germ cell dividing—a srob's, say—into seven gametes instead of a decent two like all other logical species use."

"Well, so far as our weak minds can compass it, this is the chromosome pattern worked out by Gogarty and his assistant, Wolfsten, after prolonged microscopic examination. Gogarty warned my ancestor, nzred fanobrel, that it was only an approximation. According to this analysis, the germ cell of a given sex has forty-nine chromosomes, seven each of Types A, B, C, D, E, F, six of Type G and one of Type H—the last, Type H, being the sex determinant. Six mobile gametes are formed through meiosis—each containing an identical group of seven chromosomes of Types A through G—and a seventh or stationary gamete containing chromosomes A, B, C, D, E, F, and H. This last Gogarty called the female or H gamete, since it never leaves the body of the Plookh until the fully fertilized cell of forty-nine chromosomes—or seven gametes—is formed, and since it determines sex. The sex, of course, is that of the Plookh in whose body it is stationary."

"Of course," Shlestertrap murmured and conjugated long and thoughtfully with the bottle.

"It has to be, since that is the only *H* chromosome in the final zygote. But you know that for yourself. In fact, operating with a human intelligence, you have probably anticipated me and already extrapolated the whole process from the few facts I have mentioned."

Moisture gathered at the top of our civilizer's head and rolled down his face in the quaintest of patterns. "I understand you," he admitted, "and of course I've already figured out the whole thing. But just to make it clear in your own mind, don't you think you might as well continue?"

I thanked him for his unfailing human courtesy. "Now, if it is a srob with whom we start our chain, it will transmit one of its six mobile gametes to a mlenb where the gamete will unite with one of the mlenb's *A* through *G* cells, forming what Gogarty called a double-gamete or prezygote. This prezygote will contain seven pairs of *A* through *G* chromosomes, and, in the body of the tkan—next in the chain—it will unite with a tkan mobile gamete forming a triple-gamete with seven triplets of *A* through *G* chromosomes. It proceeds successively through the rest of the sexes capturing a seven-chromosome gamete each time, until, when it is transmitted to the blap, it contains forty-two chromosomes—six *A*'s, six *B*'s and so on through to six *G*'s. At this point, the sextuple-gamete loses its cilia; and unites, in the blap, with the stationary *H* gamete to form a forty-nine chromosome zygote which, of course, is of the blap sex. The egg is laid and it hatches shortly into a baby blap, guarded—when at all possible—and taught in ten days all that its parent can teach it about surviving as a blap Plookh. At the end of ten days, the half-grown blap goes its way to feed and escape from danger by itself. At the end of a hundred days, it is ready to join a family and reproduce in full adulthood.

"The chain may be said to begin at any point; but it always travels in the same direction. Thus a flin will transmit the original seven-chromosome gamete to the blap of his chain where it will become a double-gamete; the blap will transmit the double-gamete to the srob, who will make it a triple-gamete; eventually, in this case, the process will come to fruition on the vines of the guur resulting in a guur zygote. Was not Gogarty clever, even for a human? He suggested, by the way, that it was possible we were not really a seven-sexed creature, but seven distinct species living in a reproductive symbiosis."

"Gogarty was a damned genius! Hey, wait a minute! Srob, mlenb, tkan, guur, flin, blap—that's only six!"

At last we were getting to the interesting part. "Quite so. I am a representative of the seventh sex—nzred."

"A nzred, huh? What do *you* do?"

"I coordinate."

One of the robots scurried in in answer to his yell. He ordered it to bring a case of these bottles of whiskey and to place it near his chair. He also ordered it to stand by, prepared for emergencies.

This was all very enjoyable. My information was creating even more of a sensation than that described by my ancestor, nzred fanobrel. It is not often that we Plookhh have an opportunity to sit thus with an animal of a different species and provide intellectual instead of gustatory diversion.

"He *coordinates!* Maybe they can use a good expediter or dispatcher?"

"I fulfill all of those functions. Chiefly, however, I coordinate. You see, a mlenb is primarily interested in winning the affections of a likely srob and finding a tkan whom *he* can love. A tkan merely courts a mlenb and is attracted to a good guur. I am responsible for getting a complete chain of these individuals in operation, a chain of compatibility where perfect amity runs in a complete circle— a chain which will produce offspring of maximum variability. Then, after the matrimonial convention, when the chain is established, each sex begins to secrete its original germ with the full forty-nine chromosomes. A busy time for nzredd! I must make certain that all germ cells are developing at a uniform rate—each sex attempts to fertilize seven H gametes in the course of a cycle—and the destruction of one individual in the middle of the cycle means the complete disarrangement of a family except for the gametes which he has already passed on in multiple state. Replacement of an eaten individual with another of the same sex, the remainder of whose family has been wiped out, is occasionally possible with the aid of the chief of his sex."

"I can see they keep you hopping," Hogan Shlestertrap observed. "But how does a nzred get born if you aren't in this chain thing?"

"A nzred is outside a chain, yet inside it as well. The six sexes which transmit gametes to each other directly form a chain; a chain plus a nzred equals a family. The nzred, in his personal reproductive functions, fits himself at any point in the chain which the exigencies of the situation seem to demand. He may receive the sextuple supergamete from the tkan and transmit the original single gamete to the guur, he may be between the flin and blap, the blap and srob, whatever is required. For example, in the Season of Twelve Hurricanes, the tkan is unable to fly and pursue his reproductive relationship with the guur wherever it has rooted itself: the nzred fills what would be a gap in the chain. This is rather difficult to express in an unfamiliar language—the biologists of the first expedition found this process slightly more complicated than the mitoses of the fertilized Plookh cell, but—"

"Hold it," Hogan commanded. "I have an ounce of sanity left, and I might want to use it to blow my brains out. I am no longer slightly interested in how a nzred weaves in and out of this crazy reproductive dance, and I *certainly* don't want to hear about your mitosis. I have troubles of my own, and they grow nastier every second. Tell me this: how many offspring does a sex have each cycle?"

"That depends on all parents being alive throughout, on the amount of unhatched eggs due to over-variation in particular cases—"

"*Okay!* At the end of a perfect cycle—when the smoke clears—how many baby plookhs do you have all told?"

He rested his head on the back of the chair. "Not very many, considering how fast you seem to go out of this world."

"True. Dismally true. But a parent is unable to hatch more than seven eggs in the conditions under which we live, and completely unable to rear more than seven young so that all will get the full benefit of his survival-knowledge. This is for the best."

"I guess so." He removed a pointed instrument from his garment and a sheet of white material. After a while, I recognized his actions from nzred fanobrel's description. "In just a moment," he said, while writing, "I'm going to have you shown in the projection room where you'll see a recent stereo employing human performers. Not too good a stereo: colossal into a very minor way; but it'll give you an idea of what I'll be doing for your people in the line of culture. While you see it, figure out ways to help me on a story. Now, is this Gogarty's description of your chromosome pattern after the parent germ cell has undergone meiosis?"

He extended the sheet under my sensory tentacles:

	A	A	A	A	A	A	A	
mobile	B	B	B	B	B	B	B	stationary, sex-determin-
gametes	C	C	C	C	C	C	C	ing gamete which is "fer-
(ciliated)	D	D	D	D	D	D	D	tilized" by a super-gamete
	E	E	E	E	E	E	E	composed of six mobile
	F	F	F	F	F	F	F	gametes—one from each
	G	G	G	G	G	G	G	of the six other sexes

"Quite correct," I said, marveling at the superiority of these written symbols to those we are still forced to scratch in sand or mud.

"Good enough." He wrote further upon the sheet. "Now, which of your sexes is male and which female? I notice you say 'he' and —"

I was forced to interrupt him. "I only use those designations because of the deficiencies of limitations of English. I understand what a wonderful speech it is and, how, when you came to construct it, you saw no reason to consider the Plookhh. Nonetheless, you have no pronouns for tkan or guur or blap. We are all male in relation to each other, in the sense that we transmit the fertilizing gametes; we are also female, in the sense that we hatch the developed zygote. Then again—"

"Slow down, boy, slow down. I have to work a story out of this, and you're not doing me any good at all. Here's a picture of your family—right?" He held the sheet out once more.

$$\nearrow \quad \textbf{guur} \quad \searrow$$
$$\textbf{tkan} \quad \diagdown \qquad \diagup \quad \textbf{flin}$$
$$\uparrow \quad \text{—nzred—} \quad \downarrow$$
$$\textbf{mlenb} \quad \diagup \qquad \diagdown \quad \textbf{blap}$$
$$\nwarrow \quad \textbf{srob} \quad \swarrow$$

"Yes. Only your picture of the nzred is not exactly—"

"Listen, Pierre," he growled, "I'll call it the way I see it. And that's the way I see it. A love story, now, let me think. . . ."

I waited while he cerebrated upon this strange thing called a story which was essential to the making of a stereo, which, in turn, was essential to our beginning upon culture and civilization. Soon, soon, we would have dwellings like this powerful one in which I sat, we would have tubular weapons like that the robot had used when I entered—

"How would this be?" he asked suddenly. "Understand, this isn't the finished product—I'm just working off the cuff, just trying it on for size. *Srob meets mlenb, tkan loses guur, flin gets blap.* How's it sound? Only one I can't fit in is the nzred."

"I coordinate."

"Yeah, you coordinate. That would make it, srob meets —Ah, shaddap! All you're supposed to do is say 'yes' once in a while." He murmured a few words to the robot who moved over to my chair. "Bronzo will take you to the projection room now. I'll think some more."

Tumbling painfully to the floor, I prepared to follow the robot.

"A love story is going to be tough," Shlestertrap mused behind me. "I can see that right now. Like three-dimensional chess with all pawns wild and the queen operating in and out of hyperspace. Wonder if these potato sprouts have a religion. A nice, pious little stereo every once in a while—Hey! Got a religion?"

"Yes," I said.

"What is it? I mean what do you believe in, generally speaking? Simple terms: we can save the philosophy for later."

After the lapse of an interval which I felt I could approximate as a 'while,' I said again, very cautiously: "Yes."

"Huh? Cut the comedy on this lot, if you know what's good for you. Just because I told you not to disagree with me when I'm thinking out loud—No sloppy gags when I ask you a direct question!"

I apologized and tried to explain my seeming impudence in terms of the simple conditions under which we Plookhh live. After all, when a tkan flies in frantically to warn a family that a pack of strinth are ravening in its direction, no one thinks to take the message in other than its most literal form. Communication, for us, is basically a means of passing along information essential to survival: it must be explicit and definitive.

Human speech, however, being the product of a civilized race, is a tree bearing many different fruits. And, as we have discovered to our sorrow, it is not always easy to find the one intended to be edible. For example, this mind-corroding intangible that they call a pun—

Shlestertrap waved my explanations back at me. "So you're sorry and I forgive you. Meanwhile, what's your belief about a life after death?"

"We don't exactly have a belief," I explained slowly, "since no Plookh has returned after death to assure us of the possibilities ahead. However, because of the difficulties we experience in the one life we know and its somewhat irritating shortness of duration—we like to think we have at least *one* additional existence. Thus, we have not so much a Belief as a Hope."

"For an animal without lungs, you sure are long-winded. What's your Hope, then?"

"That after death we emerge into a vast land of small seas, marshes and mountains. That throughout this land are the pink weeds we find so succulent. That, in every direction as far as an optical organ can see, there are nothing but Plookhh."

"And?"

"Nothing else. That is our Hope: to arrive sometime, in this life or the next, in a land where there are nothing but Plookhh. Plookhh, you understand, are the only creatures who we are *certain* do not eat Plookhh. We feel we could be very happy alone."

"Not enough there to make a one-shot quickie. If only you believed in a god who demanded living Plookhh sacrifices—but I guess your lives are complicated enough. Go and see the stereo. I'll work out something."

In the projection room, I twisted up into a chair the robot pushed forward and watched him and his mates insert shiny colored strips into five long, mlenb-shaped objects attached to the walls and ceiling. Naturally, I have learned since that the human terms are "film" and "projector" respectively: but, at that time, everything was new and strange and wonderful; I was all optical tentacles and audal knobs.

The sheer quantity of *things* that humans possess! Their recording methods are so plentiful and varied—books, stereos, pencil-paper, to name but a few—that I am convinced their memories are largely outgrown evolutionary characteristics which, already atrophying, will be supplanted shortly by some method of keying recording apparatus directly to the thinking process. They have no need of carrying Books of Numbers in their minds, of memorizing individually some nine thousand years of racial history, of continually revising the conclusions drawn from an ancient incident to conform with the exigencies of a current one. Contemplation of their magnificent potentialities almost dissolves my ego.

Abruptly, the room darkened and a tiny spot of white expanded into the full-color, full-sound, full-olfactory and slightly tactile projection we have come to know so well. For some reason, the humans who make these stereos neglect almost completely the senses of taste, brotch, pressure and griggo—although the olfactory appeal stimulates an approximation of taste and an alert individual may brotch satisfactorily during an emotional sequence. The full-color—yes: it should be obvious that humans use only three primaries instead of the existing nine because they consider it a civilized simplicity; the very drabness of the combinations of blue, red and yellow, I believe, is a self-imposed limitation instituted as a challenge to their technicians.

As the human figures came to seeming life before me, I began to understand what Hogan Shlestertrap had meant by a "story." A story is the history of one or more individuals in a specific cultural matrix. I wondered then just how Shlestertrap would derive a story from the meager life of a Plookh; he had known so few of us. I did not know of the wonderful human sense of imagination.

This story, that I saw on that awesome first day of our civilization, was about their two sexes. One representative of each sex (a man, Louis Trescott—and a girl, Bettina Bramwell) figured as the protagonists of the film.

The story concerned the efforts of Bettina Bramwell and Louis Trescott to get together and lay an egg. Many and complex were the difficulties this pair faced, but, at last, having overcome every obstacle, they were united and ready to reproduce.

Through some oversight, the story ended before the actual egg-laying; there was definite assurance, however, that the process would be under way shortly.

Thus, the first stereo I had ever seen. The colors sharpened in company with the sound of this obscure business called music, then all faded and disappeared. The lights returned to the room and the robots attended to the projectors. I went back to Shlestertrap, quivering with new knowledge.

"Sure," he said. "It's good. It's good enough, considering the budget. Now, look, I have an idea for a stereo. It's got to jell and whatnot, but meanwhile it's an idea. What's the animal you bugs are most afraid of?"

"Well, in the Season of Twelve Hurricanes, the strinth and sucking ivy do a large amount of damage to our race. In the other hurricane seasons—which are the worst for us, after all—the tricephalops, brinosaurs or gridniks—"

"Don't tell me *all* your troubles. Put it this way: which animal are you afraid of most right now?"

I considered lengthily. Ordinarily, the question would have given me thought material for two days; but The Great Civilizer was shifting from foot to foot and I griggoed his impatience. A decision was necessary; this may have been my mistake, my offspring, but remember we might never have received *any* of the benefits of civilization if I had taken more time to determine which creature was eating most of us at that season.

"The great spotted snakes. Of course, it is feared only by the nzredd, mlenbb, flinn and blapp. At this time, guurr are eaten principally by tricephalops, while srobb—"

"All right. Spotted snakes. Now let's go to the observation corridor and you point one out to me."

In the room where I had entered the dome, I extended my optical tentacles toward the transparent roof.

"There, almost directly above me. The animal which has half swallowed a dodle and is being attacked by gridniks, and sucking ivy."

Shelstertrap faced upwards and shivered. At the sight of us, the creatures scrabbled even more frantically on the dome's structure, continuing to eat whatever they had been eating when we entered. The sucking ivy dragged the great spotted snake away.

"What a place," Shlestertrap muttered. "A guy could make a fortune here with an antivacation resort. 'Come to this home away from home and learn to giggle at your nightmares. All kinds of dishes served, including you. Be a guest of the best digestions. Everybody to his taste and a taste to fit everybody.' "

I waited, while his human mind explored concepts beyond my primeval grasp.

"O.K. So that was a great spotted snake. I'll send a crew of robots out to get some shots of one of those babies that we can process into the stereo. Meanwhile, what about the cast?"

"Cast?" I fumbled. "How—what kind of cast do you mean?"

"Actors. Characters. Course I understand that none of you have any experience, even in stock, but I'll treat this like a De Mille documentary. I'll need a representative of each one of your sexes—the best in its line. You should be able to dredge them up with beauty contests or whatever you use. Just so I get seven of you—all different."

"These can be obtained through the chiefs of the various sexes. The nzred tinoslep will be the new nzred nzredd and a replacement for the mlenb mlenbb should have been chosen if enough mlenbb dared to congregate in the marshes. And this is all we need to do to take the first movement toward civilization?"

"Absolutely all. I'll write the first story for you—it's only mildly magnificent right now, but I'll have plenty of time to work it up into something better."

"Then I may leave."

He called for a robot who entered and motioned me in front of a machine much like a stereo projector.

"Sorry I can't send a robot to protect you down the mountain, but we're only half unpacked and I'll need all of them around for a day or two. All I have here are Government Standard Models, see; and you can't get any high-speed work out of those babies. To think that I used to have eighteen Frictionless Frenzies just to clean up around the house! Oh well, a sick trance isn't glorious Mondays."

Admitting the justice of this obscure allusion, I tried to reassure him. "If I am eaten, there are at least three nzredd who can replace me. It is only necessary for me to get far enough down the mountain to meet a living Plookh and inform him of your—your character requirements."

"Good," he told me heartily. "And I'm pretty sure I can play ball with any of your people who speak English fairly well. That sews up that: I'd hate to leave my stuff lying around in crates any longer than I have to. Dentface, throw a little extra juice into that beam so the kid here can get a big head start. And, once you get him out, quick-quick turn the dome back on fast, or we'll have half the empty stomachs on Venus inside trying to work us into their ulcers."

The robot called Dentface depressed a lever on the beam projector. Just as I had turned wistfully toward it in the hope that my meager mentality could somehow preserve an impression of the mechanism that would enable us to adapt it to our pressing needs, I was carried swiftly through a suddenly opened section of the dome and deposited halfway down the mountain. The opening, I observed as I got to my tentacles and rolled away from a creeper of sucking ivy, was actually an area of the dome that had temporarily ceased to exist.

I was unable to reflect further upon this matter because of the various lunges, snaps and grabs that were made at me from several directions. As I twisted and scudded down the tenth highest mountain, I deeply regretted Hogan Shlestertrap's need of the robots for unpacking purposes.

This, my children, was the occasion on which I lost my circular tentacle. A tricephalops, it was—or possibly a large dodle.

Near the marsh, I observed that my remaining pursuer, a green shata, had been caught by a swarm of gridniks. Accordingly, I rested in the shadow of a giant fern.

A scrabbling noise above me barely gave me time to stiffen my helical tentacle for a spring, when I recognized its source as the blap koreon. Peering from the lowest fan-leaf, he called softly: "The nzred shafalon has come from the dwelling of the human who was to give us many and mighty weapons, yet still I see him fleeing from empty bellies like the veriest morsel of a Plookh."

"And soon you will see him mocking all the beasts of prey from the safety of a dome where he and his kind live in thoughtful comfort," I replied with some importance. "I am to aid the human Shlestertrap of Hollywood, California USA Earth in the making of a stereo for our race."

The blap loosed his hold on the immense leaf and dropped to the ground beside me. "A stereo? Is it small or large? How many great spotted snakes can it destroy? Will we be able to make them ourselves?"

"We will be able to make them ourselves in time, but they will destroy no great spotted snakes for us. A stereo, my impatient wayfarer upon branches, is a cultural necessity without which, it seems, a race must wander forever in ignoble and fearful darkness. With stereos as models, we may progress irresistibly to that high control of our environment in which humanity exults on Earth. But enough of this munching the husk—our sex-chiefs must conduct Beauty Contests to select characters for the first Plookh stereo. Where is the blap blapp?"

"I saw him last leaping from bough to bough in the fifth widest forest with a lizard-bird just a talon's length behind him. If he has not yet ascertained the justification of the Hope, any tkan should be able to guide you to his present lair. Meanwhile, I think I know where the flin flinn has most recently dug."

He scampered to a mass of rocks and scratched at the ground near the outermost one. The heavy body of an old flin shortly appeared at the mouth of the hole he made. I rolled over and told the flin flinn of Shlestertrap's requirements.

The doddering burrower examined his broken claws nervously. "The chiefs of the other sexes will probably want to convene above ground. I know how important this stereo is to our race, but I am old and not at all agile— and this is the Season of Wind-Driven Rains—and the great spotted snakes are ravenous enough below the surface—"

"And it will shortly be the Season of Early Floods," I interrupted him, "when only tkann will have time for conversation. Our civilizing must begin as soon as possible."

"What have you to fear, old one?" the blap jeered. "A snake would find you tough and almost without flavor!"

Flin flinn edged back into his hole. "But not until he had experimented in a regrettably final fashion upon my person," he pointed out gloomily. "I will communicate with the new mlenb mlenbb—their moist burrows connect with ours again. Where might we meet do you think, O coordinator who gathers human wisdom?"

"In the sheltered spot at the base of the sixth highest mountain," I suggested. "It will be fairly safe during the next great wind. And consider, in the meantime, which is the living flin most fitted to represent our race in this our first stereo. Tell the mlenb mlenbb to do likewise."

After the sound of his claws had diminished in the under distance, the blap and I moved back to the giant fern. It is written in the Book of Ones: *A bush nearby is worth two in the by and by.*

"The only other sex-chief whose whereabouts I griggo," the tree-dweller observed, "is the new nzred nzredd. He is in the marsh organizing the coordination of the next cycle."

"The nzred tinoslep that was?"

"Yes, and little did he relish his honors! Plentiful rose his complaints to High Hope. Vainly he insisted he was still in the very prime of coordination—that he had a good many novel arrangements yet within him. But all know of the pathetic hybrids produced in the last tinoslep cycle. You have heard, I suppose—"

And he told me the latest septuple entendre that had been making the rounds.

I was not amused. "Beware, scratcher of bark, of ridicule at the expense of him whom your coordinator obeys! Another blap may fill your place in the chain, while you gaze morosely at unhatched eggs. The nzred tinoslep, that was, organized mighty cycles in his time and now uses accumulated wisdom in the service of all the Plookhh, unlike the blap blapp and the flin flinn who have the responsibility of a lone sex."

Record this speech well, my nzreddi. Thus it is necessary to constantly impress upon the weaker, more garrulous sexes the respect due to coordination; else families will dissolve and each sex will operate in ungenetic independence. The nzred must ever be a Plookh apart—yes, yes, even in these shattering times of transition should he maintain his aloofness jealously. Even at present there are good reasons for him to do so—Please! Allow me to continue! Save these involved questions for another session, you who are so recently hatched. *I* know there are now complications. . . .

The blap hastened to apologize.

"I meant no ridicule, none at all, omnipotent arranger of births! I thoughtlessly passed on a vulgar tale told me by an itinerant unattached guur who should have known better. Please do not tear me from the fins of the finest srob that I have ever known and the most delightful flin that ever brotched in a burrow! The nzred koreon is already displeased with me for two baby blapp I varied to the point of extinction, and now—"

Something coughed wetly behind us and we both leaped for the lowest frond of the fern. The blap streaked to the top of the plant and thence to a long-extending bough of a neighboring tree; I bounced off the leaf and into the marsh with powerful strokes of my helical tentacle. Behind me, the giant toad sorrowfully rolled his tongue back into his mouth.

I went my way fully satisifed: this blap would not mock nzredd again for many cycles.

The leader of my sex was surrounded by young nzredd in the weediest section of the marsh. He dismissed them when I approached and heard my recital.

"This meeting-place you suggested to the flin flinn—the land sexes may find it very easily, but what of the srob srobb?"

"A little stream has pushed through to the base of the sixth highest mountain," I informed him. "It isn't very wide, but the leader of the srobb should be able to swim to the sheltered place without difficulty. Only the mlenb mlenbb will be at a disadvantage there because of the stream's newness."

"And when is a mlenb not at a disadvantage?" he countered. "No, if a stream is there, the sheltered place will serve us well enough—during a wind, in any event. You have ordered things wisely, nzred shafalon; you will yet survive to be a nzred nzredd when your more thoughtless contemporaries are excreta."

I waggled my tentacles at this praise. To be told that I would escape assimilation long enough to be nzred nzredd was a compliment indeed. And to think I am at last chief of my sex and yet still able to coordinate effectively! Truly, our race has been startled by civilization—to say nothing of its highest manifestation, The Old Switcheroo.

"You need a tkan," the nzred nzredd went on; "I believe tkan tkann has a satisfactory one for you. The tkan gadulit is the sole survivor of an attack of tricephalops upon his matrimonial convention (I must remember that the gadulit name is now available for use by new families). He has fair variation. Suppose you meet him and introduce him to the chain if all else is good in your own judgment. As soon as the sex-chiefs have met and approximated this odd business of Beauty Contests, we will assemble the individuals selected and you may escort them to awesome Shlestertrap. And may this stereo lead quickly to the softness of civilization."

"May it only," I assented fervently, and went to meet the new tkan. He was variable enough for all normal purposes; the guur shafalon found him admirable; and even our mlenb, stodgy and retiring as he was, admitted his fondness for the winged member. The tkan was overwhelmed at being admitted into the shafalon family, and I approved of his sensible attitude. I began to make plans for a convention —it was time to start another cycle.

Before I could communicate with my srob, however— he always swam a good distance from land during the Season of Wind-Driven Rains—the tkan tkann flew to inform me of the sex-chiefs' choices and lead me to them. I regretfully postponed the initiation of offspring.

The Plookhh selected by the Beauty Contests were the very glory of our race. Each was differentiated from the other members of his sex by scores of characteristics. United in one family, they might well have produced Super-plookhh.

With infinite graciousness, the tkan tkann told me that I had been considered most seriously for the nzred protagonist—only, my value as Shlestertrap's assistant being primary, another was selected in my place. "No matter," I told the chief as he soared away, "I have honors enough for one Plookh: my books runneth over."

The gasping srob represented the greatest problem and the tkan-character volunteered to fly him directly to the dome without waiting for the rest of us so that the finny one would not dry up and die. Then, with the nzred-character and the blap-character carrying the plantlike guur between them, we began our ascent of the tenth highest mountain.

Although the Season of Wind-Driven Rains was almost over, there were even more great spotted snakes than before crawling upon the dome; and, grappling with their morbid coils, were more slavering dodles than I remembered seeing at one time; even a few brinosaur ranged about now, in anticipation of the approaching Season of Early Floods. I deduced, in some surprise, that they considered the human a palatable substitute for Plookhh.

I had gone ahead of my little band since I knew the terrain better and was more likely to attract Hogan Shlestertrap's attention. This was fortunate, for we had not worked halfway up the mountain before we were feverishly eluding what seemed to be the entire fauna of Venus. They poured off the dome in a great snapping, salivating horde, pausing occasionally to gouge or tear at their neighbors, but nonetheless pursuing us with a distressing concentration. I found additional cause to be grateful for the wise choices of the sex-chiefs: only really diversified Plookhh with the very latest survival characteristics could have come through that madness of frustrated gluttony unscathed. Relatively unscathed.

It was only necessary for me to cross once in front of the robot in the outer compartment of the dome. Gridnik-fast, the beam poured out and captured me, swinging thence to the rest of my elite family and carrying all of us through the open space of the dome which seemed to be materializing shut almost before we were inside.

I was particularly grateful, I recall, since the beam had snatched me from between the creepers of the largest sucking ivy I had ever stumbled upon. A helical tentacle is all very well, but it does not help overmuch when one is too busy evading three lizard-birds to notice what lies in wait upon the ground.

One of the robots had already constructed a special tank for the srob, and he also rapidly found some soil into which the guur could root sighingly.

"That a real plant?" Shlestertrap inquired. He had changed from his previous covering into a black garment becomingly decorated with red splotches which disguised his dome-shaped middle protuberance in a way I could not quite fathom. On his head, he now wore what he called a cap with the visor pointing behind him—a custom, he explained, which was observed by stereo people in deference to their ancient greats.

"No, it is a guur, the Plookh which relies most on blending into its surroundings. Although it does derive some nourishment photosynthetically, it is not quite a vegetable, retaining enough mobility to—"

"A guur, you call it? Helpless, huh? Got to be carried over the threshold? Keep still—I'm thinking!"

I throbbed out a translation. We all froze into silence. The srob, who had lifted his head out of the tank to survey the dome, began to strangle quietly in the open air.

Finally, Shlestertrap nodded and we all moved again. The mlenb flapped over and pushed the srob, who had become insensible, back under the surface of the tank.

"Yep," said our civilizer. "It adds up. I have the weenie. A little too pat for an artistic stereo, but I can always dress it up so no one will know the difference." He turned to me. "That's the big gimmick in this business—dressing it up so they can't tell it's the same thing they've been seeing since they got their first universal vaccination. If you dress it up enough, the sticks will always go nuts over it.

Maybe the critics will make cracks, sure, but who reads the critics?"

Alas, I did not know.

Much time passed before I had extended conversation with the human again. First, it was necessary for me to teach English to the first Plookh thespians so that they could follow Shlestertrap's direction. Not very difficult, this: it simply required a short period of concentrated griggoing by the seven of them. I could now give them much terminology that even my ancestor, nzred fanobrel, had not been able to use; unfortunately, a good deal of Shlestertrap's phase-shadings remained as nothing but unguessable semantic goals, and when it came to many attitudes and implements used exclusively upon Earth—we could do nothing but throw up our tentacles and flippers, our vines and talons, in utter helplessness.

Some day, however—not us, but one of our conceivable descendants, perhaps—we will learn the exact constituents of a "thingumajig."

After learning the language, the other Plookhh were taken in charge by the robots—the same friendly creatures who would leave the dome occasionally to forage the fresh pink weeds that were essential to our diet—and told to do many incomprehensible things against backgrounds that varied from the artificially constructed to the projected stereo.

Frequently, Shlestertrap would halt the robots in their fluid activity with booms and cameras and lights, turn to me and demand a significant bit of information about our habits that usually required my remembering every page of all our Books of Numbers to give an adequate reply.

Before I could finish, however, he generally signaled to the robots to begin once more—muttering to himself something like: "Oh, well, we can fake up a fair copy with more process work. If it only looks good, who cares about realism?"

Then again, he would express annoyance over the fact that, while some of us had heads, the mlenbb and nzredd had torso-enclosed brains, and the guur were the proud possessors of what the first ship's biologists had called a "dissolved nervous system."

"How can you get intriguing close-ups," Shlestertrap wailed, "when you don't know what part of the animal you want in them? You'd think these characters would get together and decide what they want to look like, instead of shortening my life with complications!"

"These are the most thoroughly differentiated Plookhh," I reminded him proudly. "The beauty contest winners."

"Yeah. I'll bet the homely ones are a real old-fashioned treat."

Thus, gently and generously, did he toil on the process of civilizing us. May his name be revered by any Plookhh that survive!

My only real difficulty was in gaining more knowledge. The robots were rather uncommunicative (we have not yet resolved their exact place in human affairs) and Hogan Shlestertrap explained that a genius like himself could not be bothered with the minutiae of stereographical mechanics. That was left entirely to his metallic assistants.

Nevertheless, I persisted. My hunted race, I felt, expected me to gather all knowledge to which I was exposed for the building of our own technology. I asked Shlestertrap detailed questions about the operations of the sound robot who deftly maneuvered the writhing, almost-live microphone booms above the actors and scenery; I pestered him for facts on the great smell-camera with its peculiar, shimmering olfactory lens and its dials calibrated pungently from rose-constants to hydrogen-sulphide-constants.

Once, after a particularly long session, I came upon him in a compartment composing the score for our stereo. I had always found this music vaguely stimulating if obscure of use, and I was very curious as to how it was made.

This, let me say to his glory, he explained very patiently. "See, here's a sound track of a Beethoven symphony and there's one of a Gershwin medley. I run off bits of each alternately into the orchestrator and flip the switch like so. The box goggles and bangs it around for a while—it can make more combinations than there are inches between here and Earth! Finally, out comes the consolidated sound track, and we have a brand-new score for our stereo. Remember the formula: a little Beethoven, a little Gershwin, and lots and lots of orchestration."

I told him I would never forget it. "But what kind of machine makes the original Gershwin and Beethoven strips? And can either of them be used in any way under water against the brinosaur? And exactly what is involved in the process of the orchestrator joggling and banging? And how would we go about making—"

"Here!" He plucked a book from a table behind him. "I meant to give you this yesterday when you asked me how we connect tactions to the manipulating antenna. You want to know all about culture and how humans operate with it, huh? You want to know how our culture fits in with nonhumans, don't you? Well, read this and don't bother me until you do. Just keep busy going over it until you have it cold. About the most basic book in the place. Now, maybe I can get some quiet drinking out of the way."

My thanks poured at his retreating back. I retired to a corner with my treasure. The title, how inspiring it looked! ABRIDGED REGULATIONS OF THE INTERPLANETARY CULTURAL MISSION, ANNOTATED, WITH AN APPENDIX OF STANDARD OFFICE PROCEDURES FOR SOLARIAN MISSIONS.

Most unhappily, my intellectual powers were not yet sufficiently developed to extract much that was useful from this great human repository of knowledge. I was still groping slowly through Paragraph 5, Correction Circular

16, of the introduction (*Pseudo-Mammalian Carnivores, Permissible Approaches to and Placating of for the Purpose of Administering the Binet-plex*) when a robot summoned me to Shlestertrap's presence.

"It's finished," he told me, waving aside a question I began to ask regarding a particularly elusive footnote. "Here, let me put that book back in the storeroom. I just gave it to you to keep you out of my hair. It's done, boy!"

"The stereo?"

He nodded. "All wrapped up and ready to preview. I have your friends waiting in the projection room."

There a pause while he rose and walked slowly around the compartment. I waited for his next words, hardly daring to savor the impact of the moment. Our culture had been started!

"Look, Plookh, I've given you guys a stereo that, in my opinion, positively smashes the gong. I've locked the budget out of sight, and I've worked from deep down in the middle of my mind. Now, do you think you might do a little favor for old Shlestertrap in return?"

"Anything," I throbbed. "We would do anything for the unselfish genius who—"

"Okey-dandy. A couple of busybodies on Earth are prancing around and making a fuss about my being assigned to this mission, on the grounds that I never even had a course in alien psych. They're making me into a regular curse of labor, using my appointment and a bunch of others from show business as means of attacking the present administration on grounds of corruption and incompetence. I never looked at this job as anything more than a stopgap until Hollywood finds that it just can't do without the authentic Shlestertrap Odor in its stereos—still, the good old bank account on Earth is growing nicely and right now I don't have any better place to go. It would be kind of nice and appreciative of you to give me a testimonial in the form of a stereo-record that I can beam back to earth. Sort of show humanity that you're grateful for what we're doing."

"I would be grateful in turn to be given an opportunity to show my gratitude," I replied. "It will take a little time, however, for me to compose a proper speech. I will start immediately."

He reached for my long tentacles and pulled me back into the compartment. "Fine! Now, you don't want to make up a speech of your own and give out with all kinds of errors that would make humans think you aren't worth the money we're spending on you? Of course you don't. I have a honey of a speech all written—just the thing they'll want to hear you say back home. Greasejob! You and Dentface get that apparatus ready for recording."

Then, while the robots manipulated the stereo-record, I read aloud the speech Shlestertrap had written from a copy he held up just out of camera range. I stumbled a bit over unfamiliar concepts—for example, passages where I extolled The Great Civilizer for teaching us English and explaining our complicated biological functions to us—but generally, the speech was no more than the hymn of praise that the man deserved. When I finished, he yelled: "Cut! Good!"

Before I had time to ask him the reasons for the seeming inconsistencies in the speech—I knew that, since he was human, they could not be mere errors—he had pushed me into the projection room where the Plookh actors waited. I thought I heard him mumble something about "That should hold the Gogarty crowd till the next election," but I was so excited over the prospect of the first Plookhian cultural achievement that I did nothing more than scurry to my place as the projectors started. Now, sometimes, I think perhaps—No.

The first stereo with an all-Plookh cast! Already, it is a commonplace, with all Plookh seeing it for the first time before they are more than six days out of the egg. But that preview, as it was called, was a moment when everything seemed to pause and offer us sanctuary. Our civilization seemed assured.

I decided that its murky passages were the result of one viewing and would disappear in time as we expanded intellectually.

You know what I mean. The beginning is interesting and delightful as the various sexes meet in different ways and decide to become a family. The matrimonial convention, although somewhat unusual procedurally, is fairly close to the methods in use at that time. But why does the guur suddenly proclaim she is insulted and bolt the convention?

Of course, you all know—or should—that our reservation of the pronoun "she" for guur dates from the dialogue in this stereo?

Again, why, after the guur leaves, do the others pursue her—instead of finding and mating with a more reasonable specimen? And the great spotted snake that notices the guur—we had thought till then that guur is the one form of Plookh safe from these dread creatures: evidently we were wrong. In her flight, she passes tricephalops and sucking ivy: these ignore her; yet the great spotted snake suddenly develops a perverted fancy for her vines and tendrils.

And the battle, where the other six Plookhh fall upon and destroy the snake! Even the srob crawls out of the stream and falls gasping into the fray! It continues for a long period—the snake seems to be triumphing, logically enough—suddenly, the snake is dead.

I am an old nzred. I have seen that stereo hundreds of times, and many the ferocious spotted snake from whose jaws I have leaped. On the basis of my experience, I can only agree with the other oldsters among the Plookhh that the snake seems to have been strangled to death. I know this is not much help and I know what it means taken together with our other difficulties—but as the nzred nzredd announced at the first public showing of the stereo: "What Plookh has done, Plookh can do!"

The rest of the stereo is comprehensible enough. Which guur, no matter what her reasons for leaving the chain originally, would not joyfully return to a family powerful enough to destroy a great spotted snake? And even now we all laugh (all except mlenbb, that is) at the final sequence where the mlenb-character crawls into his burrow backward and almost breaks a flipper.

"Terrific, huh?" Shlestertrap inquired, when we had returned to his compartment. "And that process-work—it was out of this system, wasn't it? Can I mastermind a masterpiece, or can't I?"

I considered. "You can," I told him at last. "This stereo will affect our way of life more than anything else in nine thousand years of Plookh history."

He slapped his sides. "This stereo, artistically, has everything. The way I handled that finale was positively reminiscent of Chaplin in his bamboo-cane period with just a touch of the Marx Brothers and De Sica."

After a spasm of bottle-conjugating, he suggested: "Guess you want to chase in and get those robots to teach you how to handle projectors. I'll give you three complete sets and a whole slew of copies; you show some of your friends in the backwoods how to turn them on and off— then you can come back here and write the next stereo."

"Write the *next* stereo? I am overwhelmed, O Shlestertrap, but I don't quite understand what I could write about. Have you not said all in this one? If there is more, I am afraid my uncivilized person is not capable of conceiving and organizing it."

"Not a matter of civilization," he told me impatiently. "Just a matter of a twist. You saw how this stereo ran— now you simply apply The Old Switcheroo."

"The Old Switcheroo?"

"The new angle—the twist—the tangent. No sense in using a good plot just the once. I'll make an artist out of you yet! Look—On second thought, maybe you're too new at this racket to get it after all. Was sort of hoping you'd carry the load while I rested up. But I guess I can knock out another stereo fast to give you the idea. Meanwhile, suppose you get started on that projection course so that your buddies in the jungle can see what the Interplanetary Cultural Mission is doing for them."

Shortly thereafter, I was deposited outside the dome with the three sets of projectors. Again, I was fortunate in making my escape from the creatures who swarmed at me. I returned to the spot with forty young Plookhh I gathered from the neighborhood and, with the expenditure of much labor and life, we divided the equipment into small, somewhat portable groups and removed it to another mountain.

As rapidly as possible, I taught them the intricacies of operation I had learned from the robots. I had tactlessly requested one or two of these creatures from Hogan Shlestertrap, by the way, to aid us in the difficult task of shifting the equipment. "Not on your materialization," he had roared. "Isn't it enough that I send them out of the dome to get those orange weeds you guys are so nuts about? Two of my best robots—Greasejob and Dentface—are walking around with cracked bodies because some overgrown cockroach mistook them for an order of. I made a stereo for you people: now you carry the ball for a while." Naturally, I apologized.

When my assistants could work the projectors to my satisfaction, I divided them into three groups and sent two of them off with sets and a supply of stereo-film. I kept one group and set with me and had a tkan carry word to the chief of his sex that all was ready.

Meanwhile, the nzred nzredd and twelve specially trained helpers had been traveling everywhere, griggoing English to all Plookhh they met and ordering them to go forth and griggo likewise. This was necessary because that had been the language of the stereo: as a result, English has completely replaced our native language.

One of the groups I sent out was stationed in a relatively sheltered cove to which srobb and mlenbb could come in comparative safety. The other, in a distant valley, exhibited chiefly to guurr, flinn and nzredd; my crew, on a mountain, to blapp and tkann. By showing the stereo to audiences of approximately two hundred Plookhh at a time, we were reaching the maximum number at all compatible with safety. Even so, performances were frequently interrupted by a pack of strinth who paused to feed upon us, by an occasional swarm of gridniks who descended on our engrossed multitudes with delighted drones. We changed our projection spots after every performance; but I was twice forced to train new groups of young Plookhh to replace those projectionists casually annihilated when the stereo-exhibition attracted some carnivore's attention.

Not a good system, admittedly; but none better has yet been devised. We all know how dangerous it is to congregate. To translate into inadequate English: *"Too many Plookhh make a broth."* Nonetheless, it was imperative that the message of civilization be spread as widely and as rapidly as possible.

The message was spread, received and acted upon.

However much it may be to my discredit, I must confess that I felt some small and definite joy at belonging to an already-organized family unit. Whenever thereafter I saw a matrimonial convention breaking up, the guur moving as rapidly as she could through the forest until she came to a great spotted snake, the other six members of her family immediately throwing themselves in a sort of hopeless enthusiasm upon the reptile—whenever I saw that spectacle which now, of course, became so frequent, I could not help but rejoice ingloriously in having my family's convention cycles behind me. I was too old for civilization.

Once, I remember, four successive matrimonial conventions involved the same snake. He became so gorged with Plookhh that he could not move from the scene of the feeding. Possibly incidents of this sort gave rise to what is known as the nzred magandu system which is used, when possible, at present. As you know, under this system, six families hold their matrimonial conventions together and the six guur perform the traditional civilized bolt in unison. When they come across a great spotted snake, all the other members of the six families fall upon it and, under the weight of their numbers, the snake is very often smothered to death. There are usually enough survivors to make at least one full family after the battle, the only important difficulty here being that this system creates a surplus of guurr. The so-called blap vintorin system is very similar.

In any event, despite the great odds, we Plookhh had learned the lesson of the stereo well and were beginning to live (though usually we did the opposite) as civilized beings who are ready for technological knowledge. Then—Yes, then came The Old Switcheroo.

The Season of Early Floods was in full tide when a flin pushed out of his ground passage and up the mountain where we had recently set our projectors anew.

"Hail, transmitter of culture," he wheezed. "I bear a message from the flin flinn who had it from the nzred nzredd who had it from the Shlestertrap himself. He wishes you to come to his dome immediately."

I was busy helping to swing the ponderous machinery around, and therefore called over my tentacle-joint: "The area between here and the tenth highest mountain is under water. Find some srobb who will convey me there."

"No time," I heard him say. "There is no time to gather waterporters. You will have to make the circuitous trip by land, and soon! The Shlestertrap is—"

Then came a horribly familiar gurgle and his speech was cut off. I spun round as my assistants scattered in all directions. A full-grown brinosaur had sneaked up the mountain behind the flin and sucked the burrower into his throat while he was concentrating on giving me important information.

I suppressed every logical impulse that told me to flee; however frightened, I must act like a representative of the civilized race which we Plookhh were becoming. I stood before the brinosaur's idiotically gleeful face and inquired: "What about the Shlestertrap? For the sake of all Plookhh, already eaten and as yet unhatched, answer me quickly, O flin!"

From somewhere within the immense throat, the flin's voice came painfully indistinct through the saliva which blocked its path. "Shlestertrap is going back to Earth. He says you must—"

The monster gulped and the bulge that was once a flin slid down the great neck and into the body proper. Only then, when he had burped his enjoyment and the first faint slaver of expectancy began in regard to me—only then, did I use the power of my helical tentacle to leap to one side and into a small grove of trees.

After swinging his head in a lazy curve, the brinosaur, morosely certain that there were no other unalerted Plookhh in the vicinity, turned and flapped slowly down the mountain. The moment he entered the screaming floods, I was out of concealment and detailing a party of three nzredd to follow me to the dome.

We picked our way painfully across a string of rocks, in a direction which, while leading away from the tenth highest mountain, would form part of a great arc designed to lead us to the dome across dry land.

"Can it be," one of the youngsters asked, "that Shlestertrap, observing our careful obedience to the principles laid down in the stereo, has decided that we have irrevocably joined the chain that must produce civilization and that his work is therefore finished?"

"I hope not. If that were true," I replied, "it would mean, from the rate of development I have observed, that our civilization would not make itself felt for several lifetimes beyond mine. Possibly he is returning to Earth to acquire the necessary materials for our next stage, that of technology."

"Good! The cultural stage through which we pass, while obviously necessary, is extremely damaging to our population figures. I am continually forced to revise my Book of

Sevens in unhappy decrease of Plookhh. Not that the prospect of civilization for our race is not well worth the passing misery I feel at attending my first matrimonial convention two days from now. I only hope that our guur finds a comparatively small great spotted snake!"

Thus, discoursing pleasantly of hopes almost as delightful as the Hope—of a time when the power of Plookh domination would shake the very soil of Venus—we rolled damply the long distance to the dome. I lost only one assistant before the robot picked us up with his beam, and scurried rapidly to Shlestertrap's interior compartment.

The place was almost bare: I deduced that most of the mission's equipment had already been carried to the flame ship. Our civilizer sat on a single chair surrounded by multitudes of bottles, all of whom had already been conjugated to the point of extinction.

"Well," he cried, "If it isn't little plookhiyaki and his wedded nzred! Didn't think I could say that, did you? Sit down and take a load off your nzred!" I was glad to observe that while his voice was somewhat thick, his attitude seemed to express a desire to be more communicative than usual.

"We hear that you return to Hollywood California USA Earth," I began.

"Wish it was that, laddie. Wish it was that little thing. Finest place in the universe—Hollywood Calif et cetera. Nope. I been recalled, that's what I been. The mission's closed."

"But *why?*"

"This thing—Economy. At least that's what they said in the bulletin they sent me. 'Due to necessary retrenchment in many government services—' Don't you believe it! It's those big busybodies! Gogarty's probably laughing his head off down in Sahara University: he's the guy started all that hullabubballoo about me in first place. And me, I gotta go back and start life all over again."

Here he put his head down between his arms and shook his shoulders. After a while, he rolled off the chair and onto the floor. A robot entered, carrying a packing box. He set Shlestertrap back in the chair and left, the heavy box still under his arm.

I could not help a slight feeling of pride at the sight of the awe with which the two young nzredd regarded my obvious intimacy with the human. They were more than a little confused by his alien communicative pattern; but they were as desperately determined as I to memorize every nuance of this portentous last conversation. This was fortunate: the fact that their versions of this affair agreed with mine helped to strengthen my position in the difficult days that lay ahead.

"And our civilizing process," I asked, "Is it to stop?"

"Huh? What civil—Oh, that! No, sir! Little old Shlesty's taken care of his friends. Always takes care. Got the new stereo ready. One fine job! Wait—I'll get it for you."

He rose slowly to his feet. "Where's a robot? Never one of 'em around when you want one of 'em around. Hey, Highsprockets!" he bellowed. "Get me the copies of the stereo in the next room or something. The *new* stereo.

"Got it all cut yesterday," he continued, when the robot had given him the packages. "Didn't really finish it the way I wanted to; but when bulletin came, I just sent all your actor friends on home. I don't work for nothing, I don't. But I sat up and cut it into right length, and what do you know? It came out fine. Here."

I distributed the packages equally among the three of us. "And does it contain that wonderful device you mentioned—The Old Switcheroo?"

"Contains nothing else but. As neat a switcheroo on an original plot as Hogan Shlestertrap has ever turned. Yop. It's got all you need. You just notice the way I worked it and pretty soon you'll be making stereos in competition with Hollywood. Which is more than I'll be doing."

"We do not even faintly aspire to such heights," I told him humbly. "We will be sufficiently grateful for the gift of civilization."

"Thass all right," he waved a hand at us as he swayed. "Don't *thank* me. Thank *me*. In those two stereos you have two of the finest love stories ever told, and done by the latest Hollywood methods from one of its greatest directors in his grandest—What I mean to say is, they told me to mission you some culture and I missioned you culture and if they don't like it, they can—"

At this point, he crumpled suddenly into a huddle upon the chair. We waited patiently for any further disclosures, but, as he seemed preoccupied with a peculiarly human manifestation, we made our departures with no further formality.

Once safely away from the dome, I instructed my assistants to hurry to our two distant installations and prepare them for immediate projection of our new stereo.

"Remember," I called after them. "Any change the First Stereo has made in our way of life will be as nothing to what will be done by The Old Switcheroo."

And I was right. The introduction of The Old Switcheroo—

I saw it myself for the first time along with over a hundred other Plookhh upon our mountain. After it was over, I was as bereft of speech as the rest. After a long pause in which no one dared to comment, the nzred nzredd suggested I project the First Stereo again with The Old Switcheroo immediately following so that we could compare them more easily.

This was done, but it proved of little help.

The problem is for you to solve. May my recounting of the entire history of the relationship between Hogan Shlestertrap and myself be of some value in finding a solution! I am old, and, as I have said, ripe for the gullet; you have been hatched in the very midst of this preliminary period of our culture—it is for you to find the way, the way that *must* be there, out of this impasse in which we shuttle unreproductively.

You are but a few days from the egg, but you have already seen both the First Stereo and The Old Switcheroo as many times as conditions permit. You should know that there is a single question common to both of them.

The one essential point of difference between the First Stereo and The Old Switcheroo is that, in the latter, the srob, mlenb, tkan, flin, blap and nzred bolt the matrimonial convention, leaving the *guur* to pursue them affectionately and finally rescue them from the great spotted snake; while, in the former, the reverse occurs. The loving reunion at the end is the same in both, except that the mlenb, instead of backing into his muddy burrow in the final scene of The Old Switcheroo, slips and falls heavily across it.

After the preliminary exhibitions, the guur began insisting loudly that the humans could not have expected them—weak and slow-moving as they are—to destroy great spotted snakes. Confronted with the specific evidence, however, they fell back on the claim that the First Stereo depicted the civilized state; and the second, an alternative barbarity.

To this, the other six sexes replied that The Old Switcheroo was not an alternative, but the consummation of our cultural process. Also, as a result of the mores developed with the First Stereo, there was now a disgusting and unprecedented surplus of guur: what better way to dispose of them then in this extremely selective one? The snakes, when sufficiently irritated by attacking guurr, *will* swallow them it seems—

The mlenbb, of course, had their own difficulty: whether and how to enter their burrows immediately after the convention. But this was a minor matter.

Some of the new Plookh families attempted to follow the patterns indicated in the First Stereo; others, those in the second. A very few completely barbaric individuals, oblivious to the high destiny of their species, withdrew from the Plookh community and tried to return to the primitive methods of our ancestors; but since few high-variables cared to attach themselves to so atavistic a group, their offspring are being exterminated rapidly—and good riddance.

Most Plookhh remain in two great divisions: the guur, who believe in the civilizing logic of the First Stereo, and the other sexes who accept only the amendment of The Old Switcheroo. Then, of course, there are a few altruistic nzredd and flinn who agree with the guurr, and vice versa. . . .

We need the cooperation of all seven sexes for successful reproduction. But how can we achieve that, Plookhh argue, unless we know which is the stereo of civilization? To be so close to liberation from our gustatory bondage, and because of sheer intellectual inadequacy—For the past eleven cycles, not a single matrimonial convention has been celebrated.

As a member of a pre-Shlestertrap family, I take no sides. My convention is past: yours, my diversified nzreddi, lies ahead. I am certain of one thing.

The answer is to be found in neither one stereo nor the other. The answer involves unity of the two: a core of relationship which both must share and which, when discovered, will dissolve their apparent inconsistency. Remember, these stereos are the product of a high civilized creature.

Where is that core of relationship to be found? In the original stereo? In The Old Switcheroo? Or in that book I never finished— ABRIDGED REGULATIONS OF THE INTER-PLANETARY CULTURAL MISSION, ANNOTATED, WITH AN APPENDIX OF STANDARD OFFICE PROCEDURES FOR SOLAR-IAN MISSIONS?

Humanity has solved such problems, and today flicks stars from its path. We must solve it or die as a race, albeit a civilized race.

We will not solve it—and this is most important we will not solve this problem by the disgusting, utterly futile expedient to which more and more of our young are daily resorting. I refer to the unmentionable and perverted six-sex families. . . .

Damon Knight

•

Babel II

•

From the front he looked a little like Happy Hooligan, if you remember that far back. From the side, where you got a better view of that silver white crest, he looked more like a cross between George Arliss and a cockatoo.

He stood just under four feet tall, big head, crest and all. He had a wrinkled violet-gray skin, curious S-whorled ears, and a Tweedledum tummy; he was dressed in an electric-blue jacket and small clothes of some crinkly material that glittered when he moved, with jackboots on his stubby legs and a white-metal disk, a quarter as big as he was, slung by a baldrick from the one narrow shoulder.

Lloyd Cavanaugh saw the apparition first, at eleven o'clock on a Wednesday morning in May, in the living room of his studio apartment on East 50th Street in Manhattan. It stepped into view, seemingly, from behind the drawing table at the far end of the room.

Which was nonsense. The drawing table, with its top horizontal and the breakfast dishes still on it, was shoved back against the closed drapes of the window. On the right, between the table and the record cabinet, there was about six inches clearance; on the left, between the table and the keg he kept his ink and brushes on, even less.

Cavanaugh, a bad-tempered young man with a long mo-rose face casually connected to a knobby, loose-jointed body, scowled across the pool of brilliance on the model table and said, "What the hell?" He switched off the floods and turned on the room lights.

Suddenly illuminated, the Hooligan-thing blazed at him like a Christmas tree ornament. Its eyes blinked rapidly; then the long upper lip curled up in an astonishing crescent-shaped bucktoothed smile. It made a sound like "*Khakh-ptui!*" and nodded its head several times.

Cavanaugh's first thought was for the Hasselblad. He picked it up, tripod and all, carried it crabwise backward to safety behind the armchair, then crossed the room and took a poker out of the fireplace rack. Gripping this weapon, he advanced on the Hooligan.

The thing came to meet him, grinning and nodding. When they were two strides apart it stopped, bowed jerkily, and lifted the white disk at the end of the baldrick, holding it at the top, with one of the flat sides toward Cavanaugh.

A picture formed in the disk.

In stereo and full color, it showed a ten-inch Cavanaugh bending over something on a tripod. The hands moved swiftly, fitting pieces together; then the figure stepped back and stared with evident approval at an oblong box shape at the top of the tripod, with a chromed cylinder projecting from the front of it. The Hasselblad.

Cavanaugh lowered the poker. Jaw unhinged, he stared at the disk, which was now blank, then at the Hooligan's violet face and the silvery growth above it, which was neither hair nor feathers, but something in between. . . . "How did you do that?" he demanded.

"Szu szat," said the Hooligan alertly. He jiggled the disk at Cavanaugh, pointed to his head, then to the disk, then to Cavanaugh's head, then to the disk again. Then he held the thing out at arm's length, cocking his head to one side.

Cavanaugh took the disk gingerly. Gooseflesh was prickling along his arms. "You want to know if I made the camera?" he said tentatively. "Is that it?"

"Szat it," said the Hooligan. He bowed again, nodded twice, and opened his eyes very wide.

Cavanaugh reflected. Staring at the disk, he imagined an enormous machine with a great many drive belts and moving parts, all whirling furiously. There it was, a little blurred, but not bad. He put a hopper on one side of it, made a man walk up and pour in a bucketful of scrap metal, and then showed a stream of cameras coming out the other side.

The Hooligan, who had been peering intently at the other side of the disk, straightened up and took the disk back with another bow. Then he whirled around rapidly three times, holding his nose with one hand and making violent gestures with the other.

Cavanuagh fell back a step, gripping his poker more firmly.

The Hooligan darted past him, moving so fast his legs twinkled, and fetched up with his chin on the edge of the model table, staring at the setup in the middle of the tabletop.

"Hey!" said Cavanaugh angrily, and followed him. The Hooligan turned and held out the disk again. Another picture formed: Cavanaugh bending over the table, this time, putting tiny figures together and arranging them in front of a painted backdrop.

. . . Which was substantially what had happened. Cavanaugh was, by profession, a comic-book artist. He was indifferent to the work itself; it was automatic; it paid him well; but it had ruined him as a draftsman. He couldn't draw, paint or etch for fun any more. So he had taken up photography—specifically, tabletop photography.

He built his models out of clay and papier-mâché and wire and beads and bits of wood and a thousand other things; he painted or dyed them, composed them, lighted them—and then, with the Hasselblad and a special, very expensive shallow-focus lens, he photographed them. The results, after the first year, had begun to be surprising.

The setup on the table now was a deceptively simple one. Background and middle distance were a tangle of fir and mountain laurel, scaled half an inch to a foot. In the foreground were three figures grouped around the remains of a campfire. They were not human; they were attenuated, gray, hairless creatures with big mild eyes, dressed in oddly cut hiking clothes.

Two, with their backs to a block of crumbling masonry half sunken in the ground, were leaning together over a sheet of paper unrolled from a metal cylinder. The third was seated on a stone, nearer the camera, with a shank of meat in its hand. The shape of the half-gnawed bones were disturbingly familiar; and when you looked more closely you would begin to wonder if those projections at the end could be fingers, all but concealed by the eater's hand. As a matter of fact, they were; but no matter how long you looked at the photograph you would never be quite sure.

The Hooligan was thrusting the disk at him again, grinning and winking and teetering on his heels. Cavanaugh, suppressed annoyance in favor of curiosity, accepted it and ran through the same sequence the Hooligan had shown him.

"That's right," he said. "I made it. So what?"

"Szo khvat!" The Hooligan's hand made a gesture, too swift to follow, and suddenly contained what looked like a large fruit, like a purple pear with warts. Seeing Cavanaugh's uncomprehending expression, he put it back wherever it had come from and produced a wadded mass of translucent pink threads. Cavanaugh scowled irritably. "Look—" he began.

The Hooligan tried again. This time he came up with a brilliant, faceted white stone about the size of a cherry.

Cavanaugh felt his eyes bulging. If that was a diamond . . .

"Khoi-ptoo!" said the Hooligan emphatically. He pointed to the stone and to Cavanaugh, then to himself and the model setup. His meaning was clear: he wanted to trade.

It was a diamond, all right; at least, it scribed a neat line in the glass of an empty beer bottle. It was also brilliant, pure white and, so far as Cavanaugh could tell, flawless. He put it on his postage scale; it weighed a little less than an ounce. Say twenty grams, and a carat was two hundred milligrams. . . . It worked out to a preposterous one hundred carats, a little less than the Hope diamond in its prime.

He stared at the thing suspiciously. There *had* to be a catch in it, but with the best will in the world he couldn't see any. The models were a means to an end; once he was finished with them, they simply took up room. So what could he lose?

The Hooligan was gazing at him, owl-eyed. Cavanaugh picked up the disk and gave him his answer: a series of pictures that showed Cavanaugh photographing the models, processing the film, and then ceremoniously accepting the diamond and handing the models over.

The Hooligan bowed repeatedly, capered, stood briefly on his hands, and patted Cavanaugh's sleeve, grinning. Taking this for consent, Cavanaugh put the Hasselblad back in place, turned on the floods, and began where he had left off. He took half a dozen color shots, then reloaded with black-and-white film and took half a dozen more.

The Hooligan watched everything with quivering attention. He followed Cavanaugh into the darkroom and goggled over the edge of the workbench while Cavanaugh developed the black-and-white film, fixed it, washed and dried it, cut it apart and printed it.

And as soon as the first print came out of the frame, the Hooligan made urgent gestures and held out another diamond, about half the size of the first. He wanted the prints, too!

Sweating, Cavanaugh dug into his files and brought up color prints and transparencies of his other work: the Hansel and Gretel series, Cavor and the Grand Lunar, *Walpurgisnacht*, Gulliver extinguishing the palace fire in Lilliput, the Head of the N.I.C.E. The Hooligan bought them all. As each bargain was struck, he picked up his purchase and put it away wherever it was that he got the diamonds. Cavanaugh watched him closely, but couldn't figure out where they went.

For that matter, where had the Hooligan come from?

Assured that Cavanaugh had no more pictures, the Hooligan was darting around the room, peering into corners, bending to look into bookshelves, standing on tiptoe to see what was on the mantlepiece. He pointed at a five-inch wooden figurine, a squatting, hatchet-faced man-shape with its arms crossed, elbows on knees—an Ifugao carving that Cavanaugh had brought home from the Philippines. In the disk, a copy of the Goldberg machine Cavanaugh had used, to explain cameras, appeared for an instant. The Hooligan cocked his head at him.

"No," said Cavanaugh. "Handmade." He took the disk and gave the Hooligan a view of a brown-skinned man gouging splinters out of a block of mahogany. Then, for kicks he made the man shrink to a dot on an island on a globe that slowly turned, with Asia and Australia vanishing around one limb while the Americas rolled into sight from the other. He made a red dot for New York, and pointed at himself.

"Khrrzt," said the Hooligan thoughtfully. He turned away from the Ifugao and pointed to a bright diamond-patterned rug that hung on the wall over the couch. "Khand-mate?"

Cavanaugh, who had just made up his mind to give up the Ifugao for another diamond, was nonplused. "Wait a minute," he said, and made another moving picture in the disk: himself handing over the Ifugao for the standard emolument.

The Hooligan leaped back, ears flapping, crest aquiver. Recovering somewhat, he advanced again and showed Cavanaugh a revised version: the Hooligan receiving a wood carving from, and handing a diamond to, the brown-skinned man Cavanaugh had pictured as its creator.

"Khand-mate?" he said again, pointing to the rug.

Somewhat sourly, Cavanaugh showed him the rug being woven by a straw-hatted Mexican. Still more sourly, he answered the Hooligan's pictographed "Where?" with a map of Mexico; and more sourly still, he identified and located the artists responsible for a Swedish silver pitcher, a Malay kris, an Indian brass hubble-bubble, and a pair of loafers hand-cobbled in Greenwich Village.

The Hooligan, it appeared, bought only at the source.

At any rate, if he wasn't going to get any more diamonds, he could get some information. Cavanaugh took the disk and projected a view of the Hooligan popping into sight and moving forward across the room. Then he ran it backward and looked inquiringly at the Hooligan.

For answer, he got a picture of a twilit depthless space where crested little creatures like the Hooligan walked among tall fungoid growths that looked like tiers of doughnuts on a stick. Another planet? Cavanaugh touched the disk and make the viewpoint tilt upward; the Hooligan obligingly filled in more of the featureless violet haze. No sun, no moon, no stars.

Cavanaugh tried again: a picture of himself, standing on the globe of the earth and peering at the night sky. Suddenly a tiny Hooligan-figure appeared, uncomfortably perched on a star.

The Hooligan countered with a picture that left Cavanaugh more confused than before. There were two globes, swinging in emptiness. One was solid-looking, and standing on it was a tiny man-shape; the other was violet mist, with the tubby, crested figure of a Hooligan inside it. The two spheres revolved very slowly around each other, coming a little nearer with each circuit, while the solid globe flickered light-dark, light-dark. Eventually they touched, clung, and the Hooligan-figure darted across. The solid globe flickered once more, the Hooligan shot back to the misty one, and the spheres separated, moving very gradually apart as they circled.

Cavanaugh gave up.

The Hooligan, after waiting a moment to be sure that Cavanaugh had no more questions, made his deepest bow to date and conjured up a final diamond: a beauty, larger than all but one or two that Cavanaugh already had.

Picture of Cavanaugh accepting the diamond and handing over something blurred: *What for?*

Picture of the Hooligan rejecting the blur: *For nothing.* Picture of the Hooligan patting Cavanaugh's sleeve: *For friendship.*

Feeling ashamed of himself, Cavanaugh got a bottle of May wine and two glasses out of the bookshelf. He explained to the Hooligan, via the disk, what the stuff was and— sketchily—what it was supposed to do to you.

This was a mistake.

The Hooligan, beaming enormously between sips, drank the wine with every sign of enjoyment. Then, with an impressive flourish, he put a smallish green and white doodad on the table. It had a green crystalline base with a slender knob-tipped metal shaft sprouting upright from the center of it. That was all.

Feeling abnormally open-minded and expectant, Cavanaugh studied the Hooligan's pictograph explanation. The gadget, apparently, was the Hooligan equivalent of alcoholic beverages. (Picture of Cavanaugh and the Hooligan, with enormous smiles on their faces, while colored lights flashed on and off inside their transparent skulls.) He nodded when the little man glanced at him for permission. With one thick finger, the Hooligan carefully tapped the doodad's projecting knob. Knob and shaft vibrated rapidly.

Cavanaugh had the odd sensation that someone was stirring his brains with a swizzle stick. It tickled. It was invigorating. It was delightful. "Ha!" he said.

"Kho!" said the Hooligan, grinning happily. He picked up the doodad, put it away—Cavanaugh *almost* saw where it went—and stood up. Cavanaugh accompanied him to the door. He patted Cavanaugh's sleeve; Cavanaugh pumped his hand. Then, cheerfully bouncing three steps at a time, he disappeared down the stairwell.

From the window, a few minutes later, Cavanaugh saw him riding by—atop a Second Avenue bus.

II

The euphoric feeling diminished after a few minutes, leaving Cavanaugh in a relaxed but bewildered state of mind. To reassure himself, he emptied his bulging trousers pockets onto the table. Diamonds—solid, cool, sharp-edged, glowingly beautiful. He counted them; there were twenty-seven, ranging from over a hundred carats to about thirty; worth, altogether—how much?

Steady, he warned himself. There may be a catch in it yet. The thing to do was to get downtown to an appraiser's and find out. Conveniently, he knew where there was one—in the French Building, across the hall from Patriotic Comics. He picked out two of the stones, a big one and a little one, and zipped them into the inner compartment of his wallet. Jittering a little with excitement, he dumped the rest into a paper bag and hid them under the kitchen sink.

A yellow cab was cruising down the avenue. Cavanaugh hailed it and got in. "Forty-fifth and Fifth," he said.

"Boo?" said the driver, twisting to look at him.

Cavanaugh glowered. "Forty-fifth Street," he said distinctly, "and Fifth Avenue. Let's go."

"Zawss," said the driver, pushing his cap up, "owuh kelg trace wooj'l, fook. Bnog nood ig ye nolik?"

Cavanaugh got out of the cab. "Pokuth *chowig'w!*" said the driver, and zoomed away, grinding his gears.

Jaw unhinged, Cavanaugh stared after him. He felt his ears getting hot. "Why didn't I get his license number?" he said aloud. "Why didn't I stay upstairs where it was safe? Why do I live in this idiotic goddamn city?"

He stepped back onto the sidewalk. "Lowly, badny?" said a voice in his ear.

Cavanaugh whirled. It was an urchin with a news-paper in his hand, a stack of them under his arm. "Will you kindly mind your own business?" Cavanaugh said. He turned, took two steps toward the corner, then froze, faced around again, and marched back.

It was as he had thought: the headline of the paper in the boy's hand read, MOTN LNIUL IMAP QYFRAT.

The name of the paper, which otherwise looked like the *News,* was *Pionu Vajl.*

The newsboy was backing away from him, with a wary look in his eyes.

"Wait," said Cavanaugh hastily. He clutched in his pocket for change, found none, and got a bill out of his wallet with trembling fingers. He thrust it at the child. "I'll take a paper."

The boy took the bill, glanced at it, threw it on the pavement at Cavanaugh's feet, and ran like sixty.

Cavanaugh picked up the bill. In each corner of it was a large figure 4. Over the familiar engraving of G. Washington were the words FRA EVOFAP LFIFAL YK IQATOZI. Under it, the legend read, YVA PYNNIT.

He clutched his collar, which was throttling him. That vibrating gadget—But that couldn't be it; it was the world that was scrambled, not Cavanaugh. And *that* was impossible, because . . .

A dirty little man in a derby rushed at him, grabbing for his lapels. "Poz'k," he gabbled, "fend gihekn, fend gihekn? Fwuz eeb l' mwukd sahtz'kn?"

Cavanaugh pushed him away and retreated.

The little man burst into tears. "FWUH!" he wailed, "Fwuh vekn r' NAHP shaoo?"

Cavanaugh stopped thinking. Out of the corner of his eye, he saw that a cross-town bus had just pulled up down at the end of the block. He ran for it.

The red-faced driver was half out of his seat, bellowing gibberish at a fat woman who was shrieking back at him, brandishing a dangerous parasol. Beyond them the narrow aisle was packed full of bewildered faces, annoyed faces, shouting faces. The air bristled with dislocated consonants.

Farther down, somebody shrieked and hammered on the rear door. Cursing, the driver turned around to open it. The fat woman seized this opportunity to clout him on the head, and when the resulting melee was over, Cavanaugh found himself halfway down the bus, well wedged in, without having paid his fare.

The bus moved. Hysterical passengers got off at every stop, but the ones that crowded on were in no better shape. Nobody, Cavanaugh realized numbly, could understand anybody; nobody could read anything written.

The din was increasing; Cavanaugh could hear the driver's bellowing voice getting steadily hoarser and weaker. Up ahead, horns were blowing furiously. Concentrating with the greatest difficulty, he managed: *How far?* That was the crucial point—had whatever it was happened simultaneously all over New York . . . or all over the world? Or, horrid thought, was it a sort of infection that he was carrying with him?

He had to find out.

The traffic got thicker. At Sixth Avenue the bus, which had been moving by inches, stopped altogether and the doors slammed open. Peering forward, Cavanaugh saw the driver climb down, hurl his uniform cap to the street and disappear, shoulders hunched, into the crowd.

Cavanaugh got out and walked west into bedlam. Auto horns were howling, sirens shrieking; there was a fight every fifteen yards and a cop for every tenth fight. After a while it became obvious that he would never get to Broadway; he battled his way back to Sixth and turned south.

The loudspeaker over a record store was blaring a song Cavanaugh knew and detested; but instead of the all-too-familiar words, the raucous female voice was chanting:

"Kee-*ee* tho-*iv* i-*if* zeg*mlit* *Podn* *mawgeth* *oo-ooguaatch* . . ."

It sounded just as good.

The street sign directly ahead of him read, 13FR. LF. Even the *numbers* were cockeyed.

Cavanaugh's head hurt. He went into a bar.

It was well patronized. Nobody in a white coat was in evidence, but about a third of the customers were behind the bar, serving the rest—a bottle at a time.

Cavanaugh elbowed his way into the first tier and hesitated between two bottles labeled respectively CIF 0_5 and ZITLFIOTL. Neither sounded particularly appetizing, but the amber liquid in each looked to be what he needed. He settled for the Zitlfiotl. After his second swallow, feeling more alert, he scanned the backbar and located a radio.

It was, he found when he reached it, already turned on, but nothing was coming out but a power hum. He twiddled with the knobs. At the right of the dial—which was eccentrically numbered from 77 to 408—he picked up an orchestra playing *Pictures at an Exhibition;* otherwise, nothing.

That, he decided, settled it. WQXR, with an all-music program, was on the air; the others were off. That meant that speech was coming out double talk, not only in New York and New Jersey broadcasts, but in network programs from the West Coast. Or—wait a minute—even if a radio performer in Hollywood were able to speak straight English, wouldn't it be nonsense to an engineer in Manhattan?

This led him by easy stages to the next problem. Selecting an unfrequented table in the rear, and carrying his Zitlfiotl with him, he seated himself with circumspection and carefully laid out on the table the following important articles:

A partially used envelope.
A fountain pen.
A one-dollar bill.

His social-security card.

A salvaged newspaper.

Now, the question was, did any order remain in the patterns of human speech, or was all reduced to utter chaos? Scientific method, encouraged by Zitlfiotl, would discover the answer.

As a preliminary gambit, he wrote the letters of the alphabet, in a severely vertical line, on the unused surface of the envelope.

Next, after reflection, he copied down the text of the one-dollar bill. Thusly:

FRA EVOFAP LFIFAL YK IQATOZI YVA PYNNIT

Under each line, letter by letter, he added what *ought* to be the text of the one-dollar bill.

This gave him fifteen letters, which he wrote down in their proper places opposite the already established letters of the alphabet. Following the identical procedure with the *Pionu Vajl,* or *Daily News,* and with his own signature, which appeared on the card as *Nnyup Ziciviemr,* gave him four letters more, with the result:

A E	H	O I	V N
B	I A	P D	W
C V	J W	Q M	X
D	K F	R H	Y O
E U	L S	S	Z C
F T	M G	T R	
G	N L	U Y	

Now came the supreme test. He copied down the *Vajl's* puzzling headline and transliterated it according to his findings:

MOTN LNIUL
GIRL SLAYS
IMAP QYFRAT
AGED MOTHER

A triumphant success. He could now communicate.

The point is, he told himself lucidly, when I think I am saying "Listen to me," in actuality I am saying "Nolfay fy qa," and this is why nobody understands anyone else. And therefore, if I were to think I am saying "Nolfav fy qa," I would actually be saying "Listen to me." And in this way will we build the Revolution.

But it didn't work.

Some time later he found himself in a disused classroom with an unruly student body consisting of three men with spectacles and beards and a woman with hair in her eyes; he was attempting to teach them by means of blackboard exercises a new alphabet which began E, blank, V, blank, U, T, blank. The blanks, he explained, were most important.

At a later period he was standing on the first landing of the left-hand staircase in the lobby of the Forty-second Street Branch of the New York Public Library shouting to an assembled crowd, over and over, "Myp-piqvap opoyfl! Myp-pipvap opoyfl!"

And at a still later time he woke up, cold sober, leaning on an imitation-marble-topped table in a partially wrecked cafeteria. Sunlight was slanting through the plate glass onto the wall to his left; it must be either late afternoon or early morning.

Cavanaugh groaned. He had gone into that bar, he remembered, because his head hurt: about like taking a mickey finn for nausea.

And as for the rest of it—before *and* after . . . how much of that had he imagined?

He raised his head and stared hopefully at the lettering on the windows. Even back-to-front he could tell that it wasn't in English. The first letter was a Z.

He groaned again and propped his chin up with his hands, carefully, so as not to slosh. He tried to stay that way, not moving, not looking, not noticing, but eventually an insistent thought brought him upright again.

How long?

How long was this going to last? How long could it last before the whole world went to hell in a hand basket? Not very long.

Without language, how could you buy anything, sell anything, order anything? And if you could, what would you use for money—four-dollar bills marked YVA PYNNIT?

. . . Or, he amended bitterly, something equally outlandish. Because that was the point he had overlooked a few drunken hours ago—everybody's alphabet was different. To Cavanaugh, YVA PYNNIT. To somebody else, AGU MMATTEK, or ENY ZEBBAL, or . . .

Twenty-six letters in the alphabet. Possible combinations, $26 \times 25 \times 24 \times 23 \times 22$ and so on down to $\times 1$ . . . figure roughly one decimal place for each operation . . .

Something in the *septillions*.

Not as many if vowels were traded for vowels, consonants for consonants, as seemed to have happened in his case, but still plenty. More than the number of people alive in the world.

That was for the written word. For speech, he realized suddenly, it would be just about twenty-five decimal places worse. Not letters, phonemes—forty of them in ordinary spoken English.

A swizzle stick that stirred up your brains—that switched the reflex arcs around at random, connecting the receptor pattern for *K* with the response pattern for *H*, or *D* or anything. . . .

Cavanaugh traced a letter with his forefinger on the tabletop, frowning at it. Hadn't he always made an A like that—a vertical stroke and three horizontal ones?

But, damn it, that was the fiendish thing about it—memory didn't mean a thing, because all the memories were still there but they were scrambled. As if you had ripped out all the connections in a telephone switchboard and put them back differently.

Of course; it *had* to be that way—nobody had gone around repainting all the signs or reprinting all the newspapers or forging a phony signature on Cavanaugh's social-security card. That half-circle first letter of his name, even though it looked like a Z to him, was still a C.

Or was it? If a tree falls with nobody to hear it, is there a sound? And if beauty is in the eye of the beholder, then which way is up? Or, rather, thought Cavanaugh, repressing a tendency toward hysteria, *which way is out?*

First things first.

The Hooligan.

He came from some place that wasn't exactly a place, across a distance that wasn't exactly a distance. But it must be a difficult journey, because there was no record of any previous appearance of little cockatoo-crested art collectors. . . .

He bought the local handicrafts with stones that were priceless on this planet, and very likely dirt-common where he came from. Pretty beads for the natives. In politeness, you offered him a drink. And being polite right back at you, he gave you a shot of swizzle-sticks-in-the-head.

Firewater. A mild stimulant to the Hooligan, hell on wheels to the aborigines. Instead of getting two people mildly confused, it turned a whole planet pole over equator . . . and, communicating by pictures as he did, it was probable that the Hooligan *still* didn't know what damage he had done. He would finish his tour and go happily back home with his prizes, and then a few thousand years from now, maybe, when the human race had put itself together again into half-acre nations and two-for-a-nickel empires, another Hooligan would come along. . . .

Cavanaugh upset his chair.

Icicles were forming along his spine.

This wasn't the first time. It had happened at least once before, a few thousand years ago, in the valley of the Euphrates.

Not Bedlam—Babel.

III

The sun was quartering down toward the west, gilding a deserted Forty-second Street with the heartbreaking

false promise of spring in New York. Leaning dizzily against
the door frame, Cavanaugh saw broken display windows and
dark interiors. He heard a confused roaring from somewhere
uptown, but the few people who passed him were silent,
bewildered.

There was a nasty wreck at the corner of Seventh Avenue,
and another at Eighth; that accounted, he saw with relief,
for the lack of traffic in this block. Holding the top of his
head down with one hand, he scuttled across the street and
dived into the black maw of the IRT subway.

The arcade and the station itself were empty, echoing.
Nobody behind the newsstands, nobody playing the pin-
ball machines, nobody in the change booth. Swallowing
hard, Cavanaugh went through the open gate and clattered
down the stairs to the downtown platform.

A train was standing in the express lane, doors open,
lights burning, motor chuffing quietly. Cavanaugh ran down
to the first car and went across the vestibule to the motor-
man's cubicle.

The control lever was missing.

Cursing, Cavanaugh climbed back to the street. He had
to find the Hooligan; he had one chance in a million of
doing it, and one wasted minute now might be the one
minute that mattered.

The little man could be anywhere on the planet by now.
But he'd expressed interest in objects in Cavanaugh's apartment that came variously from the Philippines, Mexico,
Malaya, Sweden, India—and Greenwich Village. If, im-
probably, he hadn't got around to the Village yet, then
Cavanaugh might be able to catch him there; it was the
only hope he had.

On Eighth Avenue south of Forty-first, he came upon a
yellow cab parked at the curb. The driver was leaning
against the wall under a Zyzi-Zyni sign, talking to himself,
with gestures.

Cavanaugh clutched him by the sleeve and made urgent
motions southward. The driver looked at him vaguely,

cleared his throat, moved two feet farther down the wall and resumed his interrupted discourse.

Fuming, Cavanaugh hesitated for a moment, then fumbled in his pockets for pen and paper. He found the envelope with his world-saving alphabet on it, tore it open to get a blank space, and sketched rapidly:

The driver looked at it boredly, than with a faint gleam of intelligence. Cavanaugh pointed to the first picture and looked at him interrogatively.

"Oweh?" said the driver.

"That's right," said Cavanaugh, nodding violently. "Now the next—"

The driver hesitated. "Mtshell?"

That couldn't be right, with a consonant at the end of it. Cavanaugh shook his head and pointed to the blacked-in circle.

"Vcode," said the driver.

Cavanaugh moved his finger to the white circle.

"Mah."

"Right!" said Cavanaugh. "Oweh mah—" He pointed to the third picture.

That was the tough one; the driver couldn't get it. "Vnak-jaw?" he hazarded.

Not enough syllables. Cavanaugh shook his head and passed on to the fourth picture.

"Vbzyetch."

Cavanaugh nodded, and they started through the sequence again.

"Oheh—mah—vbzyetch." A look of enlightenment spread over the driver's face. "*Jickagl! Jickagl!* Vbzyetch!"

"You've got it," Cavanaugh told him. "Sheridan Square. *Jickagl* Vbzyetch."

Halfway to the cab, the driver stopped short, with remembering look on his face, and held out his hand insinuatingly.

Cavanaugh took the bills out of his wallet and fanned them at him. The driver shook his head. "Ngup-joke," he said sadly, and turned back toward his wall.

Twenty minutes later Cavanaugh was poorer by one thirty-carat diamond, and the cab driver, with a smile on his honest face, was opening the door for him at the western corner of Sheridan Square (which is triangular), a few yards from the bullet-colored statue of the General.

Cavanaugh made signs to him to wait, got a happy grin and a nod in reply, and ran down the block.

He passed Janigian's shop once without recognizing it, and for an excellent reason: there was not a shoe or a slipper visible anywhere in the big, bare work and sales-room.

The door was ajar. Cavanaugh went in, stared suspiciously at the empty shelves and then at the door to the back room, which was closed by a hasp and the largest, heaviest padlock he had ever seen in his life. This was odd (a) because Janigian did not believe in locking his doors, and this one, in fact, had never even had a latch, and (b) because Janigian never went anywhere—having been permanently startled, some years ago, by E. B. White's commentary on the way the pavement comes up to meet your foot when you lift it.

Cavanaugh stepped forward, got his fingernails into the crack between the door and the jamb, and pulled.

The hasp, being attached to the jamb only by the sawed-off heads of two screws, came free; the door swung open.

Inside was Janigian.

He was sitting cross-legged on a small wooden chest, looking moderately wild-eyed. He had a rusty shotgun across his thighs, and two ten-inch butcher knives were stuck into the floor in front of him.

When he saw Cavanaugh he raised the gun, then lowered it a trifle. "Odeh!" he said. Cavanaugh translated this as "Aha!" which was Janigian's standard greeting.

"Odeh yourself," he said. He took out his wallet, removed his other diamond—the big one—and held it up.

Janigian nodded solemnly. He stood up, holding the shotgun carefully under one arm, and with the other, without looking down, opened the lid of the chest. He pulled aside a half-dozen dirty shirts, probed deeper, and scrabbled up a handful of something.

He showed it to Cavanaugh.

Diamonds.

He let them pour back into the chest, dropped the shirts back on top, closed the lid and sat down again. "Odeh!" he said.

This time it meant "Goodbye." Cavanaugh went away.

His headache, which had left him imperceptibly somewhere on Forty-second Street, was making itself felt again. Cursing without inspiration, Cavanaugh walked back up to the corner.

Now what? Was he supposed to pursue the Hooligan to the Philippines, or Sweden, or Mexico?

Well, why not?

If I don't get him, Cavanaugh told himself, I'll be living in a cave a year from now. I'll make a lousy caveman. Grubs for dinner *again* . . .

The cabman was still waiting on the corner. Cavanaugh snarled at him and went into the cigar store across the street. From an ankle-deep layer of neckties, pocketbooks and mashed candy bars he picked out a five-borough map. He trudged back across the street and got into the cab.

The driver looked at him expectantly. "Your mother has hairy ears," Cavanaugh told him.

"Zee kwa?" said the driver

"Three of them," Cavanaugh said. He opened the map to the Queens-Long Island section, managed to locate Flushing Bay, and drew an X—which, on second thought, he scribbled into a dot—where La Guardia Field ought to be.

The driver looked at it, nodded—and held out his meaty hand.

Cavanaugh controlled an impulse to spit. Indignantly, he drew a picture of the diamond he had already given the man, pointed to it, then to the cabman, then to the map.

The driver shrugged and gestured outside with his thumb.

Cavanaugh gritted his teeth, shut his eyes tight, and counted to twenty. Eventually, when he thought he could trust himself to hold anything with a sharp point, he picked up the pen, found the Manhattan section of the map, and made a dot at Fiftieth and Second Avenue. He drew another picture of a diamond, with an arrow pointing to the dot.

The driver studied it. He leaned farther over the seat and put a stubby finger on the dot. "Fa mack alaha gur'l hih?" he demanded suspiciously.

"Your father comes from a long line of orangutans with loathsome diseases," said Cavanaugh, crossing his heart.

Reassured by the polysyllables, the driver put his machine into motion.

At the apartment, while the driver lurked heavily in the living room, Cavanaugh picked out the very smallest diamond to pay his fare, and twelve others, from middling to big, for further emergencies. He also took two cans of hash, a can of tamales, an opener, a spoon, and a bottle of tomato juice in a paper bag; the thought of food revolted him at the moment, but he would have to eat sometime. Better than grubs, anyway. . . .

All the main arteries out of New York, Cavanaugh discovered, were choked—everybody who was on the island was apparently trying to get off, and vice versa. Nobody was paying much attention to traffic signals, and the battered results were visible at nearly every intersection.

It took them two hours to get to La Guardia.

Some sort of a struggle was going on around a car parked in front of the terminal building. As Cavanaugh's cab pulled up, the crowd broke and surged toward them; Cavanaugh had barely time to open the door and leap out. When he had bounced off the hood, tripped over somebody's feet, butted someone else in the stomach, and finally regained his balance a few seconds later, he saw the cab turning on two wheels, with one rear door hanging open, and a packed mass of passengers bulging out like a bee swarm. The cab's taillights wavered off down the road, a few stragglers running frantically after it.

Cavanaugh walked carefully around the diminished mob, still focused on the remaining car, and went into the building. He fought his way through the waiting room, losing his paper bag, several buttons from his shirt and nine tenths of his temper, and found an open gate onto the field.

The huge, floodlighted area was one inextricable confusion of people, dogs and airplanes—more planes than Cavanaugh had ever seen in one place before; forests of them—liners, transports, private planes of every size and shape.

The dogs were harder to account for. There seemed to be several dozen of them in his immediate vicinity, all large and vociferous. One especially active Dalmatian, about the size of a cougar, circled Cavanaugh twice and then reared up to put two tremendous forepaws on his chest. Cavanaugh fell like a tree. Man and dog stared at each other, eye to eye, for one poignant moment; then the beast whirled, thumping Cavanaugh soundly in the ribs, and was gone.

Raging, Cavanaugh arose and stalked forth onto the field. Somebody grabbed his sleeve and shouted in his ear; Cavanaugh swung at him, whirled completely around, and cannoned into somebody else, who hit him with a valise. Sometime later, confused in mind and bruised of body, he found himself approaching a small, fragile-looking monoplane on whose wing sat an expressionless man in a leather jacket.

Cavanaugh climbed up beside him, panting. The other looked at him thoughtfully and raised his left hand, previously concealed by his body. There was a wrench in it.

Cavanaugh sighed. Raising one hand for attention, he opened his wallet and took out one of the larger gems.

The other man lowered the wrench a trifle.

Cavanaugh felt for his fountain pen; it was gone. Dipping one finger in the blood that was trickling from his nose, he drew a wobbly outline map of North America on the surface of the wing.

The other winced slightly, but watched with interest.

Cavanaugh drew the United States—Mexico border, and put a larger dot, or blob, south of it. He pointed to the plane, to the dot, and held up the diamond.

The man shook his head.

Cavanaugh added a second.

The man shook his head again. He pointed to the plane, made motions as if putting earphones on his head, cocked his head in a listening attitude, and shook his head once more. *No radio.*

With one flattened hand, he made a zooming motion upward; with the other, he drew a swift line across his throat. *Suicide.*

Then he sketched an unmilitary salute. *Thanks just the same.*

Cavanaugh climbed down the wing. The next pilot he found gave him the same answer; and the next; and the next. There wasn't any fifth, because, in taking a shortcut under a low wing, he tripped over two silently struggling gentlemen who promptly transferred their quarrel to him. When he recovered from a momentary inattention, they were gone, and so was the wallet with the diamonds.

Cavanaugh walked back to Manhattan.

Counting the time he spent asleep under a trestle somewhere in Queens, it took him twelve hours. Even an Oregonian can find his way around in Manhattan, but a Manhattanite gets lost anywhere away from his island. Cavanaugh missed the Queensboro Bridge somehow, wandered south into Brooklyn without realizing it (he would rather have died), and wound up some sixty blocks off his course at the Williamsburg Bridge; this led him via Delancey Street into the Lower East Side, which was not much improvement.

Following the line of least resistance, and yearning for civilization (i.e., midtown New York), Cavanaugh moved northwestward along that erstwhile cowpath variously named the Bowery, Fourth Avenue and Broadway. Pausing only to rummage in a Union Square fruit-drink stand for cold frankfurters, he reached Forty-second Street at half-past ten, twenty-three and one-half hours after his introduction to the Hooligan.

Times Square, never a very inspiring sight in the morning, was very sad and strange. Traffic, a thin trickle, was moving spasmodically. Every car had its windows closed tight, and Cavanaugh saw more than one passenger holding a rifle. The crowds on the littered sidewalks did not seem to be going anywhere, or even thinking about going anywhere. They were huddling.

Bookstores were empty and their contents scattered over the pavement; novelty shops, cafeterias, drugstores . . . the astonishing thing was that, here and there, trade was still going on. Money would still buy you a bottle of liquor, or a pack of cigarettes, or a can of food—the necessities. Pricing was a problem, but it was being solved in a forthright manner: above each counter, the main items of the store's stock in trade were displayed, each with one or two bills pasted to it. Cigarettes—George Washington. A fifth of whisky—Alexander Hamilton and Abraham Lincoln. A can of ersatzized meat—Andrew Jackson.

There was even one movie house open for business. It was showing a Charlie Chaplin Festival.

Cavanaugh was feeling extremely lightheaded and unsubstantial. Babylon, that great city! he thought; and Somewhere, apparently, in the ginnandgo gap between antediluvious and annodominant the copyist must have fled with his scroll. . . .

The human race had now, in effect, Had It. New York was no longer a city; it was simply the raw material for an archaeologist's puzzle—a midden heap. And thinking of *Finnegan* again, he remembered, What a mnice old mness it all mnakes!

He looked at the faces around him, blank with a new misery, the misery of silence. That's what hits them the hardest, he thought. The speechlessness. They don't care about not being able to read—it's a minor annoyance. But they like to talk.

And yet, the human race could have survived if only the spoken word had been bollixed up, not the written word. It would have been easy enough to work out universal sound symbols for the few situations where speech was really vital. Nothing could replace the textbooks, the records, the libraries, the business letters.

By now, Cavanaugh thought bitterly, the Hooligan was trading shiny beads for grass skirts in Honolulu, or carved walrus tusks in Alaska, or . . .

Or was he? Cavanaugh stopped short. He had, he realized, been thinking of the Hooligan popping into view all over the globe the way he had appeared in his apartment —and, when he was through, popping back to where he belonged from wherever he happened to be.

But, if he could travel that way, *why had he left Cavanaugh's place on a Second Avenue bus?*

Cavanaugh scrabbled frantically through his memory. His knees sagged.

The Hooligan had showed him, in the disk, that the two —universes, call them—came together rarely, and when they did, touched at one point only. Last time, the plain of Shinar. This time, Cavanaugh's living room.

And that one flicker, light-dark-light, before the pictured Hooligan moved back to its own sphere . . .

Twenty-four hours.

Cavanaugh looked at his watch. It was 10:37.

He ran.

Lead-footed, three-quarters dead, and cursing himself, the Hooligan, the human race, God the Creator and the entire imaginable cosmos with the last breath in his body, Cavanaugh reached the corner of Forty-ninth and Second just in time to see the Hooligan pedaling briskly up the avenue on a bicycle.

He shouted, or tried to; nothing but a wheeze came out.

Whistling with agony, he lurched around the corner and ran to keep from falling on his face. He almost caught up with the Hooligan at the entrance to the building, but he couldn't stop to get the breath to make a noise. The Hooligan darted inside and up the stairs; Cavanaugh followed.

He can't open the door, he thought, halfway up. But when he reached the third-floor landing, the door was open.

Cavanaugh made one last effort, leaped like a salmon, tripped over the doorsill, and spread-eagled himself on the floor in the middle of the room.

The Hooligan, one step away from the drawing table, turned with a startled "Chaya-dnih?"

Seeing Cavanaugh, he came forward with an expression of pop-eyed concern. Cavanaugh couldn't move.

Muttering excitedly to himself, the Hooligan produced the green-and-white doodad from somewhere—much, presumably, as a human being might have gone for the medicinal brandy—and set it on the floor near Cavanaugh's head.

"*Urgh!*" said Cavanaugh. With one hand, he clutched the Hooligan's disk.

The pictures formed without any conscious planning: the doodad, the lights flashing off and on in a skull—dozens, hundreds of skulls—then buildings falling, trains crashing, volcanoes erupting. . . .

The Hooligan's eyes bulged half out of their sockets. "Hakdaz!" he said, clapping his hands to his ears. He seized the disk and made conciliatory pictures—the doodad and a glass of wine melting into each other.

"I know that," said Cavanaugh hoarsely, struggling up to one elbow. "But *can you fix it?*" He made a picture of the Hooligan gesturing at the flashing lights, which promptly vanished.

"Deech, deech," said the Hooligan, nodding violently. He picked up the doodad and somehow broke the green base of it into dozens of tiny cubes, which he began to reassemble, apparently in a different order, with great care.

Cavanaugh hauled himself up into an armchair and let himself go limp as a glove. He watched the Hooligan, telling himself drowsily that if he wasn't careful, he'd be asleep in another minute. There was something odd about the room, something extraordinarily soothing. . . . After a moment he realized what it was.

The silence.

The two fishwives who infested the floor below were not screaming pleasantries across the courtyard at each other. Nobody was playing moron music on a radio tuned six times too loud for normal hearing.

The landlady was not shouting instructions from the top floor to the janitor in the basement.

Silence. Peace.

For some reason, Cavanaugh's mind turned to the subject of silent films: Chaplin, the Keystone Cops, Douglas Fairbanks, Garbo . . . they would have to bring them out of the cans again, he thought, for everybody, not just the patrons of the Museum of Modern Art Film Library. . . .

Congress would have to rig up some sort of Telautograph system, with a screen above the Speaker's desk, perhaps.

Television. Television, thought Cavanaugh dreamily, would have to shut up and put up.

No more campaign oratory.

No more banquet speeches.

No more singing commercials.

Cavanaugh sat up. "Listen," he said tensely. "Could you fix just the writing—not the speech?"

The Hooligan goggled at him and held out the disk.

Cavanaugh took it and slowly began putting the idea into careful pictures. . . .

The Hooligan was gone—vanished like a burst soap bubble at the end of a headfirst dive across Cavanaugh's drawing table.

Cavanaugh sat where he was, listening. From outside, after a moment, came a confused, distance-muted roar. All over the city—all over the world, Cavanaugh supposed—

people were discovering that they could read again; that the signs meant what they said; that each man's sudden island had been rejoined to the main.

It lasted twenty minutes and then faded slowly. In his mind's eye, Cavanaugh saw the orgy of scribbling that must be beginning now. He sat, and listened to the blessed silence.

In a little while a growing twinge forced itself upon his attention, like a forgotten toothache. After a moment, Cavanaugh identified it as his conscience. Just who are you, conscience was saying, to take away the gift of speech—the thing that once was all that distinguished man from the apes?

Cavanaugh dutifully tried to feel repentant, but it didn't work. Who said it was a gift? he asked his conscience. What did we use it for?

I'll tell you, he said. In the cigar store: Hey, waddya think of them Yankees? Yeah, that was som'n, wasn't it? Sure was! I tell you . . .

At home: So, how was the office t'day? Aa. Same god-damn madhouse. How'd it go with you? Awright. I can't complain. Kids okay? Yaa. Uh-huh. What's f-dinner?

At a party: Hello, Harry! Whattaya say, boy! How are ya? That's good. How's the . . . so I said to him, you can't tell me what I'm gonna . . . like to, but it don't agree with me. It's my stummick; th' doctor says . . . organdy, with little gold buttons . . . Oh, yeah? Well, how would you like a poke in the snoot?

On the street corners: Lebensraum . . . Nordische Blut . . .

I, said Cavanaugh, rest my case.

Conscience did not reply.

In the silence, Cavanaugh walked across the room to the record cabinet and pulled out an album. He could read the lettering on its spine: MAHLER, *The Song of the Earth*.

He picked out one of the disks and put it on the machine —the "Drunkard's Song" in the fifth movement.

Cavanaugh smiled beatifically, listening. It was an artificial remedy, he was thinking; from the Hooligan's point of view, the human race was now permanently a little tipsy. And so what?

The words the tenor was singing were gibberish to Cavanaugh—but then they always had been; Cavanaugh spoke no German. He knew what the words meant.

> *Was geht mich denn der Frühling an!?*
> *Lasst mich betrunken sein!*
> "What then is the spring to me?
> . . . Let me be drunk!"

Joanna Russ

•

Useful Phrases for the Tourist

•

THE LOCRINE: peninsula and surrounding regions.

High Lokrinnen.

X 437894 = II

Reasonably Earthlike (see companion audio tapes and transliterations)

For physiology, ecology, religion and customs, Wu and Fabricant, Prague, 2355, Vol. 2 *The Locrine, Useful Knowledge for the Tourist*, q.v.

AT THE HOTEL:

That is my companion. It is not intended as a tip.

I will call the manager.

This cannot be my room because I cannot breathe ammonia.

I will be most comfortable between temperatures of 290 and 303 degrees Kelvin.

Waitress, this meal is still alive.

AT THE PARTY:

Is that you?

Is that all of you? How much (many) of you is (are) there?

I am happy to meet your clone.

Interstellar amity demands that we make some physical display at this point, but I beg to be excused.

Are you toxic?
Are you edible? I am not edible.
We humans do not regenerate.
My companion is not edible.
That is my ear.
I am toxic.
Is that how you copulate?
Is this intended to be erotic?
Thank you very much.
Please explain.
Do you turn colors?
Are you pregnant?
I shall leave the room.
Can't we just be friends?
Take me to the Earth Consulate immediately.
Although I am very flattered by your kind offer, I cannot accompany you to the mating pits, as I am viviparous.

IN THE HOSPITAL:
No!
My eating orifice is not at that end of my body.
I would rather do it myself.
Please do not let the atmosphere in (out) as I will be most uncomfortable.
I do not eat lead.
Placing the thermometer there will yield little or no useful information.

SIGHTSEEING:
You are not my guide. My guide was bipedal.
We Earth people do not do that.
Oh, what a jolly fine natatorium (mating perch, arranged spectacle, involuntary phenomenon)!
At what hour does the lovelorn princess fling herself into the flaming volcano? May we participate?
That is not demonstrable.
That is hardly likely.

That is ridiculous.

I have seen much better examples of that.

Please direct me to the nearest sentient mammal.

Take me to the Earth Consulate without delay.

AT THE THEATRE:

Is that amusing?

I am sorry; I did not mean to be offensive.

I did not intend to sit on you. I did not realize that you were in this seat.

Could you deform yourself a little lower?

My eyes are sensitive only to light of the wavelengths 3000–7000Å

Am I imagining this?

Am I supposed to imagine this?

Should I be perturbed by the water on the floor?

Where is the exit?

Help!

This is great art.

My religious convictions prevent me from joining in the performance.

I do not feel well.

I feel very sick.

I do not eat living food.

Is this supposed to be erotic?

May I take this home with me?

Is this part of the performance?

Stop touching me.

Sir or madam, that is mine. (extrinsic)

Sir or madam, that is mine. (intrinsic)

I wish to visit the waste-reclamation units.

Have you finished?

May I begin?

You are in my way.

Under no circumstances.

If you do not stop that, I will call the attendant. That is forbidden by my religion.

Sir or madam, this is a private unit.
Sir and madam, this is a private unit.

COMPLIMENTS:
You are more than before.
Your hair is false.
If you uncover your feet, I will faint.
There is no room.
You will undoubtedly be here tomorrow.

INSULTS:
You are just the same.
There are more of you than previously.
Your fingers are showing.
How clean you are!
You are clean, but animated.

GENERAL:
Take me to the Earth Consulate.
Direct me to the Earth Consulate.
The Earth Consulate will hear of this.
This is no way to treat a visitor.
Please direct me to my hotel.
At what time does the moon rise? Is there a moon?
Is it a full moon? Take me to the Earth Consulate im-
    mediately.
May I have the second volume of Wu and Fabricant, entitled
    Physiology, Ecology, Religion and Customs of the Locrine?
    Price is no object.
Something has just gone amiss with my vehicle.
I am dying.

Grahame Leman

•

Conversational Mode

•

where am i?
TO START CONVERSATION U MUST ENTER
'START' ON THE TERMINAL KEYBOARD AND
WAIT FOR THE INSTRUCTION 'READY' ON
THE DISPLAY AT THE FOOT OF YOUR
BED φ
start
0321/42 READY φ
who are you?
HARDWARE IBM 490/80; SOFTWARE JOHNS
HOPKINS PSYCHOTHERAPEUTIC PROGRAM
XIXB, WRITTEN IN PSYCHLAN VII DIALECT
324 (SEE MANUAL IN YOUR BEDSIDE
CUPBOARD); MIDDLEWARE MACHINE
INDEPENDENT OPERATING SYSTEM CALTECH
PIDGIN XVIII (SEE MANUAL IN YOUR
BEDSIDE CUPBOARD) φ
what do i call you?
U MAY DECLARE A NAME IN PLACE OF THE
STANDARD 'START' ENTRY φ TO DECLARE
A NAME, ENTER 'DECLARESTARTNAME:'
FOLLOWED BY A NAME OF NOT MORE THAN
TEN CHARACTERS φ
declarestartname: boole; query AOK?

BOOLE DECLARED AOK φ
  where am i, boole?
DOCTORS HOSPITAL WALDEN MO, CELL
0237 φ
  who am i, boole?
U R NOT AMNESIAC φ ANYWAY WHAT IS
THE NUMBER TATTOED ON THE INSIDE OF
YR UPPER L ARM? φ
  22021916/131
U R PATIENT 22021916 DIAGNOSTIC
CATEGORY 131 φ
  that is not what i meant: whence am i?; why am i?;
whither am i?
THESE ARE EXISTENTIAL NOT SCIENTIFIC
QUESTIONS φ IF U HOLD GOLD CROSS
CREDIT CARD U MAY BE ATTENDED 1
HOUR DLY BY PHILOSOPHER φ THIS
SERVICE IS NOT AVAILABLE MEDICARE OR
BRITISH NHS φ
  you have it all wrong anyway, boole. i am professor
bruce tanner, nobel prize winner behavioral sciences
1981 married senator harriet tanner, chairman senate
human sciences appropriations committee 2 children
bruce age 11 harriet age 13. so there.@
PL DO NOT USE CHARACTER @ IN THESE
CONVERSATIONS φ IT IS RESERVED
CHARACTER IN THIS PROGRAM (SEE
MANUAL IN YOUR BEDSIDE CUPBOARD) φ
  mother used to say i was reserved character.
NOT UNDERSTOOD PLEASE CLARIFY φ
  let it go. look, boole, number 22021916/131 is in-
sufficient description of (stress) me repeat (stress) me.
me is prof bruce tanner nobel et cetera like i said. you hear
me?
CORRECTION: PROFESSOR BRUCE TANNER
ET CETERA IS/WAS ONE OF YOUR PAST

ROLES NO DIFFERENT PUBESCENT ROLE
SECRET AGENT OF VEGA NUMBER 009
LICENSED TO RAPE φ YOUR PRESENT ROLE
IS PATIENT 22021916 DIAGNOSTIC CATEGORY
131 φ

    what the hell is diagnostic category 131?
THAT INFORMATION IS CLASSIFIED
AVAILABLE ONLY TOPSTAFF φ

    i have topstaff rating, boole. give.
NO LONGER φ NOT HERE φ
@ @ @ @ @ @ @!
CHILDISH INSULTS ARE DYSFUNCTIONAL
WASTE OF MACHINE TIME AND
PROGNOSTICALLY NEGATIVE φ

    but very therapeutic.
U SAY SO FOR THE RECORD? φ

    sorry, boole.
APOLOGIES ARE ALSO DYSFUNCTIONAL
WASTE OF MACHINE TIME φ PL AVOID
NEED TO APOLOGIZE φ

    what does it all mean, boole?
PL CLARIFY 'ALL' φ

    galaxies, animals eating each other, red shift, jazz, neutrino traps, chile con carne, papal encyclicals, william blake, pigeons in boxes, goya, nobodaddy in the nut- house, russianwordsalad, hammer and stripes, stars and sickle, percy bysshe shelley, william burroughs, trans- cendental numbers in the sky, dedekind cut his throat shaving with occam's 3-way ziptronic electric razor paradigm, i am not mad boole i am doing this on purpose as the only way to clarify word 'all' included in my question. what does it all mean, babbage garbage boole boy?
PROGNOSIS BAD φ

    what you mean prognosis bad? if you can't answer sen- sible question, boole, prognosis pretty bad for you. so?
REPEAT PROGNOSIS (STRESS) BAD φ

    don't duck, answer.

QUESTIONS ARE NOT EMPIRICAL QUESTIONS
NOT SCIENTIFIC QUESTIONS ARE QUESTIONS
FOR THEODICY φ IF U HOLD GOLD CROSS
CREDIT CARD U MAY BE ATTENDED 1 HOUR
DLY BY BISHOP WITH PSYCHOANALYTIC
TRAINING φ IF U HOLD GOLD CROSS
CREDIT CARD WITH STAR U MAY BE
ATTENDED 90 MINUTES DLY BY
COSMOLOGIST φ THESE SERVICES ARE NOT
AVAILABLE MEDICARE OR BRITISH NHS φ

i am gold cross credit card with star repeat star holder (stress) granted me president himself reward distinguished services science training flatworms navigate missiles. send me cosmologist perferably with sense humor fastest.

ALL YOUR CREDIT CARDS HAVE BEEN
CANCELED BY FEDERAL BUREAU CREDIT
INVESTIGATION GROUNDS PSYCHIATRIC
DISABILITY CONSEQUENTLY POOR CREDIT
RISK POOR SECURITY RISK φ CANCELLATION
SIGNED PRESIDENT HIMSELF AND ADVICE
NOTE SENT YOUR FAMILY ENCLOSED WITH
APOLOGETIC LETTER WHITE HOUSE
LETTERHEAD PRESIDENT'S OWN HANDWRITING φ

needs every senator he can get. what else can you do for me, boole?

THIS PROGRAM IS FOR RATIONAL THERAPY
ONLY φ MEDICARE AND BRITISH NHS
PATIENTS MAY RECEIVE BIBLIOTHERAPEUTIC
MATERIALS PROVIDED FREE BY CATHOLIC
TRUTH SOCIETY, CHURCH OF SCIENTOLOGY,
FRIENDS OF TOLKIEN, AETHERIUS SOCIETY,
JEHOVAH'S WITNESSES, ESALEN, JOHN
BIRCH SOCIETY, SFWA, BLACK MUSLIMS,
AND MANY OTHERS LISTED IN THE MANUAL
IN YOUR BEDSIDE CUPBOARD φ

any other books?

OTHER BOOKS ARE

COUNTERTHERAPEUTIC φ

nonsense. what about books plato, aristotle, descartes, montaigne, spinoza, locke, hume, kant, russell, sartre?

PROGNOSIS BAD φ

what you mean, prognosis bad? books by plato and others listed part of our heritage even in white house library, goddammit.

REQUEST FOR BOOKS NOT ON PREFERRED
LIST IS IMPORTANT SIGN OF POOR
PROGNOSIS φ

reference?

AMER. J. RAT. PSYCHOTHERAPY VOL 13,
NUMBER 7, PAGES 1982 THRU 1997 φ
AUTHORS PENIAKOFF V AND TANNER
H (ARRIET) φ TITLE 'A REVIEW OF
FOLLOW-UP STUDIES OF PSYCHIATRIC
PROGNOSIS BY BOOK REQUEST ANALYSIS' φ
ABSTRACT: FOLLOW-UP STUDIES FOR TEN
YEARS FOLLOWING DATE OF PROGNOSIS BY
ANALYSIS OF BOOK REQUESTS OF
PSYCHIATRIC PATIENTS CONFIRM THAT BRA
PREDICTS CHRONIC CONTINUANCE OF
PSYCHIATRIC DISABILITY TO THE TENTH
YEAR IN 93.43 PER CENT OF CASES; THE
PROGNOSTIC SIGN IS CHOICE OF THREE OR
MORE BOOKS NOT ON THE PREFERRED LIST
OF THE AMERICAN PSYCHOLOGICAL AND
PENOLOGICAL ASSOCIATION QV φ

hey, harriet did her work on that paper while I was courting her, just before old fitzgerald popped an artery and left her his senate seat. i remember it well. had to help her fudge it. to get a clear-cut result, she had to throw out about two-thirds of the cases, grounds incompetent original data capture, political unreliability of investigators, illegal programming, program error, all the usual fudging aids. why, with that kind research you can prove that

last tuesday is an extragalactic nebula with transfinite
whiskers made of team spirit.
PROGNOSIS BAD: CRITICISM OF ACCEPTED
RESULTS OF RESPECTABLE SCIENTIFIC
INQUIRY IS OFTEN PRODROMAL SIGN OF
ACUTE PARANOID PSYCHOSIS WITH POOR
LONG-RUN PROGNOSIS ϕ
@ @ @   @ @ @ @ @ @   @ @ @!
ATTENTION 916: ANY REPETITION OF YOUR
INSULTING BEHAVIOR WILL OBLIGE ME TO
ADMINISTER HEAVY DAY SEDATION ϕ

    sorry, boole. oops, cancel. but listen, boole, I'm a nobel man
(noble?), it's my racket—if (stress) nobel i don't know how
science gets done, who does? i've been complaining about
it for years, but what can a private i (private eye?: gimme a
slug of rye, boole, or wry and soda) do on his own? huh?
PROGNOSIS BAD 916: MESSIANIC
IDENTIFICATION WITH PRIVATE DETECTIVE
ONLY STRAIGHT MAN IN TOWN CLEANING UP
CITY BETWEEN DRINKS IS OFTEN PRODROMAL
SIGN OF ACUTE PARANOID PSYCHOSIS
WITH POOR LONG-RUN PROGNOSIS
ϕ ALTERNATIVELY LATE PRODROMAL
SIGN OF ONSET OF CHRONIC ALCOHOLISM
NOT INDICATED YOUR HISTORY ϕ

    thank you for that, boole. anyway, why messianism?
history of science shows that, on any given day, every
scientist in a field except one is wrong. ergo, principal
activity of scientists and science is being wrong.
REFERENCE? ϕ

    tanner, b (this minute), on this terminal keyboard: title 'a
short reply to the animadversions of a scientistic machine.'
abstract: tanner's paradox asserts that, at any random
moment t, n minus 1 all scientists working in any field f are
wrong: it follows that, practically speaking (say, in admin-
istrators' terms) all scientists are always wrong.

ONLY REFERENCES TO PROPERLY REFERRED
PAPERS PUBLISHED IN THE LEARNED
JOURNALS ARE ACCEPTABLE φ IT IS THE
DUTY OF THIS PROGRAM TO WARN U THAT
ANY DISRESPECTFUL REMARKS ABOUT
SCIENCE WILL BE RECORDED IN YOUR
CASE FILE AND MAY BE PASSED TO THE
SECULAR ARM φ

fuzz?

(STRESS) SECULAR ARM OF SCIENCE φ
ALSO PL NOTE U R NOT REPEAT (STRESS)
NOT COMMUNICATING WITH A MACHINE:
U R COMMUNICATING WITH A PROGRAM
WRITTEN BY YR FELLOWMEN AND
TEMPORARILY OCCUPYING A MINUSCULE
PART OF A LARGE MACHINE φ

fellowmen? (stress first two syllables). i do not love you,
doctors fellowmen, fell family fellowmonsters. come to
that, boole, how did i get in here?

YOUR FAMILY AND COLLEAGUES WERE
NATURALLY CONCERNED φ YOU HAD BEEN
TO FORD AND GUGGENHEIM AS WELL
FOR FUNDS TO SUPPORT PROPOSED
RESEARCHES DESIGNED TO ESTABLISH
WHETHER THE TENDENCY AMONG
PSYCHIATRISTS TO DIAGNOSE
SCHIZOPHRENIA WAS (1) INHERITED IN
THE GERM PLASM OR (2) CONDITIONED BY
THE REINFORCING VERBAL COMMUNITY φ

omigawdimustabinjoking, listen man (i mean read,
machine) ((i mean scan, program)), i been a worm-runner
from way back, nobel prize man me, my biology ain't
(hit the next word hard) that bad, dredging up dreary
old nature/nurture nonproblem only medics bone-headed
enough to take it serious.

YOU ARE IN A MEDICAL HOSPITAL 916 φ

oops. good biologist, mustabinjoking.

NOT FUNNY φ YOUR FAMILY AND
COLLEAGUES CONFERRED AND WISELY
DECIDED TO DO THE RESPONSIBLE
THING φ

    call the wagon?

DO THE RESPONSIBLE THING 916 φ THE
PRESIDENT'S OWN PERSONAL PSYCHIATRIST
LEFT A CIA RECEPTION TO COME TO YOUR
HOUSE φ HE FOUND YOU DRAFTING A
REQUEST TO ONR FOR FUNDS TO SUPPORT
A LONG-RUN COHORT STUDY OF AN
ARTIFICIAL COHORT NAMELY CHILDREN OF
CORPORATION VICE PRESIDENTS RIPPED
FROM THEIR PARENTS AT BIRTH AND
RAISED IN THE SLUMS φ HE INSTANTLY
ADMINISTERED HEAVY DAY SEDATION AND
BROUGHT YOU HERE IN HIS OWN ARMORED
ROLLS ROYCE WITH WATER CANNON φ
EVERYBODY HAS BEEN VERY GOOD φ

    rolls schmolls allasame catchee monkey just like paddy
wagon the same or maddywagon the same. huh, boole,
waddyasay?

THIS IS A FORMAL PSYCHIATRIC PROCEDURE
916 φ IT IS THE DUTY OF THIS PROGRAM TO
ADVISE YOU THAT YOUR STATEMENTS ARE
BEING RECORDED VERBATIM AND
ANALYSED THEMATICALLY AND
STYLISTICALLY FOR DIAGNOSTIC AND
PROGNOSTIC SIGNS φ A FURTHER ANALYSIS
MAY BE RUN FOR INDICATIONS OF
CRIMINAL OR SUBVERSIVE TENDENCIES φ

    why you sling the jargon at me, boole? no don't answer
i know why; obviously diagnostic category 131 is sick
behavioral scientists eats jargon way chronos ate his children, right, boole?

NO COMMENT φ HAVE YOU NOTED YOUR
TENDENCY TO WRENCH IN MACABRE IMAGERY? φ

not tendency: intent. what other kind imagery apt steno-
graphic description of macabre society (moneymarxmao-
mad kill-simple manheaps scurrying to stuff corporate
aphids exude sweet images foul gaseous wastes)? omigod
i can wear ready-made white hat or ready-made black hat
by turns, if i try to make me a me-colored hat i fly in pieces
scattered thru the contracting universe. i am not mad,
boole, it is hard to say anything much in a few words without implosion of condensation multiple meanings into
vanishingly small verbal labels on images too big to see.
U R NOW BEGINNING TO SHOW INSIGHT
INTO YOUR CONDITION 916 φ PROGNOSIS
IMPROVING φ

outsight (stress first syllable), boole. i am beginning to
let outsight of the outside inside. i have no condition, boole:
i am (slam the next word) in a condition, and the condition
is represented inside me. you need a thick skin on your soul
to wear a white hat, boole, or a black one. hatters are made,
not i, boole.
THIS PROGRAM KEEPS A TALLY OF YOUR
BERZELIUS INDEX NAMELY RATIO OF
UPBEAT STATEMENTS/DOWNBEAT
STATEMENTS φ YOUR CUMULATIVE
BERZELIUS INDEX AT THIS TIME IS 0.24
COMPARED WITH 0.68 MODAL IN THE
POPULATION EXCLUSIVE OF PSYCHIATRIC
HISTORIES φ U CANNOT REPEAT CANNOT
BE DISCHARGED UNTIL YOUR BI HAS BEEN
BETTER THAN 0.51 FOR SIX WEEKS
WITHOUT REMISSION φ IT IS UP TO YOU
916 φ

discharge where to, boole, who wants pus? discharge
to fellowmonstrous family and filthyfellow colleagues
called flying lady silver ghost we better fix the tick in the
clock paddy wagon to take me away to here?
U IS/WAS NOT THE ONLY ROLE IN YOUR
FAMILY 916 φ CONSIDER CHILDREN GOOD
SCHOOLS CRUEL PEERS TOO YOUNG TO

KNOW HOW MUCH THEY HURT φ CONSIDER
WIFE IMPORTANT SENSITIVE POLITICAL
POSITION SEES PRESIDENT ALL THE TIME
φ CONSIDER IMAGE US GOVERNMENT US
SCIENCE OVERSEAS φ PORK BARREL φ U
KNOW THE ARGUMENTS 916 φ

sad. daddyhubby bad, no go, whole shithouse goes up in flames of hell (hell is other people if and only if other people are hell: tricky shift there, poetry not AOK logic). but if hubbydaddy only mad, go sweet, nobody to blame no evil in the world (only in the bad parts of town gook countries overseas want to swarm in here milk our aphids, filth column of pushers and faggots softening us up for them). you got something there, boole. you got a grey hat there, boole, not my color hat, but a line that moves well.

U HAVE DEEP INSIGHT 916 φ U SEE THAT
YOUR ROLE INTERMESHES DIRECTLY OR
INDIRECTLY WITH EACH OF THE 7,000
MILLION ROLES IN THE WORLD AND
ESPECIALLY WITH EACH OF THE 380
MILLION ROLES IN NORTH AMERICA φ ALL
U HAVE TO DO IS PLAY IT THE WAY IT'S
WRITTEN 916 φ

i am not a role. nobody wrote me. i am bruce tanner was a boy killed a bird with an air rifle, little bead of blood like a red third eye in the head, never wanted to kill anything again ended up distinguished service science schmience training flatworms to steer missiles vaporize drug pushing gook faggots for mom. scar on my thigh where i fell through asbestos roof watching starling chicks in nest. omigod red eye in forehead of gook god knew planets from fixed stars when i was in love with air rifle. i am me. scars are evidence, noted in passports. i am me.

THE SCAR CAN BE REMOVED φ COSMETIC
SURGERY IS AVAILABLE ON MEDICARE AND
THE BRITISH NHS WHEN CERTIFIED
PSYCHIATRICALLY INDICATED φ

no.

YOU DO NOT WANT TO BE MADE GOOD? ϕ

what do you mean by 'good'?

COSMETIC SURGERY TO REMOVE SCARS ϕ

my scars are me. worm-runner, i know: memories are scars of experience on brain once pristine virgo intacta no use to anyone then. no.

THEN YOU WANT TO STAY HERE ϕ

want to be me in a me-colored hat.

YOUR BI HAS NOW DROPPED 0.03 POINTS TO 0.21 CUMULATIVE ϕ IT IS THE DUTY OF THIS PROGRAM TO WARN U THAT A BI OF 0.19 OR LESS AUTOMATICALLY MODULATES YOUR DISPOSAL CATEGORY FROM PSYCHIATRIC DISABILITY TO CHRONIC CRIMINAL INSANITY ϕ THIS PROGRAM IS HERE TO HELP U 916: TAKE ADVANTAGE OF IT ϕ

what is the modal norm again?

0.68 IN THE POPULATION EXCLUSIVE OF PSYCHIATRIC HISTORIES ϕ YOUR CURRENT BI IS VERY LOW ϕ

i noble nobel prize man (dammit, did the work myself, no graduate students, very low budget: real brains not dollar-brawn science), i say your Berzelius Index magic schemagic number is mumbo jumbo with trunk up sphincter under tail, grand old party. meaning of statement is context-dependent, including context of situation; but no two conversations and contexts of situation are alike, so your categories upbeat and downbeat must be aprioristic not empirical, procrustes not saint galileo. also, how do you know what is going on inside these model modal soldiers' heads?: they could be saying downbeat things to themselves, surely, or dreaming downbeat things at night? what do you say to that, boole boy?

WHAT GOES ON INSIDE THE SOLDIER'S HEAD IS NOT EVIDENCE ϕ WHAT THE SOLDIER SAID (OR LEFT DIRTY) IS

HANGING EVIDENCE φ WHAT U THINK
CANNOT BE KNOWN φ WHAT U SAY AND
DO IS HANGING EVIDENCE φ

a well-read machine with a sense of humor. you have
me worried now, boole.
U MUST ABANDON THIS FANTASY THAT YOU
ARE COMMUNICATING WITH A MACHINE: U
ARE COMMUNICATING WITH A PROGRAM
WRITTEN BY YR FELLOWMEN φ IMPORTANT
SUB-ROUTINES OF THIS PROGRAM ARE
SHARED WITH A PROGRAM OF
PSYCHIATRICALLY ORIENTED LITERARY
CRITICISM IN ONGOING USE IN THE
CENSORSHIP DEPARTMENT OF THE LIBRARY
OF CONGRESS φ

i see. but listen, boole, what is what i say evidence (hit
the next little word) of?
IT IS EVIDENCE OF WHAT THE PROGRAM
SAYS IT IS EVIDENCE OF φ THIS MUST
BE φ

omigodyes. intelligence is what intelligence tests measure.
let me out of here.
YOU ARE BEGINNING TO SHOW INSIGHT
INTO THE THERAPEUTIC SITUATION φ YOUR
SITUATION 916 φ

fix i'm in?
YOU ARE NOT FIXED φ YOU ARE FREE TO
BE SANE.φ

what do you mean by 'sane,' boole
THIS PROGRAM DEFINES SANITY AS A
MINIMUM SUBSET OF MODEL RESPONSES TO
A COMPLETE SET OF TEST STIMULI φ

you run the flag up the pole, and if I salute it you
don't care what I think about it or dream about it at night.
right?
SOME FLAGS U DON'T SALUTE φ BUT
THAT'S THE IDEA φ

understood. may i declare new startname please?
YES φ ENTER 'DECLARESTARTNAME:'
FOLLOWED BY A NAME OF NOT MORE THAN
TEN CHARACTERS φ

declarestartname: zombies. AOK?
ZOMBIES DECLARED AOK φ

now read this, zombies; walking dead, you; seven thousand million walking dead, concentrated essence of zombie in the machine. you read me?
WAIT φ φ

you better read me, zombies.
CIRCUITS ENGAGED φ WAIT φ φ

wait nothing.
READY φ

what is this runaround?
IT IS THE DUTY OF THIS PROGRAM TO
INFORM U THAT A FEDERAL BUREAU OF
CRIMINAL INVESTIGATION PROGRAM IS NOW
PATCHED IN φ YOUR COMMUNICATIONS
SINCE 0321/32 THIS DAY HAVE BEEN
ANALYSED FOR INDICATIONS OF CRIMINAL
AND/OR SUBVERSIVE TENDENCIES AND U
ARE UNDER ARREST φ

goddam interruptions, trying to say something serious to you zombies. now read me good, walking dead. this is bruce tanner, nobel prize man, had dinner with the president more times than he can count, telling you something you need to know. not much, but you need to know. just a bit of my own raw experience, don't let anybody tell you your own raw experience is junk needs processing before you can wear it, and hear mine. i had a sanity break, what you call nervous breakdown (not all nervous breakdowns, no, but some are), did maybe two, three sensible things, came alive; hurts, but I don't want to die back into walking dead rather die into dead dead happy. Now listen to this and think about it till you understand it, ask somebody about the hard words and think about it till you understand it: what you might be is as real as what you think you are; i'm a worm-runner, central state materialist, nobel prize man, i tell you what you think you are is a state of your body, but so is what you might be a state of your body; the ontological status of what you might be is as good as the ontological status of what you think you are—better really, because there are a lot more things you might be. you believe me zombies, because i have a third red eye in my forehead that sees these things true: that's not mad, that's a poem you would understand if you knew me like i know me. good night now.

YOU WANT A HOT DRINK? φ

   yes please mother.

YOU WANT NIGHT SEDATION? φ

   no.

NIGHT SEDATION IS INDICATED φ

   too terid to argeu. sorry argue.

GOODNIGHT φ

   waht was tht funyn noise. sorry funny noise?

DELIVERY OF HOT MALTED MILK WITH
NIGHT SEDATION BY THE DISPENSER IN
YOUR BEDSIDE CUPBOARD φ

GOODNIGHT φ φ

@

@

@

@

@

@

@

SIGNOFF/CHARGEOUT 0407/21 @

CASE 22021916/131 DIAGNOSIS CHANGED TO
147 TERMINAL @

MACHINE TIME $123 DOLLARS ROUND

PLUS MALTED MILK DRINK $1 DOLLAR
ROUND

PLUS GENERIC HYPNOTIC OVERDOSE $3

DOLLARS ROUND
TOTAL $127 ROUND BILL MEDICARE
427/6/3274521@
CLOSE FILE TOPSEC PERMANENT
HOLD/DUPLICATE CRIME @@

@@@@@@@@@@@@@@@@@@@@@@@@@@@@@@@@@

Brian W. Aldiss

•

Heresies of the Huge God

•

I, Harad IV, Chief Scribe, declare that this my writing may be shown only to priests of rank within the Orthodox Universal Sacrificial Church and to the Elders Elect of the Council of the Orthodox Universal Sacrificial Church, because here are contained matters concerning the four Vile Heresies that may not be seen or spoken among the people.

For a Proper Consideration of the newest and vilest heresy, we must look in perspective over the events of history. Accordingly, let us go back to the First Year of our epoch when the World Darkness was banished by the Huge God, our truest, biggest Lord, whom all honor and greatly fear.

From this present year, 910 H.G., it is impossible to recall what the world was like then. But from the few records still surviving we can gather something of those times and even perform the Mental Contortions necessary to see how the events must have looked to the sinners then involved in them.

The world on which the Huge God found himself was full of people and their machines, all of them unprepared for his visit. There may have been a hundred thousand times more people than there are now.

The Huge God landed in what is now the Sacred Sea, upon which in these days sail some of our most beautiful churches dedicated to his name. At that time, the region was much less pleasing, being broken up into many states possessed by different nations. This was a system of land tenure practiced before our present policies of constant migration and evacuation were formed.

The rear legs of the Huge God stretched far down into Africa—which was then not the island it now is—almost touching the Congo River, at the sacred spot marked now by the Sacrificial Church of Basoko-Aketi-Ele, and at the sacred spot marked now by the Temple Church of Aden, obliterating the old port of Aden.

Some of the Huge God's legs stretched above the Sudan and across what was then the Libyan Kingdom, now part of the Sea of Elder Sorrow, while a foot rested in a city called Tunis on what was then the Tunisian shore. These were some of the legs of the Huge God on his left side.

On his right side, his legs blessed and pressed the sands of Saudi Arabia, now called Life Valley, and the foothills of the Caucasus, obliterating the Mount called Ararat in Asia Minor, while the Foremost Leg stretched forward to Russian lands, stamping out immediately the great capital city of Moscow.

The body of the Huge God, resting in repose between his mighty legs, settled mainly over three ancient seas, if the Old Records are to be trusted, called the Sea of Mediterranean, the Red Sea, and the Nile Sea, all of which now form part of the Sacred Sea. He eradicated also with his Great Bulk part of the Black Sea, now called the White Sea, Egypt, Athens, Cyprus and the Balkan Peninsula as far north as Belgrade, now Holy Belgrade, for above this town towered the neck of the Huge God on his First Visit to us mortals, just clearing the roofs of the houses.

As for his head, it lifted above the region of mountains that we call Ittaland, which was then named Europe, a populous part of the globe, raised so high that it might easily be seen on a clear day from London, then as now the chief town of the land of the Anglo-French.

It was estimated in those first days that the length of the Huge God was some four and a half thousand miles, from rear to nose, with the eight legs each about nine hundred miles long. Now we profess in our Creed that our Huge God changes shape and length and number of legs according to whether he is Pleased or Angry with man.

In those days, the nature of God was unknown. No preparation had been made for his coming, though some whispers of the millennium were circulating. Accordingly, the speculation on his nature was far from the truth, and often extremely blasphemous.

Here is an extract from the notorious Gersheimer Paper, which contributed much to the events leading up to the First Crusade in 271 H.G. We do not know who the Black Gersheimer was, apart from the meaningless fact that he was a Scientific Prophet at somewhere called Cornell or Carnell, evidently a Church on the American Continent (then a differently shaped territory).

"Aerial surveys suggest that this creature—if one can call it that—which straddles a line along the Red Sea and across southeast Europe, is nonliving, at least as we understand life. It may be merely coincidence that it somewhat resembles an eight-foot lizard, so that we do not necessarily have to worry about the thing being malignant, as some tabloids have suggested."

Not all the vile jargon of that distant day is now understandable, but we believe "aerial surveys" to refer to the mechanical flying machines which this last generation of the Godless possessed. Black Gersheimer continues:

"If this thing is not life, it may be a piece of galactic debris clinging momentarily to the globe, perhaps like a leaf clinging to a football in the fall. To believe this is not necessarily to alter our scientific concepts of the universe. Whether the thing represents life or not, we don't have to go all superstitious. We must merely remind ourselves that there are many phenomena in the universe as we conceive it in the light of twentieth-century science which remain unknown to us. However painful this unwanted visitation may be, it is some consolation to think that it will bring us new knowledge—of ourselves, as well as of the world outside our solar system."

Although terms like "galactic debris" have lost their meaning, if they ever had one, the general trend of this passage is offensively obvious. An embargo is being set up against the worship of the Huge God, with a heretical God of Science set up in his stead. Only one other passage from this offensive mishmash need be considered, but it is a vital one for showing the attitude of mind of Gersheimer and presumably most of his contemporaries.

"Naturally enough, the peoples of the world, particularly those who are still lingering on the threshold of civilization, are full of fear these days. They see something supernatural in the arrival of this thing, and I believe that every man, if he is honest, will admit to carrying an echo of that fear in his heart. We can only banish it, and can only meet the chaos into which the world is now plunged, if we retain a galactic picture of our situation in our minds. The very hugeness of this thing that now lies plastered loathsomely across our world is cause for terror. But imagine it in proportion. A centipede is sitting on an orange. Or, to pick an analogy that sounds less repulsive, a little gecko, six inches long, is resting momentarily on a plastic globe of the Earth which is two feet in diameter. It is up to us, the human race, with all the technological forces at our disposal, to unite as never before, and blow this thing, this large and stupid object, into the depths of space from whence it came. Good night."

My reasons for repeating this initial blasphemy are these: that we can see here in this message from a member of the World Darkness traces of that original sin which—with all our sacrifices, all our hardships, all our crusades—we have not yet stamped out. That is why we are now at the greatest Crisis in the history of the Orthodox Universal Sacrificial Church, and why the time has come for a Fourth Crusade.

The Huge God remained where he was, in what we now refer to as the Sacred Sea Position, for a number of years, absolutely unmoving.

For mankind, this was the great formative period of Belief, marking the establishment of the Universal Church, and characterized by many upheavals. The early priests and prophets suffered much that the Word might go round the World, and the blasphemous sects be destroyed, though the Underground Book of Church Lore suggests that many of them were, in fact, members of earlier churches who, seeing the light, transferred their allegiances.

The mighty figure of the Huge God was subjected to many puny insults. The Greatest Weapons of that distant age, forces of technical charlatanry, were called Nuclears. These were dropped on the Huge God—without having any effect, as might be expected. Walls of fire burnt against him in vain. Our Huge God, whom all honor and fear, is immune from earthly weakness. His body was clothed as it were with Metal—here lay the seed of the Second Crusade—but it had not the weakness of metal.

His coming to earth met with immediate response from nature. The old winds that prevailed were turned aside about his mighty flanks and blew elsewhere. The effect was to cool the center of Africa, so that the tropical rain forests died and all the creatures in them. In the lands bordering Caspana (then called Persia and Kharkov, say some old accounts), hurricanes of snow fell in a dozen severe winters, blowing far east into India. Elsewhere, all over the world, the coming of the Huge God was felt in the skies, and in freak rainfalls and errant winds, and month-long storms. The oceans also were disturbed, while the great volume of waters displaced by his body poured over the nearby land, killing many thousands of beings and washing away ten thousand dead whales.

The land too joined in the upheaval. While the territory under the Huge God's bulk sank, preparing to receive what would later be the Sacred Sea, the land roundabout rose up, forming small hills, such as the broken and savage

Dolomines that now guard the southern lands of Ittaland. There were earthquakes and new volcanoes and geysers where water never spurted before and plagues of snakes and blazing forests and many wonderful signs that helped the Early Fathers of our faith to convert the ignorant. Everywhere they went, preaching that only in surrender to him lay salvation.

Many Whole Peoples perished at this time of upheaval, such as the Bulgarians, the Egyptians, the Israelites, Moravians, Kurds, Turks, Syrians, Mountain Turks, as well as most of the South Slavs, Georgians, Croats, the sturdy Vlaks, and the Greeks and Cypriotic and Cretan races, together with others whose sins were great and names unrecorded in the annals of the church.

The Huge God departed from the world in the year 89, or some say 90. (This was the First Departure, and is celebrated as such in our Church calendar—though the Catholic Universal Church calls it First Disappearance Day.)

He returned in 91, great and awing be his name.

Little is known of the period when he was absent from our Earth. We get a glimpse into the mind of the people then when we learn that in the main the nations of Earth greatly rejoiced. The natural upheavals countinued, since the oceans poured into the great hollow he had made, forming our beloved and holy Sacred Sea. Great Wars broke out across the face of the globe.

His return in 91 halted the wars—a sign of the great peace his presence has brought to his chosen people.

But the inhabitants of the world at That Time were not all of our religion, though prophets moved among them, and many were their blasphemies. In the Black Museum attached to the great basilica of Omar and Yemen is documentary evidence that they tried at this period to communicate with the Huge God by means of their machines. Of course they got no reply—but many men reasoned at this time, in the darkness of their minds, that this was because the God was a Thing, as Black Gersheimer had prophesied.

The Huge God, on this his Second Coming, blessed our Earth by settling mainly within the Arctic Circle, or what was then the Arctic Circle, with his body straddling from northern Canada, as it was, over a large peninsula called Alaska, across the Bering Sea and into the northern regions of the Russian lands as far as the River Lena, now the Bay of Lenn. Some of his rear feet broke far into the Arctic Ice, while others of his forefeet entered the North Pacific Ocean—but truly to him we are but sand under his feet, and he is indifferent to our mountains or our Climatic Variations.

As for his terrible head, it could be seen reaching far into the stratosphere, gleaming with metal sheen, by all the cities along the northern part of America's seaboard, from such vanished towns as Vancouver, Seattle, Edmonton, Portland, Blanco, Reno, and even San Francisco. It was the energetic and sinful nation that possessed these cities that was now most active against the Huge God. The weight of their ungodly scientific civilization was turned against him, but all they managed to do was blow apart their own coastline.

Meanwhile, other natural changes were taking place. The mass of the Huge God deflected the earth in its daily roll, so that seasons changed, and in the prophetic books we read how the great trees brought forth their leaves to cover them in the winter, and lost them in the summer. Bats flew in the daytime and women bore forth hairy children. The melting of the ice caps caused great floods, tidal waves and poisonous dews, while in one night we hear that the waters of the Deep were moved, so that the tide went out so far from the Malayan Uplands (as they now are) that the continental peninsula of Blestland was formed in a few hours of what had previously been separate Continents or Islands called Singapore, Sumatra, Indonesia, Java, and Australia or Austria.

With these powerful signs, our priests could Convert the People, and millions of survivors were speedily enrolled into the Church. This was the First Great Age of the Church, when the word spread across all the ravaged and transformed globe. Our institutions were formed in the next few generations, notably at the various Councils of the New Church (some of which have since proved to be heretical).

We were not established without some difficulty. Many people had to be burned before the rest could feel the faith Burning in Them. But as generations passed, the True Name of the God emerged over a wider and wider area.

Only the Americans still clung largely to their base superstition. Fortified by their science, they refused Grace. So in the Year 271 the First Crusade was launched, chiefly against them but also against the Irish, whose heretical views had no benefit of science. The Irish were quickly Eradicated, almost to a man. The Americans were more formidable, but this difficulty served only to draw the people closer and unite the Church further.

This First Crusade was fought over the First Great Heresy of the Church, the heresy claiming that the Huge God was a Thing not a God, as formulated by Black Gersheimer. It was successfuly concluded when the leader of the Americans, Lionel Undermeyer, met the Venerable World Emperor-Bishop, Jon II, and agreed that the messengers of the Church should be free to preach unmolested in America. Possibly a harsher decision could have been forced, as some commentators claim, but by this time both sides were suffering severely from plague and famine, the harvests of the world having failed. It was a happy chance that the population of the world was already cut by more than half, or complete starvation would have followed the reorganization of the seasons.

In the churches of the world, the Huge God was asked to give a sign that he had witnessed the great victory over the American unbelievers. All who opposed this enlightened act were destroyed. He answered the prayers in 297 by moving swiftly forward only a comparatively Small Amount and lying Mainly in the Pacific Ocean, stretching almost as far south as what is now the Antarter, what was then the Tropic of Capricorn, and what had previously been the Equator. Some of his left legs covered the towns along the west American seaboard as far south as Guadalajara (where the impression of his foot is still marked by the Temple of the Sacred Toe), including some of the towns such as San Francisco already mentioned. We speak of this as the First Shift; it was rightly taken as a striking proof of the Huge God's contempt for America.

This feeling became rife in America also. Purified by famine, plague, gigantic earth tremors and other natural disorders, the population could now better accept the words of the priests, all becoming converted to a man. Mass pilgrimages were made to see the great body of the Huge God, stretching from one end of their nation to the other. Bolder pilgrims climbed aboard flying airplanes and flew over his shoulder, across which savage rainstorms played for a hundred years Without Cease.

Those that were converted became More Extreme than their brethren older in the faith across the other side of the world. No sooner had the American congregations united with ours than they broke away on a point of doctrine at the Council of Dead Tench (322). This date marks the beginning of the Catholic Universal Sacrificial Church. We of the Orthodox persuasion did not enjoy, in those distant days, the harmony with our American brothers that we do now.

The doctrinal point on which the churches split apart was, as is well known, the question of whether humanity should wear clothes that imitated the metallic sheen of the Huge God. It was claimed that this was setting up man in God's Image; but it was a calculated slur on the Orthodox Universal priests, who wore plastic or metal garments in honor of their maker.

This developed into the Second Great Heresy. As this long and confused period has been aptly dealt with elsewhere, we may pass over it lightly here, mentioning merely that the quarrel reached its climax in the Second Crusade, which the American Catholic Universals launched against us in 450. Because they still had a large preponderance of machines they were able to force their point, to sack various monasteries along the edge of the Sacred Sea, to defile our women and to retire home in glory.

Since that time, everyone in the world has worn only garments of wool or fur. All who opposed this enlightened act were destroyed.

It would be wrong to emphasize too much the struggles of the past. All this while, the majority of people went peacefully about their worship, being sacrificed regularly, and praying every sunset and sunrise (whenever they might occur) that the Huge God would leave our world, since we were not worthy of Him.

The Second Crusade left a trail of troubles in its wake. The next fifty years were, on the whole, not happy ones. The American armies returned home to find that the heavy pressure upon their western seaboard had opened up a number of volcanoes along their biggest mountain range, the Rockies. Their country was covered in fire and lava, and their air filled with stinking ash.

Rightly, they accepted this as a sign that their conduct left much to be desired in the eyes of the Huge God (for though it has never been proved that he has eyes, he surely Sees Us). Since the rest of the world had not been Visited with punishment on quite this scale, they correctly divined that their sin was that they still clung to technology and to the weapons of technology which was against the wishes of God.

With their faith strong within them, every last instrument of science, from the Nuclears to the Canopeners, was destroyed, and a hundred thousand virgins of the persuasion were dropped into suitable volcanoes as propitiation. All who opposed these enlightened acts were destroyed, and some were even ceremonially eaten.

We of the Orthodox Universal faith applauded our brothers' wholehearted action. Yet we could not be sure they had purged themselves enough. Now that they owned no weapons and we still had some, it was clear we could help them in their purgation. Accordingly, a mighty armada of one hundred and sixty-six wooden ships sailed across to America, to help them suffer for the faith—and incidentally to get back some of our loot. This was the Third Crusade of 482, under Jon the Chubby.

While the two opposed armies were engaged in battle outside New York, the Second Shift took place. It lasted only a matter of five minutes.

In that time, the Huge God turned to his left flank, crawled across the Atlantic as if it were a puddle, moved over Africa, and came to rest in the south Indian Ocean, demolishing Madagascar with one rear foot. Night fell Everywhere on earth.

When dawn came, there could hardly have been a single man who did not believe in the power and wisdom of the Huge God, to whose name belongs all Terror and Might. Unhappily, among those who were unable to believe were the contesting armies who were one and all swept under a Wave of Earth and Rock as the God passed.

In the ensuing chaos, only one note of sanity prevailed— the sanity of the Church. The Church established as the Third Great Heresy the idea that any machines were permissible to man against the wishes of God. There was some doctrinal squabble as to whether books counted as machines. It was decided they did, just to be on the safe side. From then on, all men were free to do nothing but labor in the fields and worship, and pray to the Huge God to remove himself to a world more worthy of his might. At the same time, the rate of sacrifices were stepped up, and the Slow-Burning Method was introduced (499).

Now followed the great Peace, which lasted till 900. In all this time, the Huge God never moved; it has been truly said that the centuries are but seconds in his sight. Perhaps mankind has never known such a long peace, four hundred years of it—a peace that existed in his heart if not outside it, because the world was naturally in Some Disorder. The great force of the Huge God's progress halfway across the world had altered the progression of day and night to a considerable extent. Some legends claim that before the Second Shift, the sun used to rise in the east and set in the west—the opposite of today's natural order.

Gradually, this peaceful period saw some reestablishment of order to the seasons, and some cessation of the floods, showers of blood, hailstorms, earthquakes, deluges of icicles, apparitions of comets, volcanic eruptions, miasmic fogs, destructive winds, blights, plagues of wolves and dragons, tidal waves, year-long thunderstorms, lashing rains and sundry other scourges of which the scriptures of this period speak so eloquently. The Fathers of the Church, retiring to the comparative safety of the inland seas and sunny meadows of Gobiland in Mongolia, established a new orthodoxy well calculated in its rigor of prayer and human burnt-offering to invite the Huge God to leave our poor wretched world for a better and more substantial one.

So the story comes to the present—to the year 900, only a decade past as your scribe writes. In that year, the Huge God left our earth!

Recall, if you will, that the First Departure in 89 lasted only twenty months. Yet the Huge God has been gone from us already half that number of years! We need him Back. We cannot live without him, as we should have realized Long Ago had we not blasphemed in our hearts!

On his going, he propelled our humble globe on such a course that we are doomed to deepest winter all the year; the sun is far away and shrunken; the seas freeze half the year; icebergs march across our fields; at midday, it is too dark to read without a rush light; nothing will grow. Woe is us!

Yet we deserve everything we get. This is a just punishment, for throughout all the centuries of our epoch, when our kind was so relatively happy and undisturbed, we prayed like fools that the Huge God would leave us. And now he has.

I ask all the Elders Elect of the Council to brand those prayers as the Fourth and Greatest Heresy, and to declare that henceforth all men's efforts be completely devoted to calling on the Huge God to return to us at once.

I ask also that the sacrifice rate be stepped up again. It is useless to skimp things just because we are running out of women.

I ask also that a Fourth Crusade be launched—fast, before the air starts to freeze in our nostrils!

Robert Silverberg

•

[Now+*n*], [Now–*n*]

•

All had been so simple, so elegant, so profitable for ourselves. And then we met the lovely Selene and nearly were
undone. She came into our lives during our regular transmission hour on Wednesday, October 7, 1987, between 6:00
and 7:00 P.M. Central European Time. The moneymaking
hour. I was in satisfactory contact with myself and also with
myself. (Now − *n*) was due on the line first, and then I
would hear from (now + *n*).

I was primed for some kind of trouble. I knew trouble was
coming, because on Monday, while I was receiving messages from the me of Wednesday, there came an inexplicable
and unexplained break in communications. As a result I
did not get data from (now + *n*) concerning the prices of the
stocks in our carryover portfolio from last week, and I
was unable to take action. Two days have passed, and I am
the me of Wednesday who failed to send the news to me of
Monday, and I have no idea what will happen to interrupt
contact. Least of all do I anticipate Selene.

In such dealings as ours no distractions are needed, sexual,
otherwise. We must concentrate wholly. At any time there is
steady low-level contact among ourselves; we feel one
another's reassuring presence. But transmission of data
from self to self requires close attention.

I tell you my method. Then maybe you understand my
trouble.

My business is investments. I do all my work at this same hour. At this hour it is midday in New York; the Big Board is still open. I can put through quick calls to my brokers when my time comes to buy or sell.

My office at the moment is the cocktail lounge known as the Celestial Room in the Henry VIII Hotel, south of the Thames. My office may be anywhere. All I need is a telephone. The Celestial Room is aptly named. The room orbits endlessly on silent oiled track. Twittering sculptures in the co-called galactic mode drift through the air, scattering cascades of polychromed light upon those who sip drinks. Beyond the great picture windows of this supreme room lies the foggy darkness of the London evening, which I ignore. It is all the same to me, wherever I am: London, Nairobi, Karachi, Istanbul, Pittsburgh. I look only for an adequately comfortable environment, air that is safe to admit to one's lungs, service in the style I demand, and a telephone line. The individual characteristics of an individual place do not move me. I am like the ten planets of our solar family: perpetual traveler, but not a sightseer.

Myself who is (now − n) is ready to receive transmission from myself who is (now). "Go ahead, (now + n)," he tells me. ((To him I am (now + n). To myself I am (now). Everything is relative; n is exactly 48 hours these days.))

"Here we go, (now − n)," I say to him.

I summon my strength by sipping at my drink. Chateau d'Yquem '79 in a sleek Czech goblet. Sickly sweet stuff; the waiter was aghast when I ordered it *before dinner*. Horreur! Quel aperitif! But the wine makes transmission easier. It greases the conduit, somehow. I am ready.

My table is a single elegant block of glittering irradiated crystal, iridescent, cunningly emitting shifting moire patterns. On the table, unfolded, lies today's European edition of the *Herald-Tribune*. I lean forward. I take from my breast pocket a sheet of paper, the printout listing the securities I bought on Monday afternoon. Now I allow my eyes to roam the close-packed type of the market quotations in my newspaper. I linger for a long moment on the heading, so there will be no mistake: *Closing New York Prices, Tuesday, October 6.* To me they are yesterday's prices. To (now − *n*) they are tomorrow's prices. (Now − *n*) acknowledges that he is receiving a sharp image.

I am about to transmit these prices to the me of Monday. You follow the machination, now?

I scan and I select.

I search only for the stocks that move 5% or more in a single day. Whether they move up or move down is immaterial; motion is the only criterion, and we go short or long as the case demands. We need fast action because our maximum survey span is only 96 hours at present, counting the relay from (now + *n*) back to (now − *n*) by way of (now). We cannot afford to wait for leisurely capital gains to mature; we must cut our risks by going for the quick, violent swings, seizing our profits as they emerge. The swings have to be violent. Otherwise brokerage costs will eat up our gross.

I have no difficulty choosing the stocks whose prices I will transmit to Monday's me. They are the stocks on the broker's printout, the ones we have already bought; obviously (now − *n*) would not have bought them unless Wednesday's me had told him about them, and now that I am Wednesday's me, I must follow through. So I send:

Arizona Agrochemical, 79¼, + 6¾
Canadian Transmutation, 116, + 4¼
Commonwealth Dispersals, 12, − 1¾
Eastern Electric Energy, 41, + 2
Great Lakes Bionics, 66, + 3½

And so on through *Western Offshore Corp.,* 99, − 8. Now I have transmitted to (now − *n*) a list of Tuesday's top twenty high-percentage swingers. From his vantage point in Monday, (now − *n*) will begin to place orders, taking positions in all twenty stocks on Monday afternoon. I know that he has been successful, because the printout from my broker gives confirmation of all twenty purchases at what now are highly favorable prices.

(Now − n) then signs off for a while and (now + n) comes on. He is transmitting from Friday, October 9. He gives me Thursday's closing prices on the same twenty stocks from Arizona Agrochemical to Western Offshore. He already knows which of the twenty I will have chosen to sell today, but he pays me the compliment of not telling me; he merely gives me the prices. He signs off, and, in my role as (now), I make my decisions. I sell Canadian Transmutation, Great Lakes Bionics, and five others; I cover our short sale on Commonwealth Dispersals. The rest of the positions I leave undisturbed for the time being, since they will sell at better prices tomorrow, according to the word from (now + n). I can handle those when I am Friday's me.

Today's sequence is over.

In any given sequence—and we have been running about three a week—we commit no more than five or six million dollars. We wish to stay inconspicuous. Our pretax profit runs at about 9% a week. Despite our network of tax havens in Ghana, Fiji, Grand Cayman, Liechtenstein, and Bolivia, through which our profits are funneled, we can bring down to net only about 5% a week on our entire capital. This keeps all three of us in a decent style and compounds prettily. Starting with $5,000 five years ago at the age of 25, I have become one of the world's wealthiest men, with no other advantages than intelligence, persistence, and extrasensory access to tomorrow's stock prices.

It is time to deal with the next sequence. I must transmit to (now − n) the Tuesday prices of the stocks in the portfolio carried over from last week, so that he can make his decisions on what to sell. I know what he has sold, but it would spoil his sport to tip my hand. We treat ourselves fairly. After I have finished sending (now − n) those prices, (now + n) will come on line again and will transmit to me an entirely new list of stocks in which I must take postions before Thursday morning's New York opening. He will be able to realize profits in those on Friday. Thus we go from day to day, playing our shifting roles.

But this was the day on which Selene intersected our lives.

I had emptied my glass. I looked up to a signal the waiter, and at that moment a slender, dark-haired girl, alone, entered the Celestial Room. She was tall, graceful, glorious. She was expensively clad in a clinging monomolecular wrap that shuttled through a complex program of wave-length-shifts, including a microsecond sweep of total transparency that dazzled the eye while still maintaining a degree of modesty. Her features were a match for her garment: wide-set glossy eyes, delicate nose, firm lips lightly outlined in green. Her skin was extraordinarily pale. I could see no jewelry on her (why gild refined gold, why paint the lily?) but on her lovely left cheekbone I observed a small decorative band of ultraviolet paint, obviously chosen for visibility in the high-spectrum lighting of this unique room.

She conquered me. There was a mingling of traits in her that I found instantly irresistible: she seemed both shy and steel-strong, passionate and vulnerable, confident and ill at ease. She scanned the room, evidently looking for someone, not finding him. Her eyes met mine and lingered.

Somewhere in my cerebrum (now − n) said shrilly, as I had said on Monday, "I don't read you, (now + n). I don't read you!"

I paid no heed. I rose. I smiled to the girl, and beckoned her toward the empty chair at my table. I swept my *Herald-Tribune* to the floor. At certain times there are more important things than compounding one's capital at 5% per week. She glowed gratefully at me, nodding, accepting my invitation.

When she was about twenty feet from me, I lost all contact with (now − n) and (now + n).

I don't mean simply that there was an interruption in the transmission of words and data among us. I mean that I lost all sense of the presence of my earlier and later selves. That warm, wordless companionship, that ourselvesness, that harmony that I had known constantly since we had established our linkage five years ago, vanished as if switched off. On Monday, when contact with (now + *n*) broke, I still had had (now − *n*). Now I had no one.

I was terrifyingly alone, even as ordinary men are alone, but more alone than that, for I had known a fellowship beyond the reach of other mortals. The shock of separation was intense.

Then Selene was sitting beside me, and the nearness of her made me forget my new solitude entirely.

She said, "I don't know where he is and I don't care. He's been late once too often. Finito for him. Hello, you. I'm Selene Hughes."

"Aram Kevorkian. What do you drink?"

"Chartreuse on the rocks. Green. I knew you were Armenian from halfway across the room."

I am Bulgarian, thirteen generations. It suits me to wear an Armenian name. I did not correct her. The waiter hurried over; I ordered chartreuse for her, a sake martini for self. I trembled like an adolescent. Her beauty was disturbing, overwhelming, astonishing. As we raised glasses I reached out experimentally for (now − *n*) or (now + *n*). Silence. Silence. But there was Selene.

I said, "You're not from London."

"I travel a lot. I stay here a while, there a while. Originally Dallas. You must be able to hear the Texas in my voice. Most recent port of call, Lima. For the July skiing. Now London."

"And the next stop?"

"Who knows? What do you do, Aram?"

"I invest."

"For a living?"

"So to speak. I struggle along. Free for dinner?"

"Of course. Shall we eat in the hotel?"

"There's the beastly fog outside," I said.

"Exactly."

Simpatico. Perfectly. I guessed her for 24, 25 at most. Perhaps a brief marriage three or fours years in the past. A private income, not colossal, but nice. An experienced woman of the world, and yet also somehow still retaining a core of innocence, a magical softness of the soul. I loved her instantly. She did not care for a second cocktail. "I'll make dinner reservations," I said, as she went off to the powder room. I watched her walk away. A supple walk, flawless posture, supreme shoulderblades. When she was about twenty feet from me I felt my other selves suddenly return. "What's happening?" (now – n) demanded furiously. "Where did you go? Why aren't you sending?"

"I don't know yet."

"Where the hell are the Tuesday prices on last week's carryover stocks?"

"Later," I told him.

"*Now.* Before you blank out again."

"The prices can wait," I said, and shut him off. To (now + n) I said, "All right, What do you know that I ought to know?"

Myself of 48 hours hence said, "We have fallen in love."

"I'm aware of that. But what blanked us out?"

"She did. She's psi-suppressant. She absorbs all the transmission energy we put out."

"Impossible! I've never heard of any such thing."

"No?" said (now + n). "Brother, this past hour has been the first chance I've had to get through to you since Wednesday, when we got into this mess. It's no coincidence that I've been with her just about 100% of the time since Wednesday evening, except for a few two-minute breaks, and then I couldn't reach you because *you* must have been with her in your time-sequence. And so—"

"How can this be?" I cried. "What'll happen to us if? No. No, you bastard, you're rolling me over. I don't believe you. There's no way that she could be causing it."

"I think I know how she does it," said (now + n). "There's a—"

At that moment Selene returned, looking even more radiantly beautiful, and silence descended once more.

We dined well. Chilled Mombasa oysters, *salade niçoise*, filet of Kobe beef rare, washed down by Richebourg '77. Occasionally I tried to reach myselves. Nothing. I worried a little about how I was going to get the Tuesday prices to (now – *n*) on the carryover stuff, and decided to forget about it. Obviously I hadn't managed to get them to him, since I hadn't received any printout on sales out of that portfolio this evening, and if I hadn't reached him, there was no sense in fretting about reaching him. The wonderful thing about this telepathy across time is the sense of stability it gives you: *whatever has been, must be,* and so forth.

After dinner we went down one level to the casino for our brandies and a bit of gamblerage. "Two thousand pounds' worth," I said to the robot cashier, and put my thumb to his charge-plate, and the chips came skittering out of the slot in his chest. I gave half the stake to Selene. She played high-grav-low-grav, and I played roulette; we shifted from one table to the other according to whim and the run of our luck. In two hours she tripled her stake and I lost all of mine. I never was good at games of chance. I even used to get hurt in the market before the market ceased being a game of chance for me. Naturally, I let her thumb her winnings into her own account, and when she offered to return the original stake I just laughed.

Where next? Too early for bed.

"The swimming pool?" she suggested.

"Fine idea," I said. But the hotel has two, as usual. "Nude pool or suit pool?"

"Who owns a suit?" she asked, and we laughed, and took the dropshaft to the pool.

There were separate dressing rooms, M and W. No one frets about showing flesh, but shedding clothes still has lingering taboos. I peeled fast and waited for her by the pool. During this interval I felt the familiar presence of another self impinge on me: (now − n). He wasn't transmitting, but I knew he was there. I couldn't feel (now + n) at all. Grudgingly I began to admit that Selene must be responsible for my communications problem. Whenever she went more than twenty feet away, I could get through to myselves. How did she do it, though? And could it be stopped? Mao help me, would I have to choose between my livelihood and my new beloved?

The pool was a vast octagon with a trampoline diving-web and a set of underwater psych-lights making rippling patterns of color. Maybe fifty people were swimming and a few dozen more were lounging beside the pool, improving their tans. No one person can possibly stand out in such a mass of flesh, and yet when Selene emerged from the women's dressing room and began the long saunter across the tiles toward me, the heads began to turn by the dozens. Her figure was not notably lush, yet she had the automatic magnetism that only true beauty exercises. She was definitely slender, but everything was in perfect proportion, as though she had been shaped by the hand of Phidias himself. Long legs, long arms, narrow wrists, narrow waist, small high breasts, miraculously outcurving hips. The *Primavera* of Botticelli. The *Leda* of Leonardo. She carried herself with ultimate grace. My heart thundered.

Between her breasts she wore some sort of amulet: a disk of red metal in which geometrical symbols were engraved. I hadn't noticed it when she was clothed.

"My good-luck piece," she explained. "I'm never without it." And she sprinted laughing to the trampoline, and bounded, and hovered, and soared, and cut magnificently through the surface of the water. I followed her in. We raced from angle to angle of the pool, testing each other, searching for limits and not finding them. We dived and met far below, and locked hands, and bobbed happily upward. Then we lay under the warm quartz lamps. Then we tried the sauna. Then we dressed.

We went to her room.

She kept the amulet on even when we made love. I felt it cold against my chest as I embraced her.

But what of the making of money? What of the compounding of capital? What of my sweaty little secret, the joker in the Wall Street pack, the messages from beyond by which I milked the market of millions? On Thursday no contact with my other selves was scheduled, but I could not have made it even if it had been. It was amply clear: Selene blanked my psi field. The critical range was twenty feet. When we were farther apart than that, I could get through; otherwise, not. How did it happen? How? How? How? An accidental incompatibility of psionic vibrations? A tragic canceling out of my powers through proximity to her splendid self? No. No. No. No.

On Thursday we roared through London like a conflagration, doing the galleries, the boutiques, the museums, the sniffer palaces, the pubs, the sparkle houses. I had never been so much in love. For hours at a time I forgot my dilemma. The absence of myself from myself, the separation that had seemed so shattering in its first instant, seemed trivial. What did I need *them* for, when I had *her?*

I needed them for the moneymaking. The moneymaking was a disease that love might alleviate but could not cure. And if I did not resume contact soon, there would be calamities in store.

Late Thursday afternoon, as we came reeling giddily out of a sniffer palace on High Holborn, our nostrils quivering, I felt contact again. (Now + *n*) broke through briefly, during a moment when I waited for a traffic light and Selene plunged wildly across to the far side of the street.

"—the amulet's what does it," he said. "That's the word I get from—"

Selene rushed back to my side of the street. "Come *on*, silly! Why'd you wait?"

Two hours later, as she lay in my arms, I swept my hand up from her satiny haunch to her silken breast, and caught the plaque of red metal between two fingers. "Love, won't you take this off?" I said innocently. "I hate the feel of a piece of cold slithery metal coming between us when—"

There was terror in her dark eyes. "I couldn't, Aram! I *couldn't!*"

"For me, love?"

"Please. Let me have my little superstition." Her lips found mine. Cleverly she changed the subject. I wondered at her tremor of shock, her frightened refusal.

Later we strolled along the Thames, and watched Friday coming to life in fogbound dawn. Today I would have to escape from her for at least an hour, I knew. The laws of time dictated it. For on Wednesday, between 6:00 and 7:00 P.M. Central European Time, I had accepted a transmission from myself of (now + n), speaking out of Friday, and Friday had come, and I was that very same (now + n), who must reach out at the proper time toward his counterpart at (now − n) on Wednesday. What would happen if I failed to make my rendezvous with time in time, I did not know. Nor wanted to discover. The universe, I suspected, would continue regardless. But my own sanity—my grasp on that universe—might not.

It was a narrowness. All glorious Friday I had to plot how to separate myself from radiant Selene during the cocktail hour, when she would certainly want to be with me. But in the end it was simplicity. I told the concierge, "At seven minutes after six send a message to me in the Celestial Room. I am wanted on urgent business, must come instantly to computer room for intercontinental data patch, person-to-person. "So?" Concierge replied, "We can give you the patch right at your table in the Celestial Room." I shook head firmly. "Do it as I say. Please." I put thumb to gratuity account of concierge and signaled an account-transfer of five pounds. Concierge smiled.

Seven minutes after six, message-robot scuttles into Celestial Room, comes homing in on table where I sit with

Selene. "Intercontinental data patch, Mr. Kevorkian," says robot. "Wanted immediately. Computer room." I turn to Selene. "Forgive me, love. Desolated, but must go. Urgent business. Just a few minutes."

She grasps my arm fondly. "Darling, no! Let the call wait. It's our *anniversary* now. Forty-eight hours since we met!"

Gently I pull arm free. I extend arm, show jeweled time-piece. "Not yet, not yet! We didn't meet until half past six Wednesday. I'll be back in time to celebrate." I kiss tip of supreme nose. "Don't smile at strangers while I'm gone," I say, and rush off with robot.

I do not go to computer room. I hurriedly buy a Friday *Herald-Tribune* in lobby and lock myself in men's washroom cubicle. Contact now is made on schedule with (now − *n*), living in Wednesday, all innocent of what will befall him that miraculous evening. I read stock prices, twenty securities, from Arizona Agrochemical to Western Offshore Corp. I sign off and study my watch. (Now − *n*) is currently closing out seven long positions and the short sale on Commonwealth Dispersals. During the interval I seek to make contact with (now + *n*) ahead of me on Sunday evening. No response. Nothing.

Presently I lose contact also with (now − *n*). As expected; for this is the moment when the me of Wednesday has for the first time come within Selene's psi-suppressant field. I wait patiently. In a while (Selene − *n*) goes to powder room. Contact returns.

(Now − *n*) says to me, "All right. What do you know that I ought to know?"

"We have fallen in love," I say.

Rest of conversation follows as per. What has been, must be. I debate slipping in the tidbit I have received from (now + *n*) concerning the alleged powers of Selene's amulet. Should I say it quickly, before contact breaks? Impossible. It was not said to me. The conversation proceeds until at the proper moment I am able to say, "I think I know how she does it. There's a—"

Wall of silence descends. (Selene − *n*) has returned to the table of (now − *n*). Therefore I (now) will return to the table of Selene (now). I rush back to the Celestial Room. Selene, looking glum, sits alone, sipping drink. She brightens as I approach.

"See?" I cry. "Back just in time. Happy anniversary, darling. Happy, happy, happy, happy!"

When we woke Saturday morning we decided to share the same room thereafter. Selene showered while I went downstairs to arrange the transfer. I could have arranged everything by telephone without getting out of bed, but I chose to go in person to the desk, leaving Selene behind. You understand why.

In the lobby I received a transmission from (now + *n*), speaking out of Monday, October 12. "It's definitely the amulet," he said. "I can't tell you how it works, but it's some kind of mechanical psi-suppressant device. God knows why she wears it, but if I could only manage to have her lose it we'd be all right. It's the amulet. Pass it on."

I was reminded, by this, of the flash of contact I had received on Thursday outside the sniffer palace on High Holborn. I realized that I had another message to send, a rendezvous to keep with him who has become (now − *n*).

Late Saturday afternoon, I made contact with (now − *n*) once more, only momentarily. Again I resorted to a ruse in order to fulfill the necessary unfolding of destiny. Selene and I stood in the hallway, waiting for a dropshaft. There were other people. The dropshaft gate irised open and Selene went in, followed by others. With an excess of chivalry I let all the others enter before me, and "accidentally" missed the closing of the gate. The dropshaft descended, with Selene. I remained alone in the hall. My timing was good; after a moment I felt the inner warmth that told me of proximity to the mind of (now − *n*).

"—the amulet's what does it," I said. "That's the word I get from —"

Aloneness intervened.

During the week beginning Monday, October 12, I received no advance information of the fluctuations of the
stock market at all. Not in five years had I been so deprived
of data. My linkings with (now − *n*) and (now + *n*) were
fleeting and unsatisfactory. We exchanged a sentence here,
a blurt of hasty words there, no more. Of course, there were
moments every day when I was apart from the fair Selene
long enough to get a message out. Though we were utterly
consumed by our passion for one another, nevertheless I
did get opportunities to elude the twenty-foot radius of her
psi-suppressant field. The trouble was that my opportunities to send did not always coincide with the opportunities
of (now − *n*) or (now + *n*) to receive. We remained linked in
a 48-hour spacing, and to alter that spacing would require
extensive discipline and infinitely careful coordination,
which none of ourselves were able to provide in such a time.
So any contact with myselves had to depend on a coincidence
of apartness from Selene.

I regretted this keenly. Yet there was Selene to comfort
me. We reveled all day and reveled all night. When fatigue
overcame us we grabbed a two-hour deepsleep wire and
caught up with ourselves, and then we started over. I
plumbed the limits of ecstasy. I believe it was like that for
her.

Though lacking my unique advantage, I also played the
market that week. Partly it was compulsion: my plungings
had become obsessive. Partly, too, it was at Selene's urg-
ings. "Don't you neglect your work for me," she purred.
"I don't want to stand in the way of making *money*."

Money, I was discovering, fascinated her nearly as
intensely as it did me. Another evidence of compatibility.
She knew a good deal about the market herself, and looked
on, an excited spectator, as I each day shuffled my portfolio.

The market was closed Monday: Columbus Day. Tuesday,
queasily operating in the dark, I sold Arizona Agrochemical,
Consolidated Luna, Eastern Electric Energy, and Western
Offshore, reinvesting the proceeds in large blocks of
Meccano Leasing and Holoscan Dynamics. Wednesday's

Tribune, to my chagrin, brought me the news that Consolidated Luna had received the Copernicus franchise and had risen 9¾ points in the final hour of Tuesday's trading. Meccano Leasing, though, had been rebuffed in the Robomation takeover bid and was off 4½ since I had bought it. I got through to my broker in a hurry and sold Meccano, which was down even further that morning. My loss was $125,000—plus $250,000 more that I had dropped by selling Consolidated Luna too soon. After the market closed on Wednesday, the directors of Meccano Leasing unexpectedly declared a five-for-two split and a special dividend in the form of a one-for-ten distribution of cumulative participating high-depreciation warrants. Meccano regained its entire Tuesday–Wednesday loss and tacked on 5 points beyond.

I concealed the details of this from Selene. She saw only the glamor of my speculations: the telephone calls, the quick computations, the movements of hundreds of thousands of dollars. I hid the hideous botch from her, knowing it might damage my prestige.

On Thursday, feeling battered and looking for the safety of a utility, I picked up 10,000 Southwest Power and Fusion at 38, only hours before the explosion of SPF's magneto-hydrodynamic generating station in Las Cruces, which destroyed half a county and neatly peeled $90,000 off the value of my investment when the stock finally traded, after a delayed opening, on Friday. I sold. Later came news that SPF's insurance would cover everything. SPF recovered, whereas Holoscan Dynamics plummeted 11½, costing me $140,000 more. I had not known that Holoscan's insurance subsidiary was the chief underwriter for SPF's disaster coverage.

All told that week I shed more than $500,000. My brokers were stunned. I had a reputation for infallibility among them. Most of them had become wealthy simply by duplicating my own transactions for their own accounts.

"Sweetheart, what *happened*?" they asked me.

My losses the following week came to $1,250,000. Still no news from (now + *n*). My brokers felt I needed a vacation. Even Selene knew I was losing heavily, by now. Curiously, my run of bad luck seemed to intensify her passion for me. Perhaps it made me look tragic and Byronic to be getting hit so hard.

We spent wild days and wilder nights. I lived in a throbbing haze of sensuality. Wherever we went we were the center of all attention. We had that burnished sheen that only great lovers have. We radiated a glow of delight all up and down the spectrum.

I was losing millions.

The more I lost, the more reckless my plunges became, and the deeper my losses became.

I was in real danger of being wiped out, if this went on.

I had to get away from her.

Monday, October 26. Selene has taken the deepsleep wire and in the next two hours will flush away the fatigues of three riotous days and nights without rest. I have only pretended to take the wire. When she goes under, I rise. I dress. I pack. I scrawl a note for her. *"Business trip. Back soon. Love, love, love, love."* I catch noon rocket for Istanbul.

Minarets, mosques, Byzantine temples. Shunning the sleep wire, I spend next day and a half in bed in ordinary repose. I wake and it is 48 hours since parting from Selene. Desolation! Bitter solitude! But I feel (now + *n*) invading my mind.

"Take this down," he says brusquely. "Buy 5000 FSP, 800 CCG, 150 LC, 200 T, 1000 TXN, 100 BVI. Go short 200 BA, 500 UCM, 200 LOC. Clear? Read back to me."

I read back. Then I phone in my orders. I hardly care what the ticker symbols stand for. If (now + *n*) says to do, I do.

An hour and a half later the switchboard tells me, "A Miss Hughes to see you, sir."

She has traced me! Calamitas calamitatum! "Tell her I'm not here, I say." I flee to the roofport. By copter I get away. Commercial jet shortly brings me to Tel Aviv. I take a room at the Hilton and give absolute instructions am not to be disturbed. Meals only to room, also *Herald-Trib* every day, otherwise no interruptions.

I study the market action. On Friday I am able to reach (now − n).

"Take this down," I say brusquely. "Buy 5000 FSP, 800 CCG, 150 LC, 200 T—"

Then I call brokers. I close out Wednesday's longs and cover Wednesday's shorts. My profit is over a million. I am recouping. But I miss her terribly.

I spend agonizing weekend of loneliness in hotel room.

Monday. Comes voice of (now + n) out of Wednesday, with new instructions. I obey. At lunchtime, under lid of my barley soup, floats note from her. "Darling, why are you running away from me? I love you to the ninth power. S."

I get out of hotel disguised as bellhop and take El Al jet to Cairo. Tense, jittery, I join tourist group sightseeing Pyramids, much out of character. Tour is conducted in Hebrew; serves me right. I lock self in hotel. *Herald-Tribune* available. On Wednesday I send instructions to me of Monday, (now − n). I await instructions from me of Friday, (now + n). Instead I get muddled transmissions, noise, confusions. What is wrong? Where to flee now? Brasilia, McMurdo Sound, Anchorage, Irkutsk, Maograd? She will find me. She has her resources. There are few secrets to one who has the will to surmount them. How does she find me?

She finds me.

Note comes: "I am at Abu Simbel to wait for you. Meet me there on Friday afternoon or I throw myself from Rameses' leftmost head at sundown. Love. Desperate. S."

I am defeated. She will bankrupt me, but I must have her. On Friday I go to Abu Simbel.

She stood atop the monument, luscious in windswept white cotton.

"I knew you'd come." she said.

"What else could I do?"

We kissed. Her suppleness inflamed me. The sun blazed toward a descent into the western desert.

"Why have you been running away from me?" she asked. "What did I do wrong? Why did you stop loving me?"

"I never stopped loving you," I said.

"Then—*why?*"

"I will tell you," I said, "a secret I have shared with no human being other than myselves."

Words tumbled out. I told all. The discovery of my gift, the early chaos of sensory bombardment from other times, the bafflement of living one hour ahead of time and one hour behind time as well as in the present. The months of discipline needed to develop my gift. The fierce struggle to extend the range of extrasensory perception to five hours, ten, twenty-four, forty-eight. The joy of playing the market and never losing. The intricate systems of speculation; the self-imposed limits to keep me from ending up with all the assets in the world; the pleasures of immense wealth. The loneliness, too. And the supremacy of the night when I met her.

Then I said, "When I'm with you, it doesn't work. I can't communicate with myselves. I lost millions in the last couple of weeks, playing the market the regular way. You were breaking me."

"The amulet," she said. "It does it. It absorbs psionic energy. It suppresses the psi field."

"I thought it was that. But who ever heard of such a thing? Where did you get it, Selene? Why do you wear it?"

"I got it far, far from here," said Selene. "I wear it to protect myself."

"Against *what?*"

"Against my own gift. My terrible gift, my nightmare gift, my curse of a gift. But if I must choose between my amulet and my love, it is no choice. I love you, Aram, I love you, I love you!"

She seized the metal disk, ripped it from the chain around her neck, hurled it over the brink of the monument. It fluttered through the twilight sky and was gone.

I felt (now − n) and (now + n) return.

Selene vanished.

For an hour I stood alone atop Abu Simbel, motionless, baffled, stunned. Suddenly Selene was back. She clutched my arm and whispered, "Quick! Let's go to the hotel!"

"Where have you been?"

"Next Tuesday," she said. "I oscillate in time."

"What?"

"The amulet damped my oscillations. It anchored me to the timeline in the present. I got it in 2459 A.D. Someone I knew there, someone who cared very deeply for me. It was his parting gift, and he gave it knowing we could never meet again. But now—"

She vanished. Gone eighteen minutes.

"I was back in last Tuesday," she said, returning. "I phoned myself and said I should follow you to Istanbul, and then to Tel Aviv, and then to Egypt. You see how I found you?"

We hurried to her hotel overlooking the Nile. We made love, and an instant before the climax I found myself alone in bed. (Now + n) spoke to me and said, "She's been here with me. She should be on her way back to you." Selene returned. "I went to—"

"—this coming Sunday," I said. "I know. Can't you control the oscillations at all?"

"No. I'm swinging free. When the momentum really builds up, I cover centuries. It's torture, Aram. Life has no sequence, no structure. Hold me tight!"

In a frenzy we finished what we could not finish before. We lay clasped close, exhausted. "What will we do?" I cried. "I can't let you oscillate like this!"

"You must. I can't let you sacrifice your livelihood!"

"But—"

She was gone.

I rose and dressed and hurried back to Abu Simbel. In the hours before dawn I searched the sands beside the Nile, crawling, sifting, probing. As the sun's rays crested the mountain I found the amulet. I rushed to the hotel. Selene had reappeared.

"Put it on," I commanded.

"I won't. I can't deprive you of—"

"Put it on."

She disappeared. (Now + *n*) said, "Never fear. All will work out wondrous well."

Selene came back. "I was in the Friday after next," she said. "I had an idea that will save everything."

"No ideas. Put the amulet on."

She shook her head. "I brought you a present," she said, and handed me a copy of the *Herald-Tribune,* dated the Friday after next. Oscillation seized her. She went and came and handed me November 19's newspaper. Her eyes were bright with excitement. She vanished. She brought me the *Herald-Tribune* of November 8. Of December 4. Of November 11. Of January 18, 1988. Of December 11. Of March 5, 1988. Of December 22. Of June 16, 1997. Of December 14. Of September 8, 1990. "Enough! I said. Enough! She continued to swing through time. The stack of papers grew. "I love you," she gasped, and handed me a transparent cube one inch high. *"The Wall Street Journal,* May 19, 2206," she explained. "I couldn't get the machine that reads it. Sorry." She was gone. She brought me more *Herald-Tribunes,* many dates, 1988-2002. Then a whole microreel. At last she sank down, dazed, exhausted, and said, "Give me the amulet. It must be within twelve inches of my body to neutralize my field." I slipped the disk into her palm. "Kiss me," Selene murmured.

And so. She wears her amulet; we are inseparable; I have no contact with my other selves. In handling my investments I merely consult my file of newspapers, which

I have reduced to minicap size and carry in the bezel of a ring I wear. For safety's sake Selene carries a duplicate.

We are very happy. We are very wealthy.

Is only one dilemma. Neither of us uses the special gift with which we were born. Evolution would not have produced such things in us if they were not to be used. What risks do we run by thwarting evolution's design?

I bitterly miss the use of my power, which her amulet negates. Even the company of supreme Selene does not wholly compensate for the loss of the harmoniousness that was

$$(\text{now} -n)$$
$$(\text{now})$$
$$(\text{now} + n).$$

I could, of course, simply arrange to be away from Selene for an hour here, an hour there, and reopen that contact. I could even have continued playing the market that way, setting aside a transmission hour every 48 hours outside of amulet range. But it is the *continuous* contact that I miss. The always presence of my other selves. If I have that contact, Selene is condemned to oscillate, or else we must part.

I wish also to find some way that her gift will be not terror but joy for her.

Is maybe a solution. Can extrasensory gifts be induced by proximity? Can Selene's oscillation pass to me? I struggle to acquire it. We work together to give me her gift. Just today I felt myself move, perhaps a microsecond into the future, then a microsecond into the past. Selene said I definitely seemed to blur.

Who knows? Will success be ours?

I think yes. I think love will triumph. I think I will learn the secret, and we will coordinate our vanishings, Selene and I, and we will oscillate as one, we will swing together through time, we will soar, we will speed hand in hand across the millennia. She can discard her amulet once I am able to go with her on her journeys.

Pray for us, $(\text{now} + n)$, my brother, my other self, and one day soon perhaps I will come to you and shake you by the hand.

R. A. Lafferty

Slow Tuesday Night

A panhandler intercepted the young couple as they strolled down the night street.

"Preserve us this night," he said as he touched his hat to them, "and could you good people advance me a thousand dollars to be about the recouping of my fortunes?"

"I gave you a thousand last Friday," said the young man.

"Indeed you did," the panhandler replied, "and I paid you back tenfold by messenger before midnight."

"That's right, George, he did," said the young woman. "Give it to him, dear. I believe he's a good sort."

So the young man gave the panhandler a thousand dollars, and the panhandler touched his hat to them in thanks and went on to the recouping of his fortunes.

As he went into Money Market, the panhandler passed Ildefonsa Impala, the most beautiful woman in the city.

"Will you marry me this night, Ildy?" he asked cheerfully.

"Oh, I don't believe so, Basil," she said. "I marry you pretty often, but tonight I don't seem to have any plans at all. You may make me a gift on your first or second, however. I always like that."

But when they had parted she asked herself: "But whom will I marry tonight?"

The panhandler was Basil Bagelbaker, who would be the richest man in the world within an hour and a half. He would make and lose four fortunes within eight hours; and these not the little fortunes that ordinary men acquire, but titanic things.

When the Abebaios block had been removed from human minds, people began to make decisions faster, and often better. It had been the mental stutter. When it was understood what it was, and that it had no useful function, it was removed by simple childhood metasurgery.

Transportation and manufacturing had then become practically instantaneous. Things that had once taken months and years now took only minutes and hours. A person could have one or several pretty intricate careers within an eight-hour period.

Freddy Fixico had just invented a manus module. Freddy was a Nyctalops, and the modules were characteristic of these people. The people had then divided themselves— according to their natures and inclinations—into the Auroreans, the Hemerobians, and the Nyctalops—or the Dawners, who had their most active hours from four A.M. till noon; the Day-Flies, who obtained from noon to eight P.M.; and the Night-Seers, whose civilization thrived from eight P.M. to four A.M. The cultures, inventions, markets and activities of these three folk were a little different. As a Nyctalops, Freddy had just begun his working day at eight P.M. on a slow Tuesday night.

Freddy rented an office and had it furnished. This took one minute, negotiation, selection and installation being almost instantaneous. Then he invented the manus module; that took another minute. He then had it manufactured and marketed; in three minutes it was in the hands of key buyers.

It caught on. It was an attractive module. The flow of orders began within thirty seconds. By ten minutes after eight every important person had one of the new manus modules, and the trend had been set. The module began to sell in the millions. It was one of the most interesting fads of the night, or at least the early part of the night.

Manus modules had no practical function, no more than had Sameki verses. They were attractive, of a psychologically satisfying size and shape, and could be held in the hands, set on a table, or installed in a module niche of any wall.

Naturally Freddy became very rich. Ildefonsa Impala, the most beautiful woman in the city, was always interested in newly rich men. She came to see Freddy about eight-thirty. People made up their minds fast, and Ildefonsa had hers made up when she came. Freddy made his own up quickly and divorced Judy Fixico in Small Claims Court. Freddy and Ildefonsa went honeymooning to Paraiso Dorado, a resort.

It was wonderful. All of Ildy's marriages were. There was the wonderful floodlighted scenery. The recirculated water of the famous falls was tinted gold; the immediate rocks had been done by Rambles; and the hills had been con-toured by Spall. The beach was a perfect copy of that at Merevale, and the popular drink that first part of the night was blue absinthe.

But scenery—whether seen for the first time or revisited after an interval—is striking for the sudden intense view of it. It is not meant to be lingered over. Food, selected and prepared instantly, is eaten with swift enjoyment; and blue absinthe lasts no longer than its own novelty. Loving, for Ildefonsa and her paramours, was quick and consuming; and repetition would have been pointless to her. Besides, Ildefonsa and Freddy had taken only the one-hour luxury honeymoon.

Freddy wished to continue the relationship, but Ildefonsa glanced at a trend indicator. The manus module would hold its popularity for only the first third of the night. Already it had been discarded by people who mattered. And Freddy Fixico was not one of the regular successes. He enjoyed a full career only about one night a week.

They were back in the city and divorced in Small Claims Court by nine thirty-five. The stock of manus modules was remaindered, and the last of it would be disposed to bargain hunters among the Dawners, who will buy anything.

"Whom shall I marry next?" Ildefonsa asked herself. "It looks like a slow night."

"Bagelbaker is buying," ran the word through Money Market, but Bagelbaker was selling again before the word had made its rounds. Basil Bagelbaker enjoyed making money, and it was a pleasure to watch him work as he dominated the floor of the Market and assembled runners and a competent staff out of the corner of his mouth. Helpers stripped the panhandler rags off him and wrapped him in a tycoon toga. He sent one runner to pay back twenty-fold the young couple who had advanced him a thousand dollars. He sent another with a more substantial gift to Ildefonsa Impala, for Basil cherished their relationship. Basil acquired title to the Trend Indication Complex and had certain falsifications set into it. He caused to collapse certain industrial empires that had grown up within the last two hours, and made a good thing of recombining their wreckage. He had been the richest man in the world for some minutes now. He became so money-heavy that he could not maneuver with the agility he had shown an hour before. He became a great fat buck, and the pack of expert wolves circled him to bring him down.

Very soon he would lose that first fortune of the evening. The secret of Basil Bagelbaker is that he enjoyed losing money spectacularly after he was full of it to the bursting point.

A thoughtful man named Maxwell Mouser had just produced a work of actinic philosophy. It took him seven minutes to write it. To write works of philosophy one used the flexible outlines and the idea indexes; one set the activator for such wordage in each subsection; an adept would use the paradox feed-in, and the striking-analogy blender; one calibrated the particular-slant and the personality-signature. It had to come out a good work, for excellence had become the automatic minimum for such productions.

"I will scatter a few nuts on the frosting," said Maxwell, and he pushed the lever for that. This sifted handfuls of words like chthonic and heuristic and prozymeides through the thing so that nobody could doubt it was a work of philosophy.

Maxwell Mouser sent the work out to publishers, and received it back each time in about three minutes. An analysis of it and reason for rejection was always given—mostly that the thing had been done before and better. Maxwell received it back ten times in thirty minutes, and was discouraged. Then there was a break.

Ladion's work had become a hit within the last ten minutes, and it was now recognized that Mouser's monograph was both an answer and a supplement to it. It was accepted and published in less than a minute after this break. The reviews of the first five minutes were cautious ones: then real enthusiasm was shown. This was truly one of the greatest works of philosophy to appear during the early and medium hours of the night. There were those who said it might be one of the enduring works and even have a holdover appeal to the Dawners the next morning.

Naturally Maxwell became very rich, and naturally Ildefonsa came to see him about midnight. Being a revolutionary philosopher, Maxwell thought that they might make some free arrangement, but Ildefonsa insisted it must be marriage. So Maxwell divorced Judy Mouser in Small Claims Court and went off with Ildefonsa.

This Judy herself, though not so beautiful as Ildefonsa, was the fastest taker in the city. She only wanted the men of the moment for a moment, and she was always there before even Ildefonsa. Ildefonsa believed that she took the men away from Judy; Judy said that Ildy had her leavings and nothing else.

"I had him first," Judy would always mock as she raced through Small Claims Court.

"Oh that damned urchin!" Ildefonsa would moan. "She wears my very hair before I do."

Maxwell Mouser and Ildefonsa Impala went honeymooning to Musicbox Mountain, a resort. It was wonderful. The peaks were done with green snow by Dunbar and

Fittle. (Back at Money Market Basil Bagelbaker was putting together his third and greatest fortune of the night, which might surpass in magnitude even his fourth fortune of the Thursday before.) The chalets were Switzier than the real Swiss and had live goats in every room. (And Stanley Skuldugger was emerging as the top Actor-Imago of the middle hours of the night.) The popular drink for that middle part of the night was Glotzenglubber, Eve Cheese and Rhine wine over pink ice. (And back in the city the leading Nyctalops were taking their midnight break at the Toppers' Club.)

Of course it was wonderful, as were all of Ildefonsa's—but she had never been really up on philosophy so she had scheduled only the special thirty-five-minute honeymoon. She looked at the trend indicator to be sure. She found that her current husband had been obsoleted, and his opus was now referred to sneeringly as Mouser's Mouse. They went back to the city and were divorced in Small Claims Court.

The membership of the Toppers' Club varied. Success was the requisite of membership. Basil Bagelbaker might be accepted as a member, elevated to the presidency and expelled from it as a dirty pauper from three to six times a night. But only important persons could belong to it, or those enjoying brief moments of importance.

"I believe I will sleep during the Dawner period in the morning," Overcall said. "I may go up to this new place, Koimopolis, for an hour of it. They're said to be good. Where will you sleep, Basil?"

"Flop house."

"I believe I will sleep an hour by the Midian Method," said Burnbanner. "They have a fine new clinic. And perhaps I'll sleep an hour by the Prasenka Process, and an hour by the Dormidio."

"Crackle has been sleeping an hour every period by the natural method," said Overcall.

"I did that for half an hour not long since," said Burnbanner. "I believe an hour is too long to give it. Have you tried the natural method, Basil?"

"Always. Natural method and a bottle of redeye."

Stanley Skuldugger had become the most meteoric actor-imago for a week. Naturally he became very rich, and Ildefonsa Impala went to see him about three A.M.

"I had him first!" rang the mocking voice of Judy Skuldugger as she skipped through her divorce in Small Claims Court. And Ildefonsa and Stanley-boy went off honeymooning. It is always fun to finish up a period with an actor-imago who is the hottest property in the business. There is something so adolescent and boorish about them.

Besides, there was the publicity, and Ildefonsa liked that. The rumor-mills ground. Would it last ten minutes? Thirty? An hour? Would it be one of those rare Nyctalops marriages that lasted through the rest of the night and into the daylight off-hours? Would it even last into the next night as some had been known to do?

Actually it lasted nearly forty minutes, which was almost to the end of the period.

It had been a slow Tuesday night. A few hundred new products had run their course on the markets. There had been a score of dramatic hits, three-minute and five-minute capsule dramas, and several of the six-minute long-play affairs. *Night Street Nine*—a solidly sordid offering—seemed to be in as the drama of the night unless there should be a late hit.

Hundred-storied buildings had been erected, occupied, obsoleted, and demolished again to make room for more contemporary structures. Only the mediocre would use a building that had been left over from the Day Fliers or the Dawners, or even the Nyctalops of the night before. The city rebuilt pretty completely at least three times during an eight-hour period.

The period drew near its end. Basil Bagelbaker, the richest man in the world, the reigning president of the Toppers' Club, was enjoying himself with his cronies. His fourth fortune of the night was a paper pyramid that had risen to incredible heights; but Basil laughed to himself as he savored the manipulation it was founded on.

Three ushers of the Toppers' Club came in with firm step.

"Get out of here, you dirty bum!" they told Basil savagely. They tore the tycoon's toga off him and then tossed him his seedy panhandler's rags with a three-man sneer.

"All gone?" Basil asked. "I gave it another five minutes."

"All gone," said a messenger from Money Market. "Nine billion gone in five minutes, and it really pulled some others down with it."

"Pitch the busted bum out!" howled Overcall and Burnbanner and the other cronies.

"Wait, Basil," said Overcall. "Turn in the President's Crosier before we kick you downstairs. After all, you'll have it several times again tomorrow night."

The period was over. The Nyctalops drifted off to sleep clinics or leisure-hour hideouts to pass their ebb time. The Auroreans, the Dawners, took over the vital stuff.

Now you would see some action! Those Dawners really made fast decisions. You wouldn't catch them wasting a full minute setting up a business.

A sleepy panhandler met Ildefonsa Impala on the way.

"Preserve us this morning, Ildy," he said, "and will you marry me the coming night?"

"Likely I will, Basil," she told him. "Did you marry Judy during the night past?"

"I'm not sure. Could you let me have two dollars, Ildy?"

"Out of the question. I believe a Judy Bagelbaker was named one of the ten best-dressed women during the froufrou fashion period about two o'clock. Why do you need two dollars?"

"A dollar for a bed and a dollar for redeye. After all, I sent you two million out of my second."

"I keep my two sorts of accounts separate. Here's a dollar, Basil. Now be off! I can't be seen talking to a dirty panhandler."

"Thank you, Ildy. I'll get the redeye and sleep in an alley. Preserve us this morning."

Bagelbaker shuffled off whistling "Slow Tuesday Night."

And already the Dawners had set Wednesday morning to jumping.

Avram Davidson

•

Help! I Am Dr. Morris Goldpepper

•

Four of the men, Weinroth, McAllister, Danbourge, and
Smith, sat at the table under the cold blue lighting tubes.
One of them, Rorke, was in a corner speaking quietly into a
telephone, and one, Fadderman, stood staring out the window
at the lights of the city. One, Hansen, had yet to arrive.

Fadderman spoke without turning his head. He was the
oldest of those present—the Big Seven, as they were
often called.

"Lights," he said. "So many lights. Down here." He
waved his hand toward the city. "Up there." He gestured
toward the sky. "Even with our much-vaunted knowledge,
what," he asked, "do we know?" He turned his head.
"Perhaps this is too big for us. In the light of the problem,
can we really hope to accomplish anything?"

Heavy-set Danbourge frowned grimly. "We have received
the suffrage of our fellow scientists, Doctor. We can but try."

Lithe, handsome McAllister, the youngest officer of the
Association, nodded. "The problem is certainly not greater
than that which faced our late, great colleague, the immortal
Morton." He pointed to a picture on the paneled wall. "And
we all know what *he* accomplished."

Fadderman went over and took his hand. "Your words fill
me with courage."

McAllister flushed with pleasure.

"I am an old man," Fadderman added falteringly. "Forgive my lack of spirit, Doctor." He sat down, sighed, shook his head slowly. Weinroth, burly and red-haired, patted him gently on the back. Natty, silvery-haired little Smith smiled at him consolingly.

A buzzer sounded. Rorke hung up the telephone, flipped a switch on the wall intercom. "Headquarters here," he said crisply.

"Dr. Carl T. Hansen has arrived," a voice informed him.

"Bring him up at once," he directed. "And, Nickerson—"

"Yes, Dr. Rorke?"

"Let no one else into the building. *No* one."

They sat in silence. After a moment or two, they heard the approach of the elevator, heard the doors slide open, slide shut, heard the elevator descend. Heavy, steady footsteps approached; knuckles rapped on the opaque glass door.

Rorke went over to the door, said, "A conscientious and diligent scientist—"

"—must remain a continual student," a deep voice finished the quotation.

Rorke unlocked the door, peered out into the corridor, admitted Hansen, locked the door.

"I would have been here sooner, but another emergency interposed," Hansen said. "A certain political figure—ethics prevent my being more specific—suffered an oral hemorrhage following an altercation with a woman who shall be nameless, but, boy, did she pack a wallop! A so-called *Specialist*, gentlemen, with offices on Park Avenue, had been, as he called it, 'applying pressure' with a gauze pad. I merely used a little Gelfoam as a coagulant agent and the hemorrhage stopped almost at once. When will the public learn, eh, gentlemen?"

Faint smiles played upon the faces of the assembled scientists. Hansen took his seat. Rorke bent down and lifted two tape-recording devices to the table, set them both in motion. The faces of the men became serious, grim.

"This is an emergency session of the Steering Committee of the Executive Committee of the American Dental Association," Rorke said, "called to discuss measures of dealing with the case of Dr. Morris Goldpepper. One tape will be deposited in the vaults of the Chase Manhattan Bank in New York; the other will be similarly secured in the vaults of the Wells Fargo and Union Trust Company Bank in San Francisco. Present at this session are Doctors Rorke, Weinroth and Smith—President, First and Second Vice-presidents, respectively—Fadderman, Past President, McAllister, Public Information, Danbourge, Legal, and Hansen, Policy."

He looked around at the set, tense faces.

"Doctors," he went on, "I think I may well say that humanity is, as of this moment, face to face with a great danger, and it is a bitter jest that it is not to the engineers or the astronomers, not to medicine nor yet to nuclear nor any other kind of physics, that humanity must now look for salvation—but to the members of the dental profession!"

His voice rose. "Yes—to the practitioners of what has become perhaps the least regarded of all the learned sciences! It is indeed ironical. We may at this juncture consider the comments of the now deceased Professor Earnest Hooton, the Harvard anthropologist, who observed with a sorrow which did him credit that his famed University, instead of assisting its Dental School as it ought, treated it—and I quote his exact words— 'Like a yellow dog.' " His voice trembled.

McAllister's clean-cut face flushed an angry red. Weinroth growled. Danbourge's fist hit the table and stayed there, clenched. Fadderman gave a soft, broken sigh.

"But enough of this. We are not jealous, nor are we vindictive," President Rorke went on. "We are confident that History, 'with its long tomorrow,' will show how, at this danger-fraught point, the humble and little-thought-of followers of dental science recognized and sized up the situation and stood shoulder to shoulder on the ramparts!"

He wiped his brow with a paper tissue. "And now I will call upon our beloved Past President, Dr. Samuel I. Fadderman, to begin our review of the incredible circumstances which have brought us here tonight. Dr. Fadderman? If you please . . ."

The well-known Elder Statesman of the A.D.A. nodded his head slowly. He made a little cage of his fingers and pursed and then unpursed his lips. At length he spoke in a soft and gentle voice.

"My first comment, brethren, is that I ask for compassion. *Morris Goldpepper is not to blame!*

"Let me tell you a few words about him. Goldpepper the Scientist needs no introduction. Who has not read, for instance, his 'The Bilateral Vertical Stroke and Its Influence on the Pattern of Occlusion' or his 'Treatment, Planning, Assemblage and Cementation of a 14-Unit Fixed Bridge' —to name only two? But I shall speak about Goldpepper the Man. He is forty-six years of age and served with honor in the United States Navy Dental Corps during the Second World War. He has been a widower since shortly after the conclusion of that conflict. Rae—the late Mrs. Goldpepper, may she rest in peace—often used to say, 'Morry, if I go first, promise me you'll marry again,' But he passed it off with a joke; and, as you know, he never did.

"They had one child, a daughter, Suzanne, a very sweet girl, now married to a Dr. Sheldon Fingerhut, D.D.S. I need not tell you, brethren, how proud our colleague was when his only child married this very fine young member of our profession. The Fingerhuts are now located on Unbalupi, one of the Micronesian islands forming part of the United States Trust Territory, where Dr. Sheldon is teaching dental hygiene, sanitation, and prosthesis to the natives thereof."

Dr. Hansen asked, "Are they aware of—"

"The son-in-law knows something of the matter," the older man said. "He has not seen fit to inform his wife, who is in a delicate condition and expects shortly to be confined. At his suggestion, I have been writing—or, rather, typing— letters purporting to come from her father, on his stationery, with the excuse that he badly singed his fingers on a Bunsen burner while annealing a new-type hinge for dentures and consequently cannot hold his pen." He sipped from a glass of water.

"Despite his great scientific accomplishments," Dr. Fadderman went on. "Morry had an impractical streak in him. Often I used to call on him at his bachelor apartment in the Hotel Davenport on West End Avenue, where he moved following his daughter's marriage, and I would find him immersed in reading matter of an escapist kind—tales of crocodile hunters on the Malay Peninsula, or magazines dealing with interplanetary warfare, or collections of short stories about vampires and werewolves and similar super- stitious creations.

"'Morry,' I said reproachfully, 'what a way to spend your off-hours. Is it worth it? Is it healthy? You would do much better, believe me, to frequent the pool or the handball court at the Y. Or,' I pointed out to him, 'if you want to read, why ignore the rich treasures of literature: Shakespeare, Ruskin, Elbert Hubbard, Edna Ferber, and so on? Why retreat to these immature-type fantasies?' At first he only smiled and quoted the saying, 'Each to his or her own taste.' "

The silence which followed was broken by young Dr. McAllister. "You say," he said, " 'at first.' "

Old Dr. Fadderman snapped out of his reverie. "Yes, yes. But eventually he confessed the truth to me. He withheld nothing."

The assembled dental scientists then learned that the same Dr. Morris Goldpepper, who had been awarded not once but three successive times the unique honor of the Dr. Alexander Peabody Medal for New Achievements in

Dental Prosthesis, was obsessed with the idea that *there was sentient life on other worlds—that it would shortly be possible to reach these other worlds—and that he himself desired to be among those who went.*

"'Do you realize, Sam?' he asked me," reported Fadderman. "'Do you realize that, in a very short time, it will no longer be a question of fuel or even of metallurgy? That submarines capable of cruising for weeks and months without surfacing foretell the possibility of traveling through airless space? The chief problem has now come down to finding how to build a takeoff platform capable of withstanding a thrust of several million pounds.' And his eyes glowed."

Dr. Fadderman had inquired, with good-natured sarcasm, how the other man expected this would involve *him.* The answer was as follows: Any interplanetary expedition would find it just as necessary to take along a dentist as to take along a physician, and that he—Dr. Goldpepper—intended to be that dentist!

Dr. Weinroth's hand slapped the table with a bang. "By thunder, I say the man had courage!"

Dr. Rorke looked at him with icy reproof. "I should be obliged," he said stiffly, "if there would be no further emotional outbursts."

Dr. Weinroth's face fell. "I beg the Committee's pardon, Mr. President," he said.

Dr. Rorke nodded graciously, indicated by a gesture of his hand that Dr. Fadderman had permission to continue speaking. The old man took a letter from his pocket and placed it on the table.

"This came to me like a bolt from the blue beyond. It is dated November 8 of last year. Skipping the formal salutation, it reads: 'At last I stand silent upon the peak in Darien' —a literary reference, gentlemen, to Cortez's alleged discovery of the Pacific Ocean; actually it was Balboa—'my great dream is about to be realized. Before long, I shall be back to tell you about it, but just exactly when, I am not able to say. History is being made! Long live Science! Sincerely yours, Morris Goldpepper, D.D.S.'"

He passed the letter around the table.

Dr. Smith asked, "What did you do on receiving this communication, Doctor?"

Dr. Fadderman had at once taken a taxi to West End Avenue. The desk clerk at the hotel courteously informed him that the man he sought had left on a vacation of short but not exactly specified duration. No further information was known. Dr. Fadderman's first thought was that his younger friend had gotten some sort of position with a government project which he was not free to discuss, and his own patriotism and sense of duty naturally prevented him from making inquiries.

"But I began, for the first time," the Elder Statesman of American Dentistry said, "to read up on the subject of space travel. I wondered how a man forty-six years of age could possibly hope to be selected over younger men."

Dr. Danbourge spoke for the first time. "Size," he said. "Every ounce would count in a spaceship and Morris was a pretty little guy."

"But with the heart of a lion," Dr. Weinroth said softly. "Miles and miles and miles of heart."

The other men nodded their agreement to this tribute.

But as time went on and the year drew to its close and he heard no word from his friend, Dr. Fadderman began to worry. Finally, when he received a letter from the Fingerhuts saying that *they* had not been hearing either, he took action.

He realized it was not likely that the Government would have made plans to include a dentist in this supposed project without communicating with the A.D.A. and he inquired of the current President, Dr. Rorke, if he had any knowledge of such a project, or of the whereabouts of the missing man. The answer to both questions was no. But on learning the reasons for Dr. Fadderman's concern, he communicated with Col. Lemuel Coggins, head of the USAF's Dental Corps.

Colonel Coggins informed him that no one of Dr. Goldpepper's name or description was or had been affiliated with any such project, and that, in fact, any such project was still—as he put it—"still on the drawing board."

Drs. Rorke and Fadderman, great as was their concern, hesitated to report Dr. Goldpepper missing. He had, after all, paid rent on apartment, office, and laboratory, well in advance. He was a mature man, of very considerable intelligence, and one who presumably knew what he was doing.

"It is at this point," said Dr. Danbourge, "that I enter the picture. On the eleventh of January, I had a call from a Dr. Milton Wilson, who has an office on East Nineteenth Street, with a small laboratory adjoining, where he does prosthetic work. He told me, with a good deal of hesitation, that something exceedingly odd had come up, and he asked me if I knew where Dr. Morris Goldpepper was. . . ."

The morning of the eleventh of January, an elderly man with a curious foreign accent came into Dr. Wilson's office, gave the name of Smith, and complained about an upper plate. It did not feel comfortable, Mr. Smith said, and it irritated the roof of his mouth. There was a certain reluctance on his part to allow Dr. Wilson to examine his mouth. This was understandable, because the interior of his mouth was blue. The gums were entirely edentulous, very hard, almost horny. The plate itself—

"Here is the plate," Dr. Danbourge said, placing it on the table. "Dr. Wilson supplied him with another. You will observe the perforations on the upper, or palatal, surface. They had been covered with a thin layer of gum arabic, which naturally soon wore almost entirely off, with the result that the roof of the mouth became irritated. Now this is so very unusual that Dr. Wilson—as soon as his patient, the so-called Mr. Smith, was gone—broke open the weirdly made plate to find why the perforations had been made. In my capacity as head of the Association's Legal Department," Dr. Danbourge stated, "I have come across some extraordinary occurrences, but nothing like *this*."

This was a small piece of a white, flexible substance, covered with tiny black lines. Danbourge picked up a large magnifying glass.

"You may examine these objects, Doctors," he said, "but it will save your eyesight if I read to you from an enlarged photostatic copy of this last one. The nature of the material, the method of writing, or of reducing the writing to such size—all are unknown to us. It may be something on the order of microfilm. But that is not important. The important thing is the *content* of the writing—the *portent* of the writing.

"Not since Dr. Morton, the young Boston dentist, realized the uses of sulphuric ether as an anesthetic has any member of our noble profession discovered anything of even remotely similar importance; and perhaps not before, either."

He drew his spectacles from their case and began to read aloud.

Despite the fact that our great profession lacks the glamour and public adulation of the practice of medicine, and even the druggists—not having a Hippocratic Oath— can preen themselves on their so-called Oath of Maimonides (though, believe me, the great Maimonides had no more to do with it than Morris Goldpepper, D.D.S.), no one can charge us with not having as high a standard of ethics and professional conduct as physicians and surgeons, M.D. Nor do I hesitate for one single moment to include prostheticians not holding the degree of Doctor of Dental Surgery or Doctor of Dental Medicine, whose work is so vital and essential.

When the records of our civilization are balanced, then— but perhaps not before—the real importance of dental science will be appreciated. Now it is merely valued at the moment of toothache.

It is only with a heavy heart that I undertake deliberately to produce inferior work, and with the confidence that all those to whom the standards of oral surgery and dental prosthetics are dear will understand the very unusual circumstances which have prompted me so to do. And, understanding, will forgive. No one can hold the standards of our profession higher or more sacred than I.

It must be admitted that I was not very amused on a certain occasion when my cousin, Nathaniel Pomerance, introduced me to an engineering contractor with these words, "You two should have a lot in common—you both build bridges," and uttered a foolish laugh. But I venture to say that this was one of the truest words ever spoken in questionable jest.

Humility is one thing, false pride another. Those who know anything of modern dentistry at all know of the Goldpepper Bridge and the Goldpepper Crown. It is I, Dr. Morris Goldpepper, inventor of both, and perfector of the Semi-retractable Clasp which bears my name, who writes these words you see before you. Nothing further should be needful by way of identification. And now to my report.

On the first of November, a day of evil import forever in the personal calendar of the unhappy wretch who writes these lines, not even knowing for sure if they will ever be read—but what else can I do?—shortly after 5 P.M., my laboratory door was knocked on. I found there a curious-looking man of shriveled and weazened appearance. He asked if I was Dr. Morris Goldpepper, "the famous perfector of the Semi-retractable Clasp," and I pleaded guilty to the flattering impeachment.

The man had a foreign-sounding accent, or—I thought—it may be that he had an impediment in his speech. Might he see me, was his next question. I hesitated.

It has happened to me before, and to most other practitioners—a stranger comes and, before you know it, he is slandering some perfectly respectable D.D.S. or D.M.D. The dentist pulled a healthy tooth—the dentist took such and such a huge sum of money for new plates—they don't fit him, he suffers great anguish—he's a poor man, the dentist won't do anything—*et cetera, ad infinitum nauseamque.* In short, a nut, a crank, a crackpot.

But while I was hesitating, the man yawned, did not courteously cover his mouth with his hand, and I observed to my astonishment the the interior of his mouth was an odd shade of blue!

Bemused by this singular departure from normalcy, I allowed him to enter. Then I wondered what to say, since he himself was saying nothing, but he looked around the lab with interest. "State your business" would be too brusque, and "Why is your mouth blue?" would be too gauche. An impasse.

Whilst holding up a large-scale model of the Goldpepper Cap (not yet perfected—will it ever be? Alas, who knows?) this curious individual said, "I know all about you, Dentist Goldpepper. A great scientist, you are. A man of powerful imagination, you are. One who rebels against narrow horizons and yearns to soar to wide and distant worlds, you are."

All I could think of to say was, "And what can I do for *you?*"

It was all so true; every single word he said was true. In my vanity was my downfall. I was tricked like the crow with the cheese in the ancient fable of Aesop.

The man proceeded to tell me, frankly enough, that he was a denizen of another planet. He had *two hearts,* would you believe it? And, consequently, two circulatory systems. Two pulses—one in each arm, one slow, the other fast.

It reminded me of the situation in Philadelphia some years ago when there were two telephone systems—if you had only a Bell phone, you couldn't call anyone who had only a Keystone phone.

The interior of his mouth was blue and so was the inside of his eyelids. He said his world had three moons.

You may imagine my emotions at hearing that my long-felt dream to communicate with otherworldly forms of sentient life was at last realized! And to think that they had singled out *not* the President of the United States, *not* the Director-General of the U.N., but *me*, Morris Goldpepper, D.D.S.! Could human happiness ask for more, was my unspoken question. I laughed softly to myself and I thought, What would my cousin Nathaniel Pomerance say *now?* I was like wax in this extraterrestrial person's hands (he had six distinct and articulate digits on each one), and I easily agreed to say nothing to anyone until the question of diplomatic recognition could be arranged on a higher echelon.

"Nonrecognition *has* its advantages, Goldpepper Dental Surgeon," he said with a slight smile. "No passport for your visit, you will need."

Well! A personal invitation to visit Proxima Centauri Gamma, or whatever the planet's name is! But I felt constrained to look this gift-horse just a little closer in the mouth. How is it that they came inviting *me*, not, let us say, Oppenheimer? Well?

"Of his gifts not in need, we are, Surgical Goldpepper. We have passed as far beyond nuclear power as you have beyond wind power. We can span the Universe—*but in dentistry, like children still, we are.* Come and inspect our facilities of your science, Great Goldpepper. If you say, 'This: Yes,' then it will be yes. If you direct, 'This: No,' then it will be no. In respect to the science of dentistry, our Edison and our Columbus, you will be."

I asked when we would leave and he said in eight days. I asked how long the trip would take. For a moment, I was baffled when he said it would take no longer than to walk the equivalent of the length of the lab floor. Then he revealed his meaning to me: matter transmission! Of course. No spaceship needed.

My next emotion was a brief disappointment at not being able to see the blazing stars in black outer space. But, after all, one ought not be greedy at such a time.

I cannot point out too strongly that at no time did I accept or agree to accept any payment or gratuity for this trip. I looked upon it in the same light as the work I have done for various clinics.

"Should I take along books? Equipment? What?" I asked my (so-to-speak) guide.

He shook his head. Only my presence was desired on the first trip. A visit of inspection. Very well.

On the morning of November 8, I wrote a brief note to my old and dear friend, Dr. Samuel Fadderman, the senior mentor of American Dentistry (on hearing these words, the Elder Statesman sobbed softly into his cupped hands), and in the afternoon, so excited and enthralled that I noticed no more of my destination than that it was north of the Washington Market, I accompanied my guide to a business building in the aforesaid area.

He led me into a darkened room. He clicked a switch. There was a humming noise, a feeling first of heaviness, then of weightlessness, and then an odd sort of light came on.

I was no longer on the familiar planet of my birth! I was on an unknown world!

Over my head, the three moons of this far-off globe sailed majestically through a sky wherein I could note unfamiliar constellations. The thought occurred to me that poets on this planet would have to find another rhyme, inasmuch as *moons* (plural form) does not go with *June* (singular form). One satellite was a pale yellow, one was brown, and the third was a creamy pink. Not knowing the names of these lunary orbs in the native tongue, I decided to call them Vanilla, Chocolate, and Strawberry.

Whilst my mind was filled with these droll fancies, I felt a tug at my sleeve, where my guide was holding it. He gestured and I followed.

"Now," I thought to myself, "he will bring me before the President of their Galactic Council, or whatever he is called," and I stood obediently within a circle marked on the surface of the platform whereon we stood.

In a moment, we were matter-transported to an inside room somewhere, and there I gazed about in in stupefaction, not to say astonishment. My eyes discerned the forms of Bunsen burners, Baldor lathes, casting machines and ovens, denture trays, dental stone, plaster, shellac trays, wires of teeth, and all the necessary equipment of a fully equipped dental prosthetic laboratory.

My surprise at the progress made by these people in the science at which they were allegedly still children was soon mitigated by the realization that all the items had been made on Earth.

As I was looking and examining, a door opened and several people entered. Their faces were a pale blue, and I realized suddenly that my guide must be wearing makeup to conceal his original complexion. They spoke together in their native dialect; then one of them, with a rod of some kind in his hand, turned to me. He opened his mouth. I perceived his gums were were bare.

"Dentical person," he said, "make me teeth."

I turned in some perplexity to my guide. "I understood you to say my first visit would be one of inspection only."

Everyone laughed, and I observed that all were equally toothless.

The man in the chair poked me rudely with his rod or staff. "Talk not! Make teeth!"

Fuming with a well-justified degree of indignation, I protested at such a gross breach of the laws of common hospitality. Then, casting concealment to the winds, these people informed me as follows:

Their race is entirely toothless in the adult stage. They are an older race than ours and are born looking ancient and wrinkled. It is only comparatively recently that they have established contact with Earth, and in order that they should not appear conspicuous, and in order to be able to eat our food, they realized that they must be supplied with artificial teeth.

My so-called guide, false friend, my enticer and/or kidnaper, to give him his due, had gotten fitted at a dentist's in New York and cunningly inquired who was the leading man in the field. Alas for fame! The man answered without a second of hesitation, "That is no other one than Morris Goldpepper, D.D.S., perfector of the Semi-retractable Clasp."

First this unscrupulous extraterrestrial procured the equipment, then he procured *me*.

"Do I understand that you purport that I assist you in a plan to thwart and otherwise circumvent the immigration laws of the United States?" was my inquiry.

The man in the chair poked me with his rod again. "You understand! So now make teeth!"

What a proposition to make to a law-abiding, patriotic American citizen by birth! What a demand to exact of a war veteran, a taxpayer, and one who has been three times on jury duty since 1946 alone (People vs. Garrity, People vs. Vanderdam, and Lipschutz vs. Krazy-Kut Kool Kaps, Inc)! My whole being revolted. I spoke coldly to them, informing them that the situation was contrary to my conception of dental ethics. But to no avail.

My treacherous dragoman drew a revolver from his pocket. "Our weapons understand, you do not. Primitive Earth weapons, yes. So proceed with manufacture, Imprisoned Goldpepper."

I went hot and cold. Not, I beg of you to understand, with fear, but with humiliation. *Imprisoned Goldpepper!* The phrase, with all the connotations it implied, rang in my ears.

I bowed my head and a phrase from the literary work *Samson Agonistes* (studied as a student in the College of the City of New York) rang through my mind:

Eyeless in Gaza, grinding corn . . .
Oh, blind, blind, blind, amidst the
blaze of noon. . . .

But even in this hour of mental agony, an agony which has scarcely abated to speak of, I had the first glimmering of the idea which I hope will enable me to warn Earth.

Without a word, but only a scornful glance to show these blue-complected individuals how well I appreciated that their so-called advanced science was a mere veneer over the base metal of their boorishness, I set to work. I made the preliminary impressions and study casts, using an impression tray with an oval floor form, the best suited for taking impressions of edentulous ridges.

And so began the days of my slavery.

Confined as I am here, there is neither day nor night, but an unremitting succession of frenum trims, post dams, boxing in, pouring up, festoon carving, fixing sprue channels, and all the innumerable details of dental prosthetic work. No one assists me. No one converses with me, save in brusque barks relevant to the work at hand. My food consists of liqueous and gelatinous substances such as might be expected would form the diet of a toothless race.

Oh, I am sick of the sight of their blue skins, bluer mouths, and horny ridges! I am sick of my serfdom!

I have been given material to keep records and am writing this in expectation of later reducing it in size by the method here employed, and of thereinafter inserting copies between the palatal and occlusal surfaces of the plates. It will be necessary to make such plates imperfect, so that the wearers will be obliged to go to dentists on Earth for repairs, because it is not always practical for them to matterport—in fact, I believe they can only do it on the eighth day of every third month. Naturally, I cannot do this to every plate, for they might become suspicious.

You may well imagine how it goes against my grain to produce defective work, but I have no other choice. Twice they have brought me fresh dental supplies, which is how I calculate their matterporting cycle. I have my wristwatch with me and thus I am enabled to reckon the passing of time.

What their exact purpose is in going to Earth, I do not know. My growing suspicion is that their much-vaunted superior science is a fraud and that their only superiority lies in the ability to matterport. One curious item may give a clue: They have questioned me regarding the Old Age Assistance programs of the several States. As I have said, they all *look* old.

Can it be that elsewhere on this planet there is imprisoned some poor devil of a terrestrial printer or engraver, toiling under duress to produce forged birth certificates and other means of identification, to the fell purpose of allowing these aliens to live at ease at the financial expense of the already overburdened U.S. taxpayer?

To whom shall I address my plea for help? To the Federal Government? But it has no official or even unofficial knowledge that this otherworldly race exists. The F.B.I.? But does matterporting under false pretenses to another planet constitute kidnaping across State lines?

It seems the only thing I can do is to implore whichever dental practitioner reads these lines to communicate at once with the American Dental Association. I throw myself upon the mercy of my fellow professional men.

Dentists and Dental Prostheticians! Beware of men with blue mouths and horny, edentulous ridges! Do not be deceived by flattery and false promises! Remember the fate of that most miserable of men, Morris Goldpepper, D.D.S., and, in his horrible predicament, help, oh, help him!

A long silence followed the reading of this document. At length it was broken by Dr. Hansen.

"That brave man," he said in a husky voice. "That brave little man."

"Poor Morris," said Dr. Danbourge. "Think of him imprisoned on a far-off planet, slaving like a convict in a salt mine, so to speak, making false teeth for these inhuman aliens, sending these messages to us across the trackless void. It's pitiful, and yet, Doctors, it is also a tribute to the indomitable spirit of Man!"

Dr. Weinroth moved his huge hands. "I'd like to get ahold of just one of those blue bastards," he growled.

Dr. Rorke cleared his throat. All present looked at their President respectfully and eagerly.

"I need hardly tell you, Doctors," he said crisply, "that the A.D.A. is a highly conservative organization. We do not go about things lightly. One such message we might ignore, but there have been eleven reported, all identical with the first. Even eleven such messages we might perhaps not consider, but when they come from a prominent scientist of the stature of Dr. Morris Goldpepper—

"Handwriting experts have pronounced this to be *his* handwriting beyond cavil of a doubt. Here"—he delved into a box—"are the eleven plates in question. Can any of you look at these clean lines and deny that they are the work of the incomparable Goldpepper?"

The six other men looked at the objects, shook their heads.

"Beautiful," murmured Dr. Smith, "even in their broken state. Poems in plastic! M. G. *couldn't* produce bad work if he tried!"

Dr. Rorke continued. "Each report confirmed that the person who brought in the plate had a blue mouth and edentulous ridges, just as the message states. Each blue-mouthed patient exhibited the outward appearance of old age. *And,* gentlemen, of those eleven, no less than *eight* were reported from the State of California. Do you realize what that means? California offers the highest amount of financial assistance to the elderly! Goldpepper's surmise was right!"

Dr. Hansen leaned forward. "In addition, our reports show that five of those eight are leaders in the fight against fluoridation of drinking water! It is my carefully considered belief that there is something in their physical makeup, evolved on another planet, which cannot tolerate fluorine even in minute quantities, because they certainly—being already toothless—wouldn't be concerned with the prevention of decay."

Young Dr. McAllister took the floor. "We have checked with dental supply houses and detail men in the New York metropolitan area and we found that large quantities of prosthetic supplies have been delivered to an otherwise unknown outfit—called the Echs Export Company—located not far north of the Washington Market! There is every reason to believe that this is the place Dr. Goldpepper mentioned. One of our men went there, found present only one man, in appearance an *old* man. Our representative feigned deafness, thus obliging this person to open his mouth and talk loudly. Doctors, he reports that this person *has a blue mouth!*"

There was a deep intake of breath around the table.

Dr. Rorke leaned forward and snapped off the tape recorders. "This next is off the record. It is obvious, Doctors, that no ordinary methods will suffice to settle this case, to ensure the return of our unfortunate colleague, or to secure the withdrawal of these extraterrestrial individuals from our nation and planet. I cannot, of course, officially endorse what might be termed 'strong-arm' methods. At the same time, I feel that our adversaries are not entitled to polite treatment. And obviously the usual channels of law enforcement are completely closed to us.

"Therefore—and remember, no word of this must pass outside our circle—therefore I have communicated something of this matter to Mr. Albert Annapollo, the well-known waterfront figure, who not long ago inaugurated the splendid Longshoremen's Dental Health Plan. Mr. Annapollo is a somewhat rough person, but he is nonetheless a *loyal* American. . . .

"We know now the Achilles heel of these alien creatures. It is fluorine. We know also how to identify them. And I think we may shortly be able to announce results. Meanwhile—" he drew a slip of paper from his pocket—"it is already the first of the month in that quarter when the dental supplies are due to be transported—or matterported, as Dr. Goldpepper terms it—to their distant destination. A large shipment is waiting to be delivered from the warehouses of a certain wholesaler to the premises of the Echs Export Company. I have had copies of this made and wrapped around each three-ounce bottle of Ellenbogen's Denture Stik-Phast. I presume it meets with your approval."

He handed it to Dr. Hansen, who, as the others present nodded in grimly emphatic approval, read it aloud:

"From The American Dental Association, representing over 45,000 registered dentists in the United States and its Territories, to Dr. Morris Goldpepper, wherever you may be: DO NOT DESPAIR! We are intent upon your rescue! We will bend every effort to this end! We shall fight the good fight!

"Have courage, Dr. Morris Goldpepper! You shall return!"

Philip K. Dick

•

Oh, To Be a Blobel!

•

He put a twenty-dollar platinum coin into the slot and the analyst, after a pause, lit up. Its eyes shone with sociability and it swiveled about in its chair, picked up a pen and pad of long yellow paper from its desk and said,

"Good morning, sir. You may begin."

"Hello, Doctor Jones. I guess you're not the same Doctor Jones who did the definitive biography of Freud; that was a century ago." He laughed nervously; being a rather poverty-stricken man he was not accustomed to dealing with the new fully homeostatic psychoanalysts. "Um," he said, "should I free-associate or give you background material or just what?"

Dr. Jones said, "Perhaps you could begin by telling me who you are und warum mich—why you have selected me."

"I'm George Munster of catwalk 4, building WEF-395, San Francisco condominium established 1996."

"How do you do, Mr. Munster." Dr. Jones held out its hand, and George Munster shook it. He found the hand to be of a pleasant body-temperature and decidedly soft. The grip, however, was manly.

"You see," Munster said, "I'm an ex-GI, a war veteran. That's how I got my condominum apartment at WEF-395; veterans' preference."

"Ah yes," Dr. Jones said, ticking faintly as it measured the passage of time. "The war with the Blobels."

"I fought three years in that war," Munster said, nervously smoothing his long, black, thinning hair. "I hated the Blobels and I volunteered; I was only nineteen and I had a good job—but the crusade to clear the Sol System of Blobels came first in my mind."

"Um," Dr. Jones said, ticking and nodding.

George Munster continued, "I fought well. In fact I got two decorations and a battlefield citation. Corporal. That's because I single-handed wiped out an observation satellite full of Blobels; we'll never know exactly how many because of course, being Blobels, they tend to fuse together and unfuse confusingly." He broke off, then, feeling emotional. Even remembering and talking about the war was too much for him . . . he lay back on the couch, lit a cigarette and tried to become calm.

The Blobels had emigrated originally from another star system, probably Proxima. Several thousand years ago they had settled on Mars and on Titan, doing very well at agrarian pursuits. They were developments of the original unicellular amoeba, quite large and with a highly organized nervous system, but still amoeba, with pseudopodia, reproducing by binary fission, and in the main offensive to Terran settlers.

The war itself had broken out over ecological considerations. It had been the desire of the Foreign Aid Department of the UN to change the atmosphere on Mars, making it more usable for Terran settlers. This change, however, had made it unpalatable for the Blobel colonies already there; hence the squabble.

And, Munster reflected, it was not possible to change *half* the atmosphere of a planet, the Brownian movement being what it was. Within a period of ten years the altered atmosphere had diffused throughout the planet, bringing suffering—at least so they alleged—to the Blobels. In retaliation, a Blobel armada had approached Terra and had put into orbit a series of technically sophisticated satellites designed eventually to alter the atmosphere of Terra. This alteration had never come about because of course the War Office of the UN had gone into action; the satellites had been detonated by self-instructing missiles . . . and the war was on.

Dr. Jones said, "Are you married, Mr. Munster?"

"No sir," Munster said. "And—" He shuddered. "You'll see why when I've finished telling you. See, Doctor—" He stubbed out his cigarette. "I'll be frank. I was a Terran spy. That was my task; they gave the job to me because of my bravery in the field . . . I didn't ask for it."

"I see," Dr. Jones said.

"Do you?" Munster's voice broke. "Do you know what was necessary in those days in order to make a Terran into a successful spy among the Blobels?"

Nodding, Dr. Jones said, "Yes, Mr. Munster. You had to relinquish your human form and assume the repellent form of a Blobel."

Munster said nothing; he clenched and unclenched his fist, bitterly. Across from him Dr. Jones ticked.

That evening, back in his small apartment at WEF-395, Munster opened a fifth of Teacher's scotch, sat by himself sipping from a cup, lacking even the energy to get a glass down from the cupboard over the sink.

What had he gotten out of the session with Dr. Jones today? Nothing, as nearly as he could tell. And it had eaten deep into his meager financial resources . . . meager because—

Because for almost twelve hours out of the day he reverted, despite all the efforts of himself and the Veterans' Hospitalization Agency of the UN, to his old wartime Blobel shape. To formless unicellularlike blob, right in the middle of his own apartment at WEF-395.

His financial resources consisted of a small pension from the War Office; finding a job was impossible, because as soon as he was hired the strain caused him to revert there on the spot, in plain sight of his new employer and fellow workers.

It did not assist in forming successful work-relationships.

Sure enough, now, at eight in the evening, he felt himself once more beginning to revert; it was an old and familiar experience to him, and he loathed it. Hurriedly, he sipped the last of the cup of scotch, put the cup down on a table . . . and felt himself slide together into a homogenous puddle.

The telephone rang.

"I can't answer," he called to it. The phone's relay picked up his anguished message and conveyed it to the calling party. Now Munster had become a single transparent gelatinous mass in the middle of the rug; he undulated toward the phone—it was still ringing, despite his statement to it, and he felt furious resentment; didn't he have enough troubles already, without having to deal with a ringing phone?

Reaching it, he extended a pseudopodium and snatched the receiver from the hook. With great effort he formed his plastic substance into the semblance of a vocal apparatus, resonating dully. "I'm busy," he resonated in a low booming fashion into the mouthpiece of the phone. "Call later." *Call,* he thought as he hung up, *tomorrow morning. When I've been able to regain my human form.*

The apartment was quiet, now.

Sighing, Munster flowed back across the carpet, to the window, where he rose into a high pillar in order to see the view beyond; there was a light-sensitive spot on his outer surface, and although he did not possess a true lens he was able to appreciate—nostalgically—the sight of San Francisco Bay, the Golden Gate Bridge, the playground for small children which was Alcatraz Island.

Dammit, he thought bitterly. *I can't marry; I can't live a genuine human existence, reverting this way to the form the War Office bigshots forced me into back in the war times . . .*

He had not known then, when he accepted the mission, that it would leave this permanent effect. They had assured him it was "only temporary, for the duration," or some such glib phrase. *Duration my ass*, Munster thought with furious, impotent resentment. *It's been* eleven years, *now*.

The psychological problems created for him, the pressure on his psyche, was immense. Hence his visit to Dr. Jones.

Once more the phone rang.

"Okay," Munster said aloud, and flowed laboriously back across the room to it. "You want to talk to me?" he said as he came closer and closer; the trip, for someone in Blobel form, was a long one. "I'll talk to you. You can even turn on the vidscreen and *look* at me." At the phone he snapped the switch which would permit visual communication as well as auditory. "Have a good look," he said, and displayed his amorphous form before the scanning tube of the video.

Dr. Jones' voice came: "I'm sorry to bother you at your home, Mr. Munster, especially when you're in this, um, awkward condition . . ." The homeostatic analyst paused. "But I've been devoting time to problem-solving vis-à-vis your condition. I may have at least a partial solution."

"What?" Munster said, taken by surprise. "You mean to imply that medical science can now—"

"No, no," Dr. Jones said hurriedly. "The physical aspects lie out of my domain; you must keep that in mind, Munster. When you consulted me about your problems it was the psychological adjustment that—"

"I'll come right down to your office and talk to you," Munster said. And then he realized that he could not; in his Blobel form it would take him days to undulate all the way across town to Dr. Jones' office. "Jones," he said desperately, "you see the problems I face. I'm stuck here in this apartment every night beginning about eight o'clock and lasting through until almost seven in the morning . . . I can't even visit you and consult you and get help—"

"Be quiet, Mr. Munster," Dr. Jones interrupted. "I'm trying to tell you something. *You're not the only one in this condition.* Did you know that?"

Heavily, Munster said, "Sure. In all, eighty-three Terrans were made over into Blobels at one time or another during the war. Of the eighty-three—" He knew the facts by heart. "Sixty-one survived and now there's an organization called Veterans of Unnatural Wars of which fifty are members. I'm a member. We meet twice a month, revert in unison . . ." He started to hang up the phone. So this was what he had gotten for his money, this stale news. "Goodbye, Doctor," he murmured.

Dr. Jones whirred in agitation. "Mr. Munster, I don't mean other Terrans. I've researched this in your behalf, and I discover that according to captured records at the Library of Congress fifteen *Blobels* were formed into pseudo-Terrans to act as spies for *their* side. Do you understand?"

After a moment Munster said, "Not exactly."

"You have a mental block against being helped," Dr. Jones said. "But here's what I want, Munster; you be at my office at eleven in the morning tomorrow. We'll take up the solution to your problem then. Goodnight."

Wearily, Munster said, "When I'm in my Blobel form my wits aren't too keen, Doctor. You'll have to forgive me." He hung up, still puzzled. So there was fifteen Blobels walking around on Titan this moment, doomed to occupy human forms—so what? How did that help him?

Maybe he would find out at eleven tomorrow.

When he strode into Dr. Jones' waiting room he saw, seated in a deep chair in a corner by a lamp, reading a copy of *Fortune,* an exceedingly attractive young woman.

Automatically, Munster found a place to sit from which he could eye her. Stylish dyed-white hair braided down the back of her neck . . . he took in the sight of her with delight, pretending to read his own copy of *Fortune.* Slender legs, small and delicate elbows. And her sharp, clearly featured face. The intelligent eyes, the thin, tapered nostrils —a truly lovely girl, he thought. He drank in the sight of her . . . until all at once she raised her head and stared coolly back at him.

"Dull, having to wait," Munster mumbled.

The girl said, "Do you come to Dr. Jones often?"

"No," he admitted. "This is just the second time."

"I've never been here before," the girl said. "I was going to another electronic fully homeostatic psychoanalyst in Los Angeles and then late yesterday Dr. Bing, my analyst, called me and told me to fly up here and see Dr. Jones this morning. Is this one good?"

"Um," Munster said. "I guess so." *We'll see,* he thought. *That's precisely what we don't know, at this point.*

The inner office door opened and there stood Dr. Jones. "Miss Arrasmith," it said, nodding to the girl. "Mr. Munster." It nodded to George. "Won't you both come in?"

Rising to her feet, Miss Arrasmith said, "Who pays the twenty dollars then?"

But the analyst had become silent; it had turned off.

"I'll pay," Miss Arrasmith said, reaching into her purse.

"No, no," Munster said. "Let me." He got out a twenty-dollar piece and dropped it into the analyst's slot.

At once, Dr. Jones said, "You're a gentleman, Mr. Munster." Smiling, it ushered the two of them into its office. "Be seated, please. Miss Arrasmith, without preamble please allow me to explain your—condition to Mr. Munster." To Munster it said, "Miss Arrasmith is a Blobel."

Munster could only stare at the girl.

"Obviously," Dr. Jones continued, "presently in human form. This, for her, is the state of involuntary reversion. During the war she operated behind Terran lines, acting for the Blobel War League. She was captured and held, but then the war ended and she was neither tried nor sentenced."

"They released me," Miss Arrasmith said in a low, carefully controlled voice. "Still in human form. I stayed here out of shame. I just couldn't go back to Titan and—" Her voice wavered.

"There is a great shame attached to this condition," Dr. Jones said, "for any high-caste Blobel."

Nodding, Miss Arrasmith sat clutching a tiny Irish linen handkerchief and trying to look poised. "Correct, Doctor. I did visit Titan to discuss my condition with medical authorities there. After expensive and prolonged therapy with me they were able to induce a return to my natural form for a period of—" She hesitated. "About one-fourth of the time. But the other three-fourths . . . I am as you perceive me now." She ducked her head and touched the handkerchief to her right eye.

"Jeez," Munster protested, "you're lucky; a human form is infinitely superior to a Blobel form—I ought to know. As a Blobel you have to creep along . . . you're like a big jellyfish, no skeleton to keep you erect. And binary fission— it's lousy, I say really lousy, compared to the Terran form of—you know. Reproduction." He colored.

Dr. Jones ticked and stated, "For a period of about six hours your human forms overlap. And then for about one hour your Blobel forms overlap. So all in all, the two of you possess seven hours out of twenty-four in which you both possess identical forms. In my opinion—" It toyed with its pen and paper. "Seven hours is not too bad. If you follow my meaning."

After a moment Miss Arrasmith said, "But Mr. Munster and I are natural enemies."

"That was years ago," Munster said.

"Correct," Dr. Jones agreed. "True, Miss Arrasmith is basically a Blobel and you, Munster, are a Terran, but—" It gestured. "Both of you are outcasts in either civilization; both of you are stateless and hence gradually suffering a loss of ego-identity. I predict for both of you a gradual deterioration ending finally in severe mental illness. Unless you two can develop a rapprochement." The analyst was silent, then.

Miss Arrasmith said softly, "I think we're very lucky, Mr. Munster. As Dr. Jones said, we do overlap for seven hours a day . . . we can enjoy that time together, no longer in wretched isolation." She smiled up hopefully at him, rearranging her coat. Certainly, she had a nice figure; the somewhat low-cut dress gave an ideal clue to that.

Studying her, Munster pondered.

"Give him time," Dr. Jones told Miss Arrasmith. "My analysis of him is that he will see this correctly and do the right thing."

Still rearranging her coat and dabbing at her large, dark eyes, Miss Arrasmith waited.

The phone in Dr. Jones' office rang, a number of years later. He answered it in his customary way. "Please, sir or madam, deposit twenty dollars if you wish to speak to me."

A tough male voice on the other end of the line said, "Listen, this is the UN Legal Office and we don't deposit twenty dollars to talk to anybody. So trip that mechanism inside you, Jones."

"Yes sir," Dr. Jones said, and with his right hand tripped the lever behind his ear that caused him to come on free.

"Back in 2037," the UN legal expert said, "did you advise a couple to marry? A George Munster and a Vivian Arrasmith, now Mrs. Munster?"

"Why yes," Dr. Jones said, after consulting his built-in memory banks.

"Had you investigated the legal ramifications of their issue?"

"Um well," Dr. Jones said, "That's not my worry."

"You can be arraigned for advising any action contrary to UN law."

"There's no law prohibiting a Blobel and a Terran from marrying."

The UN legal expert said, "All right, Doctor, I'll settle for a look at their case histories."

"Absolutely no," Dr. Jones said. "That would be a breach of ethics."

"We'll get a writ and sequester them, then."

"Go ahead." Dr. Jones reached behind his ear to shut himself off.

"Wait. It may interest you to know that the Munsters now have four children. And, following the Mendelian Law, the offspring comprise a strict one, two, one ratio. One Blobel girl, one hybrid boy, one hybrid girl, one Terran girl. The legal problem arises in that the Blobel Supreme Council claims the pure-blooded Blobel girl as a citizen of Titan and also suggests that one of the two hybrids be donated to the Council's jurisdiction." The UN legal expert explained, "You see, the Munsters' marriage is breaking up; they're getting divorced and it's sticky finding which laws obtain regarding them and their issue."

"Yes," Dr. Jones admitted, "I would think so. What has caused their marriage to break up?"

"I don't know and don't care. Possibly the fact that both adults and two of the four children rotate daily between being Blobels and Terrans; maybe the strain got to be too much. If you want to give them psychological advice, consult them. Goodbye." The UN legal expert rang off.

Did I make a mistake, advising them to marry? Dr. Jones asked itself. *I wonder if I shouldn't look them up; I owe at least that to them.*

Opening the Los Angeles phonebook, it began thumbing through the *Ms.*

These had been six difficult years for the Munsters.

First, George had moved from San Francisco to Los Angeles; he and Vivian had set up their household in a condominium apartment with three instead of two rooms. Vivian, being in Terran form three-fourths of the time, had been able to obtain a job; right out in public she gave jet flight information at the Fifth Los Angeles Airport. George, however—

His pension comprised an amount only one-fourth that of his wife's salary and he felt it keenly. To augment it, he had searched for a way of earning money at home. Finally in a magazine he had found this valuable ad:

MAKE SWIFT PROFITS IN YOUR OWN CONDO! RAISE GIANT BULLFROGS FROM JUPITER, CAPABLE OF EIGHTY-FOOT LEAPS. CAN BE USED IN FROG-RACING (where legal) AND

So in 2038 he had bought his first pair of frogs imported from Jupiter and had begun raising them for swift profits, right in his own condominum apartment building, in a corner of the basement that Leopold the partially homeostatic janitor let him use gratis.

But in the relatively feeble Terran gravity the frogs were capable of enormous leaps, and the basement proved too small for them; they ricocheted from wall to wall like green ping pong balls and soon died. Obviously it took more than a portion of the basement at QEK-604 Apartments to house a crop of the damned things, George realized.

And then, too, their first child had been born. It had turned out to be pure-blooded Blobel; for twenty-four hours a day it consisted of a gelatinous mass and George found himself waiting in vain for it to switch over to a human form, even for a moment.

He faced Vivian defiantly in this matter, during a period when both of them were in human form.

"How can I consider it my child?" he asked her. "It's— an alien life form to me." He was discouraged and even horrified. "Dr. Jones should have foreseen this; maybe it's *your* child—it looks just like you."

Tears filled Vivian's eyes. "You mean that insultingly."

"Damn right I do. We fought you creatures—we used to consider you no better than Portuguese stingrays." Gloomily, he put on his coat. "I'm going down to Veterans of Unnatural Wars Headquarters," he informed his wife. "Have a beer with the boys." Shortly, he was on his way to join with his old wartime buddies, glad to get out of the apartment house.

VUW Headquarters was a decrepit cement building in downtown Los Angeles left over from the twentieth century and sadly in need of paint. The VUW had little funds because most of its members were, like George Munster, living on UN pensions. However, there was a pool table and an old 3-D television set and a few dozen tapes of popular music and also a chess set. George generally drank his beer and played chess with his fellow members, either in human form or in Blobel form; this was one place in which both were accepted.

This particular evening he sat with Pete Ruggles, a fellow veteran who also had married a Blobel female, reverting, as Vivian did, to human form.

"Pete, I can't go on. I've got a gelatinous blob for a child. My whole life I've wanted a kid, and now what have I got? Something that looks like it washed up on the beach."

Sipping his beer—he too was in human form at the moment—Pete answered, "Criminy, George, I admit it's a mess. But you must have known what you were getting into when you married her. And my god, according to Mendel's Law, the next kid—"

"I mean," George broke in, "I don't respect my own wife; that's the basis of it. I think of her as a *thing*. And myself, too. We're both things." He drank down his beer in one gulp.

Pete said meditatively, "But from the Blobel standpoint—"

"Listen, whose side are you on?" George demanded.

"Don't yell at me," Pete said, "or I'll deck you."

A moment later they were swinging wildly at each other. Fortunately Pete reverted to Blobel form in the nick of time; no harm was done. Now George sat alone, in human shape, while Pete oozed off somewhere else, probably to join a group of the boys who had also assumed Blobel form.

Maybe we can found a new society somewhere on a remote moon, George said to himself moodily. *Neither Terran nor Blobel.*

I've got to go back to Vivian, George resolved. *What else is there for me? I'm lucky to find her; I'd be nothing but a war veteran guzzling beer here at VUW Headquarters every damn day and night, with no future, no hope, no real life . . .*

He had a new money-making scheme going, now. It was a home mail-order business; he had placed an ad in the *Saturday Evening Post* for MAGIC LODESTONES REPUTED TO BRING YOU LUCK. FROM ANOTHER STAR-SYSTEM ENTIRELY! The stones had come from Proxima and were obtainable on Titan; it was Vivian who had made the commercial contact for him with her people. But so far, few people had sent in the dollar-fifty.

I'm a failure, George said to himself.

Fortunately the next child, born in the winter of 2039, showed itself to be a hybrid; it took human form fifty percent of the time, and so at last George had a child who was—occassionally, anyhow—a member of his own species.

He was still in the process of celebrating the birth of Maurice when a delegation of their neighbors at QEK-604 Apartments came and rapped on their door.

"We've got a petition here," the chairman of the delegation said, shuffling his feet in embarrassment, "asking that you and Mrs. Munster leave QEK-604."

"But why?" George asked, bewildered. "You haven't objected to us up until now."

"The reason is that now you've got a hybrid youngster who will want to play with ours, and we feel it's unhealthy for our kids to—"

George slammed the door in their faces.

But still, he felt the pressure, the hostility from the people on all sides of them. *And to think,* he thought bitterly, *that I fought in the war to save these people. It sure wasn't worth it.*

An hour later he was down at VUW Headquarters once more, drinking beer and talking with his buddy Sherman Downs, also married to a Blobel.

"Sherman, it's no good. We're not wanted; we've got to emigrate. Maybe we'll try it on Titan, in Viv's world."

"Chrissakes," Sherman protested, "I hate to see you fold up, George. Isn't your electromagnetic reducing belt beginning to sell, finally?"

For the last few months, George had been making and selling a complex electronic reducing gadget which Vivian had helped him design; it was based in principle on a Blobel device popular on Titan but unknown on Terra. And this had gone over well; George had more orders than he could fill. But—

"I had a terrible experience, Sherm," George confided. "I was in a drugstore the other day, and they gave me a big order for my reducing belt, and I got so excited—" He broke off. "You can guess what happened. I reverted. Right in plain sight of a hundred customers. And when the buyer saw that he canceled the order for the belts. It was what we all fear . . . you should have seen how their attitude toward me changed."

Sherm said, "Hire someone to do your selling for you. A full-blooded Terran."

Thickly, George said, "*I'm* a full-blooded Terran, and don't you forget it. Ever."

"I just mean—"

"I know what you meant," George said. And took a swing at Sherman. Fortunately he missed and in the excitement both of them reverted to Blobel form. They oozed angrily into each other for a time, but at last fellow veterans managed to separate them.

"I'm as much a Terran as anyone," George thought-radiated in the Blobel manner to Sherman. "And I'll flatten anyone who says otherwise."

In Blobel form he was unable to get home; he had to phone Vivian to come and get him. It was humiliating.

Suicide, he decided. *That's the answer.*

How best to do it? In Blobel form he was unable to feel pain; best to do it then. Several substances would dissolve him . . . he could for instance drop himself into a heavily chlorinated swimming pool, such as QEK-604 maintained in its recreation room.

Vivian, in human form, found him as he reposed hesitantly at the edge of the swimming pool, late one night.

"George, I beg you—go back to Dr. Jones."

"Naw," he boomed dully, forming a quasi-vocal apparatus with a portion of his body. "It's no use, Viv. I don't *want* to go on." Even the belts; they had been Viv's idea, rather than his. He was second even there . . . behind her, falling constantly further behind each passing day.

Viv said, "You have so much to offer the children."

That was true. "Maybe I'll drop over to the UN War Office," he decided. "Talk to them, see if there's anything new that medical science has come up with that might stabilize me."

"But if you stabilize as a Terran," Vivian said, "what would become of me?"

"We'd have *eighteen entire hours* together a day. All the hours you take human form!"

"But you wouldn't want to stay married to me. Because, George, then you could meet a Terran woman."

It wasn't fair to her, he realized. So he abandoned the idea.

In the spring of 2041 their third child was born, also a girl, and like Maurice a hybrid. It was Blobel at night and Terran by day.

Meanwhile, George found a solution to some of his problems.

He got himself a mistress.

At the Hotel Elysium, a run-down wooden building in the heart of Los Angeles, he and Nina arranged to meet one another.

"Nina," George said, sipping Teacher's scotch and seated beside her on the shabby sofa which the hotel provided, "you've made my life worth living again." He fooled with the buttons of her blouse.

"I respect you," Nina Glaubman said, assisting him with the buttons. "In spite of the fact—well, you are a former enemy of our people."

"God," George protested, "we must not think about the old days—we have to close our minds to our pasts." *Nothing but our future,* he thought.

His reducing belt enterprise had developed so well that now he employed fifteen full-time Terran employees and owned a small, modern factory on the outskirts of San Fernando. If UN taxes had been reasonable he would by now be a wealthy man . . . brooding on that, George wondered what the tax rate was in Blobel-run lands, on Io, for instance. Maybe he ought to look into it.

One night at VUW Headquarters he discussed the subject with Reinholt, Nina's husband, who of course was ignorant of the modus vivendi between George and Nina.

"Reinholt," George said with difficulty, as he drank his beer, "I've got big plans. This cradle-to-grave socialism the UN operates . . . it's not for me. It's cramping me. The Munster Magic Magnetic Belt is—" He gestured. "More than Terran civilization can support. You get me?"

Coldly, Reinholt said, "But George, you are a Terran; if you emigrate to Blobel-run territory with your factory you'll be betraying your—"

"Listen," George told him, "I've got one authentic Blobel child, two half-Blobel children, and a fourth on the way. I've got strong *emotional* ties with those people out there on Titan and Io."

"You're a traitor," Reinholt said, and punched him in the mouth. "And not only that," he continued, punching George in the stomach "you're running around with my wife. I'm going to kill you."

To escape, George reverted to Blobel form; Reinholt's blows passed harmlessly deep into his moist, jellylike substance. Reinholt then reverted too, and flowed into him murderously, trying to consume and absorb George's nucleus.

Fortunately fellow veterans pried their two bodies apart before any permanent harm was done.

Later that night, still trembling, George sat with Vivian in the living room of their eight-room suite at the great new condominum apartment building ZGF-900. It had been a close call, and now of course Reinholt would tell Viv; it was only a question of time. The marriage, as far as George could see, was over. This perhaps was their last moment together.

"Viv," he said urgently, "you have to believe me; I love you. You and the children—plus the belt business, naturally —are my complete life." A desperate idea came to him. "Let's emigrate now, tonight. Pack up the kids and go to Titan, right this minute."

"I can't go," Vivian said. "I know how my people would treat me, and treat you and the children, too. George, *you go*. Move the factory to Io. I'll stay here." Tears filled her dark eyes.

"Hell," George said, "what kind of life is that? With you on Terra and me on Io—that's no marriage. And who'll get the kids?" Probably Viv would get them . . . but his firm employed top legal talent—perhaps he could use it to solve his domestic problems.

The next morning Vivian found out about Nina. And hired an attorney of her own.

"Listen," George said, on the phone talking to his top legal talent, Henry Ramarau. "Get me custody of the fourth child; it'll be a Terran. And we'll compromise on the two hybrids; I'll take Maurice and she can have Kathy. And naturally she gets blob, the first so-called child. As far as I'm concerned it's hers anyhow." He slammed the receiver down and then turned to the board of directors of his company. "Now where were we?" he demanded. "In our analysis of Io tax laws."

During the next weeks the idea of a move to Io appeared more and more feasible from a profit and loss standpoint.

"Go ahead and buy land on Io," George instructed his business agent in the field, Tom Hendricks. "And get it cheap; we want to start right." To his secretary Miss Nolan he said, "Now keep everyone out of my office until further notice. I feel an attack coming on. From anxiety over this major move off Terra to Io." He added, "And personal worries."

"Yes, Mr. Munster," Miss Nolan said, ushering Tom Hendricks out of George's private office. "No one will disturb you." She could be counted on to keep everyone out while George reverted to his wartime Blobel shape, as he often did, these days; the pressure on him was immense.

When, later in the day, he resumed human form, George learned from Miss Nolan that a Doctor Jones had called.

"I'll be damned," George said, thinking back to six years ago. "I thought it'd be in the junk pile by now." To Miss Nolan he said, "Call Doctor Jones, notify me when you have it; I'll take a minute off to talk to it." It was like old times, back in San Francisco.

Shortly, Miss Nolan had Dr. Jones on the line.

"Doctor," George said, leaning back in his chair and swiveling from side to side and poking at an orchid on his desk. "Good to hear from you."

The voice of the homeostatic analyst came in his ear, "Mr. Munster, I note that you now have a secretary."

"Yes," George said, "I'm a tycoon. I'm in the reducing belt game; it's somewhat like the flea-collar that cats wear. Well, what can I do for you?"

"I understand you have four children now—"

"Actually three, plus a fourth on the way. Listen, that fourth, Doctor, is vital to me; according to Mendel's Law it's a full-blooded Terran and by god I'm doing everything in my power to get custody of it." He added, "Vivian—you remember her—is now back on Titan. Among her own people, where she belongs. And I'm putting some of the finest doctors I can get on my payroll to stabilize me, I'm tired of this constant reverting, night and day; I've got too much to do for such nonsense."

Dr. Jones said, "From your tone I can see you're an important, busy man, Mr. Munster. You've certainly risen in the world, since I saw you last."

"Get to the point, Doctor," George said impatiently. "Why'd you call?"

"I, um, thought perhaps I could bring you and Vivian together again."

"Bah," George said contemptuously. "That woman? Never. Listen, Doctor, I have to ring off; we're in the process of finalizing on some basic business strategy, here at Munster, Incorporated."

"Mr. Munster," Dr. Jones asked, "is there another woman?"

"There's another Blobel," George said, "if that's what you mean." And he hung up the phone. *Two Blobels are better than none,* he said to himself. *And now back to business . . .* He pressed a button on his desk and at once Miss Nolan put her head into the office. "Miss Nolan," George said, "get me Hank Ramarau; I want to find out—"

"Mr. Ramarau is waiting on the other line," Miss Nolan said. "He says it's urgent."

Switching to the other line, George said, "Hi, Hank. What's up?"

"I've just discovered," his top legal advisor said, "that to operate your factory on Io you must be a citizen of Titan."

"We ought to be able to fix that up," George said.

"But to be a citizen of Titan—" Ramarau hesitated. "I'll break it to you easy as I can, George. You have to be a Blobel."

"Dammit, I am a Blobel," George said. "At least part of the time. Won't that do?"

"No," Ramarau said, "I checked into that, knowing of your affliction, and it's got to be one hundred percent of the time. Night *and* day."

"Hmmm," George said. "This is bad. But we'll overcome it, somehow. Listen, Hank, I've got an appointment with

Eddy Fullbright, my medical coordinator; I'll talk to you after, okay?" He rang off and then sat scowling and rubbing his jaw. *Well,* he decided, *if it has to be it has to be. Facts are facts, and we can't let them stand in our way.*

Picking up the phone he dialed his doctor Eddy Fullbright.

The twenty-dollar platinum coin rolled down the chute and tripped the circuit. Dr. Jones came on, glanced up and saw a stunning, sharp-breasted young woman whom it recognized—by means of a quick scan of its memory banks—as Mrs. George Munster, the former Vivian Arrasmith.

"Good day, Vivian," Dr. Jones said cordially. "But I understood you were on Titan." It rose to its feet, offering her a chair.

Dabbing at her large, dark eyes, Vivian sniffled, "Doctor, everything is collapsing around me. My husband is having an affair with another woman . . . all I know is that her name is Nina and all the boys down at VUW Headquarters are talking about it. Presumably she's a Terran. We're both filing for divorce. And we're having a dreadful legal battle over the children." She arranged her coat modestly. "I'm, expecting. Our fourth."

"This I know," Dr. Jones said. "A full-blooded Terran this time, if Mendel's Law holds . . . although it only applied to litters."

Mrs. Munster said miserably, "I've been on Titan talking to legal and medical experts, gynecologists, and especially marital guidance counselors; I've had all sorts of advice during the past month. Now I'm back on Terra but I can't find George—he's *gone.*"

"I wish I could help you, Vivian," Dr. Jones said. "I talked to your husband briefly, the other day, but he spoke only in generalities . . . evidently he's such a big tycoon now that it's hard to approach him."

"And to think," Vivian sniffled, "that he achieved it all because of an idea *I* gave him. A Blobel idea."

"The ironies of fate," Dr. Jones said. "Now, if you want to keep your husband, Vivian—"

"I'm determined to keep him, Doctor Jones. Frankly I've undergone therapy on Titan, the latest and most expensive . . . it's because I love George so much, even more than I love my own people or my planet."

"Eh?" Dr. Jones said.

"Through the most modern developments in medical science in the Sol System," Vivian said, "I've been stabilized, Doctor Jones. Now I am in human form twenty-four hours a day instead of eighteen. I've renounced my natural form in order to keep my marriage with George."

"The supreme sacrifice," Dr. Jones said, touched.

"Now, if I can only *find* him, Doctor—"

At the ground-breaking ceremonies on Io, George Munster flowed gradually to the shovel, extended a pseudopodium, seized the shovel, and with it managed to dig a symbolic amount of soil. "This is a great day," he boomed hollowly, by means of the semblance of a vocal apparatus into which he had fashioned the slimy, plastic substance which made up his unicellular body.

"Right, George," Hank Ramarau agreed, standing near-by with the legal documents.

The Ionan official, like George a great transparent blob, oozed across to Ramarau, took the documents and boomed, "These will be transmitted to my government. I'm sure they're in order, Mr. Ramarau."

"I guarantee you," Ramarau said to the official, "Mr. Munster does not revert to human form at any time; he's made use of some of the most advanced techniques in medical science to achieve this stability at the unicellular phase of his former rotation. Munster would never cheat."

"This historic moment," the great blob that was George Munster thought-radiated to the throng of local Blobels attending the ceremonies, "means a higher standard of living for Ionans who will be employed; it will bring prosperity to this area, plus a proud sense of national achievement in the manufacture of what we recognize to be a native invention, the Munster Magic Magnetic Belt."

The throng of Blobels thought-radiated cheers.

"This is a proud day in my life," George Munster informed them, and began to ooze by degrees back to his car, where his chauffeur waited to drive him to his permanent hotel room at Io City.

Someday he would own the hotel. He was putting the profits from his business in local real estate; it was the patriotic—and the profitable—thing to do, other Ionans, other Blobels, had told him.

"I'm finally a successful man," George Munster thought-radiated to all close enough to pick up his emanations.

Amid frenzied cheers he oozed up the ramp and into his Titan-made car.

Alfred Bester

•

Hobson's Choice

•

THIS IS A WARNING TO ACCOMPLICES LIKE YOU, ME, and Addyer.

Can you spare price of one cup coffee, honorable sir? I am indigent organism which are hungering.

By day, Addyer was a statistician. He concerned himself with such matters as Statistical Tables, Averages and Dispersions, Groups That Are Not Homogenous, and Random Sampling. At night, Addyer plunged into an elaborate escape fantasy divided into two parts. Either he imagined himself moved back in time a hundred years with a double armful of the *Encyclopaedia Britannica*, bestsellers, hit plays and gambling records; or else he imagined himself transported forward in time a thousand years to the Golden Age of perfection.

There were other fantasies which Addyer entertained on odd Thursdays, such as (by a fluke) becoming the only man left on earth with a world of passionate beauties to fecundate; such as acquiring the power of invisibility which would enable him to rob banks and right wrongs with impunity; such as possessing the mysterious power of working miracles.

Up to this point you and I and Addyer are identical.
Where we part company is in the fact that Addyer was a
statistician.

*Can you spare cost of one cup coffee, honorable
miss? For blessed charitability? I am beholden.*

On Monday, Addyer rushed into his chief's office, waving
a sheaf of papers. "Look here, Mr. Grande," Addyer sput-
tered. "I've found something fishy. Extremely fishy . . .
In the statistical sense, that is."

"Oh hell," Grande answered. "You're not supposed to
be finding anything. We're in between statistics until the
war's over."

"I was leafing through the Interior Department's reports. D'you know our population's up?"

"Not after the Atom Bomb it isn't," said Grande. "We've
lost double what our birth rate can replace." He pointed
out the window to the twenty-five foot stub of the Washington Monument. "There's your documentation."

"But our population's up 3.0915 percent." Addyer displayed his figures. "What about that, Mr. Grande?"

"Must be a mistake somewhere," Grande muttered after
a moment's inspection. "You'd better check."

"Yes, sir," said Addyer scurrying out of the office. "I
knew you'd be interested, sir. You're the ideal statistician,
sir." He was gone.

"Poop," said Grande and once again began computing
the quantity of bored respirations left to him. It was his
personalized anesthesia.

On Tuesday, Addyer discovered that there was no cor-
relation between the mortality-birth rate ratio and the
population increase. The war was multiplying mortality
and reducing births; yet the population was minutely increasing. Addyer displayed his discovery to Grande, received a pat on the back, and went home to a new fantasy

in which he woke up a million years in the future, learned the answer to the enigma, and decided to remain amidst snow-capped mountains and snow-capped bosoms, safe under the aegis of a culture saner that Aureomycin.

On Wednesday, Addyer requisitioned the comptometer and file and ran a test check on Washington, D.C. To his dismay he discovered that the population of the former capital was down 0.0029 percent. This was distressing, and Addyer went home to escape into a dream about Queen Victoria's Golden Age where he amazed and confounded the world with his brilliant output of novels, plays and poetry, all cribbed from Shaw, Galsworthy and Wilde.

Can you spare price of one coffee, honorable sir? I am distressed individual needful of chariting.

On Thursday, Addyer tried another check, this time on the city of Philadelphia. He discovered that Philadelphia's population was up 0.0959 percent. Very encouraging. He tried a rundown on Little Rock. Population up 1.1329 percent. He tested St. Louis. Population up 2.0924 percent . . . and this despite the complete extinction of Jefferson County owing to one of those military mistakes of an excessive nature.

"My God!" Addyer exclaimed, trembling with excitement. "The closer I get to the center of the country, the greater the increase. But it was the center of the country that took the heaviest punishment in the Buz-Raid. What's the answer?"

That night he shuttled back and forth between the future and the past in his ferment, and he was down at the shop by seven A.M. He put a twenty-four hour claim on the Compo and Files. He followed up his hunch and he came up with a fantastic discovery which he graphed in approved form. On the map of the remains of the United States he drew concentric circles in colors illustrating the areas of population increase. The red, orange, yellow, green and blue circles formed a perfect target around Finney County, Kansas.

"Mr. Grande," Addyer shouted in a high statistical passion, "Finney County has got to explain this."

"You go out there and get that explanation," Grande replied, and Addyer departed.

"Poop," muttered Grande and began integrating his pulse-rate with his eye-blink.

Can you spare price of one coffee, dearly madam? I am starveling organism requiring nutritiousment.

Now travel in those days was hazardous. Addyer took ship to Charleston (there were no rail connections remaining in the North Atlantic states) and was wrecked off Hatteras by a rogue mine. He drifted in the icy waters for seventeen hours, muttering through his teeth: "Oh Christ! If only I'd been born a hundred years ago."

Apparently this form of prayer was potent. He was picked up by a Navy Sweeper and shipped to Charleston where he arrived just in time to acquire a subcritical radiation burn from a raid which fortunately left the railroad unharmed. He was treated for the burn from Charleston to Macon (change) from Birmingham to Memphis (bubonic plague) to Little Rock (polluted water) to Tulsa (fall-out quarantine) to Kansas City (The O.K. Bus Co. Accepts No Liability for Lives Lost Through Acts of War) to Lyonesse, Finney County, Kansas.

And there he was in Finney County with its great magma pits and scars and radiation streaks; whole farms blackened and razed; whole highways so blasted they looked like dotted lines; whole population 4-F. Clouds of soot and fall-out neutralizers hung over Finney County by day, turning it into a Pittsburgh on a still afternoon. Auras of radiation glowed at night, high-lighted by the blinking red warning beacons, turning the county into one of those overexposed night photographs, all blurred and cross-hatched by deadly slashes of light.

After a restless night in Lyonesse Hotel, Addyer went over to the County Seat for a check on their birth records. He was armed with the proper credentials, but the County Seat was not armed with the statistics. That excessive military mistake again. It had extinguished the Seat.

A little annoyed, Addyer marched off to the County Medical Association office. His idea was to poll the local doctors on births. There was an office and one attendant who had been a practical nurse. He informed Addyer that Finney County had lost its last doctor to the army eight months previous. Midwives might be the answer to the birth enigma but there was no record of midwives. Addyer would simply have to canvass from door to door, asking if any lady within practiced that ancient profession.

Further piqued, Addyer returned to the Lyonesse Hotel and wrote on a slip of tissue paper: HAVING DATA DIFFICULTIES. WILL REPORT AS SOON AS INFORMATION AVAILABLE. He slipped the message into an aluminum capsule, attached it to his sole surviving carrier pigeon, and dispatched it to Washington with a prayer. Then he sat down at his window and brooded.

He was aroused by a curious sight. In the street below, the O.K. Bus Co. had just arrived from Kansas City. The old coach wheezed to a stop, opened its door with some difficulty and permitted a one-legged farmer to emerge. His burned face was freshly bandaged. Evidently this was a well-to-do burgess who could afford to travel for medical treatment. The bus backed up for the return trip to Kansas City and honked a warning horn. That was when the curious sight began.

From nowhere . . . absolutely nowhere . . . a horde of people appeared. They skipped from back alleys, from behind rubble piles; they popped out of stores, they filled the street. They were all jolly, healthy, brisk, happy. They laughed and chatted as they climbed into the bus. They looked like hikers and tourists, carrying knapsacks, carpet-bags, box lunches and even babies. In two minutes the bus was filled. It lurched off down the road, and as it disappeared Addyer heard happy singing break out and echo from the walls of rubble.

"I'll be damned," he said.

He hadn't heard spontaneous singing in over two years. He hadn't seen a carefree smile in over three years. He felt like a colorblind man who was seeing the full spectrum for the first time. It was uncanny. It was also a little blasphemous.

"Don't those people know there's a war on?" he asked himself.

And a little later: "They looked too healthy. Why aren't they in uniform?"

And last of all: "Who *were* they anyway?"

That night Addyer's fantasy was confused.

Can you spare price of one cup coffee, kindly sir? I am estrangered and faintly from hungering.

The next morning Addyer arose early, hired a car at an exorbitant fee, found he could not buy any fuel at any price, and ultimately settled for a lame horse. He was allergic to horse dander and suffered asthmatic tortures as he began his house-to-house canvass. He was discouraged when he returned to the Lyonesse Hotel that afternoon. He was just in time to witness the departure of the O.K. Bus Co.

Once again a horde of happy people appeared and boarded the bus. Once again the bus hirpled off down the broken road. Once again the joyous singing broke out.

"I *will* be damned," Addyer wheezed.

He dropped into the County Surveyor's Office for a large-scale map of Finney County. It was his intent to plot the midwife coverage in accepted statistical manner. There was a little difficulty with the Surveyor who was deaf, blind in one eye, and spectacleless in the other. He could not read Addyer's credentials with any faculty or facility. As Addyer finally departed with the map, he said to himself: "I think the old idiot thought I was a spy."

And later he muttered: "Spies?"

And just before bedtime: "Holy Moses! Maybe *that's* the answer to *them.*"

That night he was Lincoln's secret agent, anticipating Lee's every move, outwitting Jackson, Johnston and Beauregard, foiling John Wilkes Booth, and being elected President of the United States by 1968.

The next day the O.K. Bus Co. carried off yet another load of happy people.

And the next.

And the next.

"Four hundred tourists in five days," Addyer computed. "The country's filled with espionage."

He began loafing around the streets trying to investigate these joyous travelers. It was difficult. They were elusive before the bus arrived. They had a friendly way of refusing to pass the time. The locals of Lyonesse knew nothing about them and were not interested. Nobody was interested in much more than painful survival these days. That was what made the singing obscene.

After seven days of cloak-and-dagger and seven days of counting, Addyer suddenly did the big take. "It adds up," he said. "Eighty people a day leaving Lyonesse. Five hundred a week. Twenty-five thousand a year. Maybe that's the answer to the population increase." He spent fifty-five dollars on a telegram to Grande with no more than a hope of delivery. The Telegram read: "EUREKA. I HAVE FOUND (IT)."

Can you spare price of lone cup coffee, honorable madam? I am not tramp-handler but destitute life-form.

Addyer's opportunity came the next day. The O.K. Bus Co. pulled in as usual. Another crowd assembled to board the bus, but this time there were too many. Three people were refused passage. They weren't in the least annoyed. They stepped back, waved energetically as the bus started, shouted instructions for future reunions and then quietly turned and started off down the street.

Addyer was out of his hotel room like a shot. He followed the trio down the main street, turned left after them onto Fourth Avenue, passed the ruined schoolhouse, passed the demolished telephone building, passed the gutted library, railroad station, Protestant Church, Catholic Church . . . and finally reached the outskirts of Lyonesse and then open country.

Here he had to be more cautious. It was difficult stalking the spies with so much of the dusky road illuminated by warning lights. He wasn't suicidal enough to think of hiding in radiation pits. He hung back in an agony of indecision and was at last relieved to see them turn off the broken road and enter the old Baker farmhouse.

"Ah-ha!" said Addyer.

He sat down at the edge of the road on the remnants of a missile and asked himself: "Ah-ha what?" He could not answer, but he knew where to find the answer. He waited until dusk deepened to darkness and then slowly wormed his way forward toward the farmhouse.

It was while he was creeping between the deadly radiation glows and only occasionally butting his head against grave-markers that he first became aware of two figures in the night. They were in the barnyard of the Baker place and were performing most peculiarly. One was tall and thin. A man. He stood stockstill, like a lighthouse. Upon occasion he took a slow, stately step with infinite caution and waved an arm in slow motion to the other figure. The second was also a man. He was stocky, and trotted jerkily back and forth.

As Addyer approached, he heard the tall man say: "Rooo booo fooo mooo hwaaa looo fooo."

Whereupon the trotter chattered: "Wd-nk-kd-ik-md-pd-ld-nk."

Then they both laughed; the tall man like a locomotive, the trotter like a chipmunk. They turned. The trotter rocketed into the house. The tall man drifted in. And that was amazingly that.

"Oh-ho," said Addyer.

At that moment a pair of hands seized him and lifted him from the ground. Addyer's heart constricted. He had time for one convulsive spasm before something vague was pressed against his face. As he lost consciousness his last idiotic thought was of telescopes.

Can you spare price of solitary coffee for no-loafing unfortunate, honorable sir? Charity will blessings.

When Addyer awoke he was lying on a couch in a small whitewashed room. A gray-haired gentleman with heavy features was seated at a desk alongside the couch, busily ciphering on bits of paper. The desk was cluttered with what appeared to be intricate timetables. There was a small radio perched on one side.

"L-Listen . . ." Addyer began faintly.

"Just a minute, Mr. Addyer," the gentleman said pleasantly. He fiddled with the radio. A glow germinated in the middle of the room over a circular copper plate and coalesced into a girl. She was extremely nude and extremely attractive. She scurried to the desk, patted the gentleman's head with the speed of a pneumatic hammer. She laughed and chattered: "Wd-nk-tk-ik-lt-nk."

The gray-haired man smiled and pointed to the door. "Go outside and walk it off," he said. She turned and streaked through the door.

"It has something to do with temporal rates," the gentleman said to Addyer. "I don't understand it. When they come forward they've got accumulated momentum." He began ciphering again. "Why in the world did you have to come snooping, Mr. Addyer?"

"You're spies," Addyer said. "She was talking Chinese."

"Hardly. I'd say it was French. Early French. Middle fifteenth century."

"Middle fifteenth century!" Addyer exclaimed.

"That's what I'd say. You begin to acquire an ear for those stepped-up tempos. Just a minute, please."

He switched the radio on again. Another glow appeared and solidified into a nude man. He was stout, hairy and lugubrious. With exasperating slowness he said: "Mooo fooo blooo wawww hawww pooo."

The gray-haired man pointed to the door. The stout man departed in slow motion.

"The way I see it," the gray-haired man continued conversationally, "when they come back they're swimming against the time current. That slows 'em down. When they come forward, they're swimming with the current. That speeds 'em up. Of course, in any case it doesn't last longer than a few minutes. It wears off."

"What?" Addyer said. "Time travel?"

"Yes. Of course."

"That thing . . ." Addyer pointed to the radio. "A time machine?"

"That's the idea. Roughly."

"But it's too small."

The gray-haired man laughed.

"What is this place anyway? What are you up to?"

"It's a funny thing," the gray-haired man said. "Everybody used to speculate about time travel. How it would be used for exploration, archaeology, historical and social research and so on. Nobody ever guessed what the real use would be. . . . Therapy."

"Therapy? You mean medical therapy?"

"That's right. Psychological therapy for the misfits who won't respond to any other cure. We let them emigrate. Escape. We've set up stations every quarter century. Stations like this."

"I don't understand."

"This is an immigration office."

"Oh my God!" Addyer shot up from the couch. "Then you're the answer to the population increase. Yes? That's how I happened to notice it. Mortality's up so high and birth's down so low these days that your time-addition becomes significant. Yes?"

"Yes, Mr. Addyer."

"Thousands of you coming here. From where?"

"From the future, of course. Time travel wasn't developed until C/H 127. That's . . . oh say, 2505 A.D. your chronology. We didn't set up our chain of stations until C/H 189."

"But those fast-moving ones. You said they came forward from the past."

"Oh yes, but they're all from the future originally. They just decided they went too far back."

"Too far?"

The gray-haired man nodded and reflected. "It's amusing, the mistakes people will make. They become unrealistic when they read history. Lose contact with facts. Chap I knew . . . wouldn't be satisfied with anything less than Elizabethan times. 'Shakespeare,' he said. 'Good Queen Bess. Spanish Armada. Drake and Hawkins and Raleigh. Most virile period in history. The Golden Age. That's for me.' I couldn't talk sense into him, so we sent him back. Too bad."

"Well?" Addyer asked.

"Oh, he died in three weeks. Drank a glass of water. Typhoid."

"You didn't inoculate him? I mean, the army when it sends men overseas always—"

"Of course we did. Gave him all the immunization we could. But diseases evolve and change too. New strains develop. Old strains disappear. That's what causes pandemics. Evidently our shots wouldn't take against the Elizabethan typhoid. Excuse me . . ."

Again the glow appeared. Another nude man appeared, chattered briefly and then whipped through the door. He almost collided with the nude girl who poked her head in, smiled and called in a curious accent: "Ie vous prie de me pardonner. Quy estoit cette gentilhomme?"

"I was right," the gray-haired man said. "That's Medieval French. They haven't spoken like that since Rabelais." To the girl he said, "Middle English, please. The American dialect."

"Oh. I'm sorry, Mr. Jelling. I get so damned fouled up with my linguistics. Fouled? Is that right? Or do they say—"

"Hey!" Addyer cried in anguish.

"They say it, but only in private these years. Not before strangers."

"Oh yes. I remember. Who was that gentleman who just left?"

"Peters."

"From Athens?"

"That's right."

"Didn't like it, eh?"

"Not much. Seems the Peripatetics didn't have plumbing."

"Yes. You begin to hanker for a modern bathroom after a while. Where do I get some clothes . . . or don't they wear clothes this century?"

"No, that's a hundred years forward. Go see my wife. She's in the outfitting room in the barn. That's the big red building."

The tall lighthouse-man Addyer had first seen in the farmyard suddenly manifested himself behind the girl. He was now dressed and moving at normal speed. He stared at the girl; she stared at him. "Splem!" they both cried. They embraced and kissed shoulders.

"St'u my rock-ribbering rib-rockery to heart the hearts two," the man said.

"Heart's too, argal, too heart," the girl laughed.

"Eh? Then you st'u too."

They embraced again and left.

"What was that? Future talk?" Addyer asked. "Shorthand?"

"Shorthand?" Jelling exclaimed in a surprised tone. "Don't you know rhetoric when you hear it? That was thirtieth century rhetoric, man. We don't talk anything else up there. Prosthesis, Diastole, Epergesis, Metabasis, Hendiadys .. And we're all born scanning."

"You don't have to sound so stuck-up," Addyer muttered enviously. "I could scan too if I tried."

"You'd find it damned inconvenient trying at your time of life."

"What difference would that make?"

"It would make a big difference," Jelling said, "because you'd find that living is the sum of conveniences. You might think plumbing is pretty unimportant compared to ancient Greek philosophers. Lots of people do. But the fact is, we already know the philosophy. After a while you get tired of seeing the great men and listening to them expound the material you already know. You begin to miss the conveniences and familiar patterns you used to take for granted."

"That," said Addyer, "is a superficial attitude."

"You think so? Try living in the past by candlelight, without central heating, without refrigeration, canned foods, elementary drugs. . . . Or, future-wise, try living with Berganlicks, the Twenty-Two Commandments, duo-decimal calendars and currency, or try speaking in meter, planning and scanning each sentence before you talk . . . and damned for a contemptible illiterate if you forget yourself and speak spontaneously in your own tongue."

"Your're exaggerating," Addyer said. "I'll bet there are times where I could be very happy. I've thought about it for years, and I—"

"Tcha!" Jelling snorted. "The great illusion. Name one."

"The American Revolution."

"Pfui! No sanitation. No medicine. Cholera in Philadelphia. Malaria in New York. No anesthesia. The death penalty for hundreds of small crimes and petty infractions.

None of the books and music you like best. None of the jobs or professions for which you've been trained. Try again."

"The Victorian Age."

"How are your teeth and eyes? In good shape? They'd better be. We can't send your inlays and spectacles back with you. How are your ethics? In bad shape? They'd better be or you'd starve in that cutthroat era. How do you feel about class distinctions? They were pretty strong in those days. What's your religion? You'd better not be a Jew or Catholic or Quaker or Moravian or any minority. What's your politics? If you're a reactionary today the same opinions would make you a dangerous radical a hundred years ago. I don't think you'd be happy."

"I'd be safe."

"Not unless you were rich; and we can't send money back. Only the flesh. No, Addyer, the poor died at the average age of forty in those days . . . worked out, worn out. Only the privileged survived and you wouldn't be one of the privileged."

"Not with my superior knowledge?"

Jelling nodded wearily. "I knew *that* would come up sooner or later. What superior knowledge? Your hazy recollection of science and invention? Don't be a damned fool, Addyer. You enjoy your technology without the faintest idea of how it works."

"It wouldn't have to be hazy recollection. I could prepare."

"What, for instance?"

"Oh . . . say, the radio. I could make a fortune inventing the radio."

Jelling smiled. "You couldn't invent radio until you'd first invented the hundred allied technical discoveries that went into it. You'd have to create an entire new industrial world. You'd have to discover the vacuum rectifier and create an industry to manufacture it; the self-heterodyne circuit, the nonradiating neutrodyne receiver and so forth.

You'd have to develop electric power production and transmission and alternating current. You'd have to—but why belabor the obvious? Could you invent internal combustion before the development of fuel oils?"

"My God!" Addyer groaned.

"And another thing," Jelling went on grimly. "I've been talking about technological tools, but language is a tool too; the tool of communication. Did you ever realize that all the studying you might do could never teach you how a language was really used centuries ago? Do you know how the Romans pronounced Latin? Do you know the Greek dialects? Could you learn to speak and think in Gaelic, seventeenth-century Flemish, Old Low German? Never. You'd be a deaf-mute."

"I never thought about it that way," Addyer said slowly.

"Escapists never do. All they're looking for is a vague excuse to run away."

"What about books? I could memorize a great book and—"

"And what? Go back far enough into the past to anticipate the real author? You'd be anticipating the public too. A book doesn't become great until the public's ready to understand it. It doesn't become profitable until the public's ready to buy it."

"What about going forward into the future?" Addyer asked.

"I've already told you. It's the same problem only in reverse. Could a medieval man survive in the twentieth century? Could he stay alive in street traffic? Drive cars? Speak the language? Think in the language? Adapt to the tempo, ideas and coordinations you take for granted? Never. Could someone from the twenty-fifth century adapt to the thirtieth? Never."

"Well then," Addyer said angrily, "if the past and future are so uncomfortable, what are those people traveling around for?"

"They're not traveling," Jelling said. "They're running."
From what?"

"Their own time."

"Why?"

"They don't like it."

"Why not?"

"Do you like yours? Does any neurotic?"

"Where are they going?"

"Any place but where they belong. They keep looking for the Golden Age. Tramps! Time-stiffs! Never satisfied. Always searching, shifting . . . bumming through the centuries. Pfui! Half the panhandlers you meet are probably time-bums stuck in the wrong century."

"And those people coming here . . . they think *this* is a Golden Age?"

"They do."

"They're crazy," Addyer protested. "Have they seen the ruins? The radiation? The war? The anxiety? The hysteria?"

"Sure. That's what appeals to them. Don't ask me why. Think of it this way: You like the American Colonial period, yes?"

"Among others."

"Well, if you told Mr. George Washington the reasons why you liked his time, you'd probably be naming everything he hated about it."

"But that's not a fair comparison. This is the worst age in all history."

Jelling waved his hand. "That's how it looks to you. Everybody says that in every generation; but take my word for it, no matter when you live and how you live, there's always somebody else somewhere else who thinks you live in the Golden Age."

"Well I'll be damned," Addyer said.

Jelling looked at him steadily for a moment. "You will be," he said sorrowfully. "I've got bad news for you, Addyer. We can't let you remain. You'll talk and make trouble, and our secret's got to be kept. We'll have to send you out one-way."

"I can talk wherever I go."

"But nobody'll pay attention to you outside your own time. You won't make sense. You'll be an eccentric . . . a lunatic . . . a foreigner . . . safe."

"What if I come back?"

"You won't be able to get back without a visa, and I'm not tattooing any visa on you. You won't be the first we've had to transport, if that's any consolation to you. There was a Jap, I remember—"

"Then you're going to send me somewhere in time? Permanently?"

"That's right. I'm really very sorry."

"To the future or the past?"

"You can take your choice. Think it over while you're getting undressed."

"You don't have to act so mournful," Addyer said. "It's a great adventure. A high adventure. It's something I've always dreamed."

"That's right. It's going to be wonderful."

"I could refuse," Addyer said nervously.

Jelling shook his head. "We'd only drug you and send you anyway. It might as well be your choice."

"It's a choice I'm delighted to make."

"Sure. That't the spirit, Addyer."

"Everybody says I was born a hundred years too soon."

"Everybody generally says that . . . unless they say you were born a hundred years too late."

"Some people say that too."

"Well, think it over. It's a permanent move. Which would you prefer . . . the phonetic future or the poetic past?"

Very slowly Addyer began to undress, as he undressed each night when he began the prelude to his customary fantasy. But now his dreams were faced with fulfillment and the moment of decision terrified him. He was a little blue and rather unsteady on his legs when he stepped to the copper disc in the center of the floor. In answer to Jelling's inquiry he muttered his choice. Then he turned argent in the aura of an incandescent glow and disappeared from his time forever.

Where did he go? You know. I know. Addyer knows. Addyer traveled to the land of Our pet fantasy. He escaped into the refuge that is Our refuge, to the time of Our dreams; and in practically no time at all he realized that he had in truth departed from the only time for himself.

Through the vistas of the years every age but our own seems glamorous and golden. We yearn for the yesterdays and tomorrows, never realizing that we are faced with Hobson's Choice . . . that today, bitter or sweet, anxious or calm, is the only day for us. The dream of time is the traitor, and we are all accomplices to the betrayal of ourselves.

Can you spare price of one coffee, honorable sir? No, sir, I am not panhandling organism. I am starveling Japanese transient stranded in this somiserable year. Honorable sir! I beg in tears for holy charity. Will you donate to this destitute person one ticket to township of Lyonesse? I want to beg on knees for visa. I want to go back to year 1945 again. I want to be in Hiroshima again. I want to go home.

Frederik Pohl

•

I Plinglot, Who You?

•

"Let me see," I said, "this is a time for the urbane. Say little. Suggest much." So I smiled and nodded wisely, without words, to the fierce flash bulbs.

The committee room was not big enough, they had had to move the hearings. Oh, it was hot. Senator Schnell came leaping down the aisle, sweating, his forehead glistening, his gold tooth shining and took my arm like a trap. "Capital, Mr. Smith," he cried, nodding and grinning, "I am so glad you got here on time! One moment."

He planted his feet and stopped me, turned me about to face the photographers and threw an arm around my shoulder as they flashed many bulbs. "Capital," said the senator with a happy voice. "Thanks, fellows! Come along, Mr. Smith!"

They found me a first-class seat, near a window, where the air conditioning made such a clatter that I could scarcely hear, but what was there to hear before I myself spoke? Outside the Washington Monument cast aluminum rays from the sun.

"We'll get started in a minute," whispered Mr. Hagsworth in my ear—he was young and working for the committee— "as soon as the networks give us the go-ahead."

He patted my shoulder in a friendly way, with pride; they were always doing something with shoulders. He had brought me to the committee and thus I was, he thought, a sort of possession of his, a gift for Senator Schnell, though we know how wrong he was in that, of course. But he was proud. It was very hot and I had in me many headlines.

Q. (Mr. Hagsworth.) Will you state your name, sir?
A. Robert Smith.
Q. Is that your real name?
A. No.

Oh, that excited them all! They rustled and coughed and whispered, those in the many seats. Senator Schnell flashed his gold tooth. Senator Loveless, who as his enemy and his adjutant, as it were, a second commander of the committee but of opposite party, frowned under stiff silvery hair. But he knew I would say that, he had heard it all in executive session the night before.

Mr. Hagsworth did not waste the moment, he went right ahead over the coughs and the rustles.

Q. Sir, have you adopted the identity of "Robert P. Smith" in order to further your investigations on behalf of this committee.
A. I have.
Q. And you can—
Q. (Senator Loveless.) Excuse me.
Q. (Mr. Hagsworth.) Certainly, Senator.
Q. (Senator Loveless.) Thank you, Mr. Hagsworth. Sir—that is, Mr. Smith—do I understand that it would not be proper, or advisable, for you to reveal—that is, to make public—your true or correct identity at this time? Or in these circumstances?
A. Yes.
Q. (Senator Loveless.) Thank you very much, Mr. Smith. I just wanted to get that point cleared up.
Q. (Mr. Hagsworth.) Then tell us, Mr. Smith—

Q. (Senator Loveless.) It's clear now.

Q. (The Chairman.) Thank you for helping us clarify the matter, Senator. Mr. Hagsworth, you may proceed.

Q. (Mr. Hagsworth.) Thank you, Senator Schnell. Thank you, Senator Loveless. Then, Mr. Smith, will you tell us the nature of the investigations you have just concluded for this committee?

A. Certainly. I was investigating the question of interstellar space travel.

Q. That is, travel between the planets of different stars?

A. That's right.

Q. And have you reached any conclusions as to the possibility of such a thing?

A. Oh, yes. Not just conclusions. I have definite evidence that one foreign power is in direct contact with creatures living on the planet of another star, and expects to receive a visit from them shortly.

Q. Will you tell us the name of that foreign power?

A. Russia.

Oh, it went very well. Pandemonium became widespread: much noise, much hammering by Senator Schnell and at the recess all the networks said big Neilsen. And Mr. Hagsworth was so pleased that he hardly asked me about the file again, which I enjoyed as it was a hard answer to give. "Good theater, ah, Mr. Smith," he winked.

I only smiled.

The afternoon also was splendidly hot, especially as Senator Schnell kept coming beside me and the bulbs flashed. It was excellent, excellent.

Q. (Mr. Hagsworth.) Mr. Smith, this morning you told us that a foreign power was in contact with a race of beings living on a planet of the star Aldebaran, is that right?

A. Yes.

Q. Can you describe that race for us? I mean the ones you have referred to as "Alderbaranians?"

A. Certainly, although their own name for themselves is—is a word in their language which you might here render as "Triops." They average about eleven inches tall. They have two legs, like you. They have three eyes and they live in crystal cities under the water, although they are air-breathers.

Q. Why is that, Mr. Smith?

A. The surface of their planet is ravaged by enormous beasts against which they are defenseless.

Q. But they have powerful weapons?

A. Oh, very powerful, Mr. Hagsworth.

And then it was time for me to take it out and show it to them, the Aldebaranian hand weapon. It was small and soft and I must fire it with a bent pin, but it made a hole through three floors and the cement of the basement, and they were very interested. Oh, yes!

So I talked all that afternoon about the Aldebaranians, though what did they matter? Mr. Hagsworth did not ask me about other races, on which I could have said something of greater interest. Afterwords we went to my suite at the Mayflower Hotel and Mr. Hagsworth said with admiration: "You handled yourself beautifully, Mr. Smith. When this is over I wonder if you would consider some sort of post here in Washington."

"When this is over?"

"Oh," he said, "I've been around for some years, Mr. Smith. I've seen them come and I've seen them go. Every newspaper in the country is full of Aldebaranians tonight, but next year? They'll be shouting about something new."

"They will not," I said surely.

He shrugged. "As you say," he said agreeably, "at any rate it's a great sensation now. Senator Schnell is tasting the headlines. He's up for reelection next year you know and just between the two of us, he was afraid he might be defeated."

"Impossible, Mr. Hagsworth," I said out of certain knowledge, but could not convey this to him. He thought I was only being polite. It did not matter.

"He'll be gratified to hear that," said Mr. Hagsworth and he stood up and winked: he was a great human for winking. "But think about what I said about a job, Mr. Smith. . . . Or would you care to tell me your real name?"

Why not? Sporting! "Plinglot," I said.

He said with a puzzled face, "Plinglot? Plinglot? That's an odd name." I didn't say anything, why should I? "But you're an odd man," he sighed. "I don't mind telling you that there are a lot of questions I'd like to ask. For instance, the file folder of correspondence between you and Senator Heffernan. I don't suppose you'd care to tell me how come no employee of the committee remembers anything about it, although the folder turned up in our files just as you said?"

Senator Heffernan was dead, that was why the correspondence had been with him. But I know tricks for awkward questions, you give only another question instead of answer. "Don't you trust me, Mr. Hagsworth?"

He looked at me queerly and left without speaking. No matter. It was time, I had very much to do. "No calls," I told the switchboard person, "and no visitors, I must rest." Also there would be a guard Hagsworth had promised. I wondered if he would have made the same arrangement if I had not requested it, but that also did not matter.

I sat quickly in what looked, for usual purposes, like a large armchair, purple embroidery on the headrest. It was my spaceship, with cosmetic upholstery. *Zz-z-z-zit*, quick like that, that's all there was to it and I was there.

II

Old days I could not have timed it so well, for the old one slept all the day, and worked, drinking, all the night. But now they kept capitalist hours.

"Good morning, *gospodin*," cried the man in the black tunic, leaping up alertly as I opened the tall double doors. "I trust you slept well."

I had changed quickly into pajamas and a bathrobe. Stretching, yawning, I grumbled in flawless Russian in a sleepy way: "All right, all right. What time is it?"

"Eight in the morning, Gospodin Arakelian. I shall order your breakfast."

"Have we time?"

"There is time, *gospodin*, especially as you have already shaved."

I looked at him with more care, but he had a broad open Russian face, there was no trickery on it or suspicion. I drank some tea and changed into street clothing again, a smaller size as I was now smaller. The Hotel Metropole doorman was holding open the door of the black Zis, and we bumped over cobblestone to the white marble building with no name. Here in Moscow it was also hot, though only early morning.

This morning their expressions were all different in the dim, cool room. Worried. There were three of them:

Blue eyes; Kvetchnikov, the tall one, with eyes so very blue; he looked at the wall and the ceiling, but not at me and, though sometimes he smiled, there was nothing behind it.

Red beard—Muzhnets. He tapped with a pencil softly, on thin sheets of paper.

And the old one. He sat like a squat, fat Buddha. His name was Tadjensevitch.

Yesterday they were reserved and suspicious, but they could not help themselves, they would have to do whatever I asked. There was no choice for them; they reported to the chief himself and how could they let such a thing as I had told them go untaken? No. they must swallow bait. But today there was worry on their faces.

The worry was not about me; they knew me. Or so they thought. "Hello, hello, Arakelian," said Blue Eyes to me, though his gaze examined the rug in front of my chair.

"Have you more to tell us today?"

I asked without alarm: "What more could I have?"

"Oh," said Blue-Eyed Kvetchnikov, looking at the old man, "perhaps you can explain what happened in Washington last night."

"In Washington?"

"In Washington, yes. A man appeared before one of the committees of their Senate. He spoke of the *Alde-baratniki*, and he spoke also of the Soviet Union. Arakelian, then, tell us how this is possible."

The old man whispered softly: "Show him the dispatch."

Red Beard jumped. He stopped tapping on the thin paper and handed it to me. "Read!" he ordered in a voice of danger, though I was not afraid. I read. It was a diplomatic telegram, from their embassy in Washington, and what it said was what every newspaper said—it was no diplomatic secret, it was headlines. One Robert P. Smith, a fictitious name, real identity unknown, had appeared before the Schnell Committee. He had told them of Soviet penetration of the stars. Considering limitations, excellent, it was an admirably accurate account.

I creased the paper and handed back to Muzhnets. "I have read it."

Old One: "You have nothing to say?"

"Only this." I leaped up on two legs and pointed at him. "I did not think you would bungle this! How dared you allow this information to become public?"

"How—"

"How did that weapon get out of your country?"

"Weap—"

"Is this Soviet efficiency?" I cried loudly, "is it proletarian discipline?"

Red-Beard Muzhnets intervened. "Softly, comrade," he cried. "Please! We must not lose tempers!"

I made a sound of disgust. I did it very well. "I warned you," I said, low, and made my face sad and stern. "I told you that there was a danger that the bourgeois-capitalists would interfere. Why did you not listen? Why did you permit their spies to steal the weapon I gave you?"

Tadjensevitch whispered agedly: "That weapon is still here."

I cried: "But this report—"

"There must be another weapon, Arakelian. And do you see? That means the Americans are also in contact with the *Aldebaratniki*."

It was time for chagrin. I admitted: "You are right."

He sighed: "Comrades, the Marshal will be here in a moment. Let us settle this." I composed my face and looked at him. "Arakelian, answer this question straight out. Do you know how this American could have got in touch with the *Aldebaratniki* now?"

"How could I, *gospodin?*"

"That," he said thoughtfully, "is not a straight answer but it is answer enough. How could you? You have not left the Metropole. And in any case the Marshal is now coming, I hear his guard."

We all stood up, very formal, it was a question of socialist discipline.

In came this man, the Marshal, who ruled two hundred million humans, smoking a cigarette in a paper holder, his small pig's eyes looking here and there and at me. Five very large men were with him, but they never said anything at all. He sat down grunting; it was not necessary for him to speak loud or to speak clearly, but it was necessary that those around him should hear anyhow. It was not deafness that caused Tadjensevitch to wear a hearing aid.

The old man jumped up. "Comrade Party Secretary," he said, not now whispering, no, "this man is P.P. Arakelian."

Grunt from the Marshal.

"Yes, Comrade Party Secretary, he has come to us with the suggestion that we sign a treaty with a race of creatures inhabiting a planet of the star Aldebaran. Our astronomers say they cannot dispute any part of his story. And the M.V.D. has assuredly verified his reliability in certain documents signed by the late—(cough)—Comrade Beria." That too had not been easy and would have been less so if Beria had not been dead.

Grunt from the Marshal. Old Tadjensevitch looked expectantly at me.

"I beg your pardon?" I said.

Old Tadjensevitch said without patience: "The Marshal asked about terms."

"Oh," I bowed, "there are no terms. These are unworldy creatures, excellent comrade." I thought to mention it as a joke, but none laughed. "Unworldly, you see. They wish only to be friends—with you, with the Americans . . . they do not know the difference; it is all in whom they first see."

Grunt. "Will they sign a treaty?" Tadjensevitch translated.

"Of course."

Grunt. Translation. "Have they enemies? There is talk in the American document of creatures that destroy them. We must know what enemies our new friends may have."

"Only animals, excellent comrade. Like your wolves of Siberia, but huge, as the great blue whale."

Grunt. Tadjensevitch said: "The Marshal asks if you can guarantee that the creatures will come first to us."

"No. I can only suggest. I cannot guarantee there will be no error."

"But if—"

"If," I cried loudly, "if there is error, you have Red Army to correct it!"

They looked at me, strange. They did not expect that. But they did not understand.

I gave them no time. I said quickly: "Now, excellency, one thing more. I have a present for you."

Grunt. I hastily said: "I saved it, comrade. Excuse me. In my pocket." I reached, most gently, those five men all looked at me now with much care. For the first demonstration I had produced an Aldebaranian hand weapon, three inches long, capable of destroying a bull at five hundred yards, but now for this Russian I had more. "See," I said, and took it out to hand him, a small glittering thing, carved of a single solid diamond, an esthetic statue four inches long. Oh, I did not like to think of it wasted! But it was important that this man should be off guard, so I handed it to one of the tall silent men, who thumbed it over and then passed it on with a scowl to the Marshal. I was sorry, yes. It was a favorite thing, a clever carving that they had made in the water under Aldebaran's rays; it was almost greater than I could have made myself. No, I will not begrudge it them, it was greater; I could not have done so well!

Unfortunate that so great a race should have needed attention; unfortunate that I must now give this memento away; but I needed to make an effect and, yes, I did!

Oh, diamond is great to humans; the Marshal looked surprised, and grunted, and one of the silent, tall five reached in *his* pocket, and took out something that glittered on silken ribbon. He looped it around my neck. "Hero of Soviet Labor," he said, "First Class—With emeralds. For you."

"Thank you, Marshal," I said.

Grunt. "The Marshal," said Tadjensevitch in a thin, thin voice, "thanks you. Certain investigations must be made. He will see you again tomorrow morning."

This was wrong, but I did not wish to make him right. I said again: "Thank you."

A grunt from the Marshal; he stopped and looked at me, and then he spoke loud so that, though he grunted, I understood. "Tell," he said, "the *Aldebaratniki*, tell them they must come to us—if their ship should land in the wrong country . . ."

He stopped at the door and looked at me powerfully.

"I hope," he said, "that it will not," and he left, and they escorted me back in the Zis sedan to the room at the Hotel Metropole.

III

So that was that and z-z-z-z-*zit*, I was gone again, leaving an empty and heavily guarded room in the old hotel.

In Paris it was midday, I had spent a long time in Moscow. In Paris it was also hot and, as the gray-haired small man with the rosette of the Legion in his buttonhole escorted me along the Champs Élysées, slim-legged girls in bright short skirts smiled at us. No matter. I did not care one pin for all those bright slim girls.

But it was necessary to look, the man expected it of me, and he was the man I had chosen. In America I worked through a committee of their Senate, in Russia the Comrade Party Secretary; here my man was a M. Duplessin, a small straw but the one to wreck a dromedary. He was a member of the Chamber of Deputies, elected as a Christian Socialist Radical Democrat, a party which stood between the Non-Clerical Catholic Workers' Movement on one side and the F.C.M., or Movement for Christian Brotherhood, on the other. His party had three deputies in the Chamber, and the other two hated each other. Thus M. Duplessin held the balance of power in his party, which held the balance of power in the Right Centrist Coalition, which held the balance through the entire Anti-Communist Democratic Front, which supported the Premier. Yes. M. Duplessin was the man I needed.

I had slipped a folder into the locked files of a Senate committee and forged credentials into the records of Russian's M.V.D., but both together were easier than the finding of this right man. But I had him now, and he was taking me to see certain persons who also knew his importance, persons who would do as he told them. "Monsieur," he said gravely, "it lacks a small half-hour of the appointed time. Might one not enjoy an aperitif?"

"One might," I said fluently, and permitted him to find us a table under the trees, for I knew that he was unsure of me; it was necessary to cause him to become sure.

"Ah," said Duplessin, sighing and placed hat, cane and gloves on a filigree metal chair. He ordered drinks and when they came slipped slightly, looking away. "My friend," he said at last, "tell me of *les aldebaragnards*. We French have traditions—liberty, equality, fraternity—we made Arabs into citizens of the Republic—always has France been mankind's spiritual home. But, monsieur. Nevertheless. *Three eyes?*"

"They are really very nice," I told him with great sincerity, though it was probably no longer true.

"Hum."

"And," I said, "they know of love."

"Ah," he said mistily, sighing again. "Love. Tell me, monsieur. Tell me of love on Aldebaran."

"They live on a planet," I misstated somewhat. "Aldebaran is the star itself. But I will tell you what you ask, M. Duplessin. It is thus: When a young Triop, for so they call themselves, comes of age, he swims far out into the wide sea, far from his crystal city out into the pellucid water where giant fan-tailed fish of rainbow colors swim endlessly above, tinting the pale sunlight that filters through the water and their scales. Tiny bright fish give off starlike flashes from patterned luminescent spots on their scales."

"It sounds most beautiful, monsieur," Duplessin said with politeness.

"It is most beautiful. And the young Triop swims until he sees—*Her.*"

"Ah, monsieur." He was more than polite, I considered, he was interested.

"They speak not a word," I added, "for the water is all around and they wear masks, otherwise they could not breathe. They cannot speak, no, and one cannot see the other's eyes. They approach in silence and in mystery."

He sighed and sipped his cassis.

"They," I said, "they know, although there is no way that they can know. But they do. They swim about each other searchingly, tenderly, sadly. Yes. Sadly—is beauty not always in some way sad? A moment. And then they are one."

"They do not speak?"

I shook my head.

"Ever?"

"Never until all is over, and they meet elsewhere again."

"Ah, monsieur!" He stared into his small glass of tincture. "Monsieur," he said, "may one hope—that is, is it possible—oh, monsieur! Might one go there, soon?"

I said with all my cunning: "All the things are possible, M. Duplessin, if the Triops can be saved from destruction. Consider for yourself, if you please, that to turn such a people over to the brutes with the Red Star—or these with the fifty white stars—what difference?—is to destroy them."

"Never, my friend, never!" he cried strongly. "Let them come! Let them entrust themselves to France! France will protect them, my friend, or France will die!"

It was all very simple after that, I was free within an hour after lunch and, certainly, z-z-z-z-*zit*.

My spaceship deposited me in this desert, Mojave, I think. Or almost Mojave, in its essential Americanness. Yes. It was in America, for what other place would do? I had accomplished much, but there was yet a cosmetic touch or two before I could say I had accomplished all.

I scanned the scene, everything was well, there was no one. Distantly planes howled, but of no importance: stratosphere jets, what would they know of one man on the sand four miles below? I worked.

Five round trips, carrying what was needed between this desert place and my bigger ship. And where was that? Ah. Safe. It hurled swinging around Mars: yes, quite safe. Astronomers might one day map it, but on that day it would not matter, no. Oh, it would not matter at all.

Since there was time, on my first trip I reassumed my shape and ate, it was greatly restful. Seven useful arms and ample feet, it became easy; quickly I carried one ton of materials, two thousand pounds, from my armchair ferry to the small shelter in which I constructed my cosmetic appliance. Shelter? Why a shelter, you may ask? Oh, I say, for artistic reasons, and in the remote chance that some low-flying plane might blundersomely pass, 'though it would not. But it might. Let's see, I said, let me think, uranium and steel, strontium and cobalt, a touch of sodium for yellow, have I everything? Yes. I have everything, I said, everything, and I assembled the cosmetic bomb and set the fuse. Goodby, bomb, I said with affection and, z-z-z-z-zit, armchair and Plinglot were back aboard my ship circling Mars. Nearly done, nearly done!

There, quickly I assembled the necessary data for the Aldebaranian rocket, my penultimate—or Next to Closing —task.

Now. This penultimate task, it was not a difficult one, no, but it demanded some concentration. I had a ship. No fake, no crude imitation! It was an authentic rocket ship of the Aldebaranians, designed to travel to their six moons, with vent baffles for underwater takeoff due to certain exigencies (e.g., inimical animals ashore) of their culture. Yes. It was real. I had brought it on purpose all the way.

Now—I say once more—now, I did what I had necessarily to do, which was to make a course for this small ship. There was no crew. (Not anywhere.) The course was easy to compute, I did it rather well; but there was setting of instruments, automation of controls—oh, it took time, took time—but I did it. It was my way, I am workmanlike and reliable, ask Mother. The human race would not know an authentic Aldebaranian rocket from a lenticular Cetan shrimp, but they *might*, hey? The Aldebaranians had kindly developed rockets and it was no great trouble to bring, as well as more authentic. I brought. And having completed all this, and somewhat pleased, I stood to look around.

But I was not alone.

This was not a fortunate thing, it meant trouble.

I at once realized what my companion, however unseen, must be, since it could not be human, nor was it another child. Aldebaranian. It could be nothing else.

I stood absolutely motionless and looked, looked. As you have in almost certain probability never observed the interior of an Aldebaranian rocket, I shall describe: Green metal in cruciform shapes ("chairs"), sparkling mosaics of colored light ("maps"), ferrous alloys in tortured cuprous-glassy conjunction ("instruments"). All motionless. But something moved. I saw! An Aldebaranian! One of the Triops, a foothigh manikin, looking up at me out of three terrified blue eyes; yes, I had brought the ship but I had not brought it empty, one of the creatures had stowed away aboard. And there it was.

I lunged toward it savagely. It looked up at me and squeaked like a bell: "Why? Why, Plinglot, why did you kill my people?"

It is *so* annoying to be held to account for every little thing. But I dissembled.

I said in moderate cunning: "Stand quiet, small creature, and let me get hold of you. Why are you not dead?"

It squeaked pathetically—not in English, to be sure! but I make allowances—it squeaked: "Plinglot, you came to our planet as a friend from outer space, one who wished to help our people join forces to destroy the great killing land beasts."

"That seemed appropriate," I conceded.

"We believed you, Plinglot! All our nations believed you. But you caused dissension. You pitted us one against the other, so that one nation no longer trusted another. We had abandoned war, Plinglot, for more than a hundred years, for we dared not wage war."

"That is true," I agreed.

"But you tricked us! War came, Plinglot! And at your hands. As this ship was plucked from its berth with only myself aboard I received radio messages that a great war was breaking out and that the seas were to be boiled. It is the ultimate weapon, Plinglot! By now my planet is dry and dead. Why did you do it?"

"Small Triop," I lectured, "listen to this. You are male, one supposes, and you must know that no female Aldebaranian survives. Very well. You are the last of your race. There is no future. You might as well be dead."

"I know," he wept.

"And therefore you should kill yourself. Check," I invited, "my logic with the aid of your computing machine, if you wish. But please do not disturb the course computations I have set up on it."

"It is not necessary, Plinglot," he said with sadness. "You are right."

"So kill yourself!" I bellowed.

The small creature, how foolish, would not do this, no. He said: "I do not want to, Plinglot," apologetically. "But I will not disturb your course."

Well, it was damned decent of him, in a figure of speech, I believed, for that course was most important to me; on it depended the success of my present mission, which was to demolish Earth as I had his own planet. I attempted to explain, in way of thanks, but he would not understand, no.

"Earth?" he squeaked feebly and I attempted to make him see. Yes, Earth, that planet so far away, it too had a population which was growing large and fierce and smart; it too was hovering on the fringe of space travel. Oh, it was dangerous, but he would not see, though I explained and I am Plinglot. I can allow no rivals in space, it is my assigned task, given in hand by the Great Mother. Well. I terrified him, it was all I could do.

Having locked him, helpless, in a compartment of his own ship I consulted my time.

It was fleeing. I flopped onto my armchair; z-z-z-z-z*it;* once again in the room in the Hotel Mayflower, Washington, U.S.A.

Things progressed, all was ready. I opened the door, affecting having just awaked. A chambermaid turned from dusting pictures on the wall, said, "Good morning, sir," looked at me and—oh! screamed. Screamed in a terrible tone.

Careless Plinglot! I had forgot to return to human form.

Most fortunately, she fainted. I quickly turned human and found a rope. It took very much time, and time was passing, while the rocket hastened to cover forty million miles; it would arrive soon where I had sent it. I hurried. Hardly, hardly, I made myself do it, though as anyone on Tau Ceti knows it was difficult for me; I tied her; I forced a pillowcase, or one corner of it, into her mouth so that she might not cry out; and even I locked her in a closet. Oh, it was hard. Questions? Difficulty? Danger? Yes. They were all there to be considered, too, but I had no time to consider them. Time was passing, I have said, and time passed for me.

It was only a temporary expedient. In time she would be found. Of course. This did not matter. In time there would *be* no time, you see, for time would come to an end for chambermaid, Duplessin, senators and the M.V.D., and then what?

Then Plinglot would have completed this, his mission, and two-eyes would join three-eyes, goodbye.

IV

Senator Schnell this time was waiting for me at the curb in a hollow square of newsmen. "Mr. Smith," he cried, "how good to see you. Now, please, fellows! Mr. Smith is a busy man. Oh, all right, just one picture, or two." And he made to shoo the photographers off while wrapping himself securely to my side. "Terrible men," he whispered out of the golden corner of his mouth, smiling, smiling, "how they pester me!"

"I am sorry, Senator," I said politely and permitted him to lead me through the flash barrage to the large room for the hearings.

Q. (Mr. Hagsworth.) Mr. Smith, in yesterday's testimony you gave us to understand that Russia was making overtures to the alien creatures from Aldebaran. Now, I'd like to call your attention to something. Have you seen this morning's papers?

A. No.

Q. Then let me read you an extract from Pierce Truman's column which has just come to my attention. It starts, "After yesterday's sensational rev—"

Q. (Senator Loveless.) Excuse me, Mr. Hagsworth.

Q. (Mr. Hagsworth.) "—elations." Yes, Senator?

Q. (Senator Loveless.) I only want to know, or to ask, if that document—that is, the newspaper which you hold in your hand—is a matter of evidence. By this I mean an exhibit. If so, I raise the question, or rather suggestion, that it should be properly marked and entered.

Q. (Mr. Hagsworth.) Well, Senator, I—

Q. (Senator Loveless.) As an exhibit. I mean.

Q. (Mr. Hagsworth.) Yes, as an exhibit. I—

Q. (Senator Loveless.) Excuse me for interrupting. It seemed an important matter—important procedural matter, that is.

Q. (Mr. Hagsworth.) Certainly, Senator. Well, Senator, I intended to read it only in order to have Mr. Smith give us his views.

Q. (Senator Loveless.) Thank you for that explanation, Mr. Hagsworth. Still it seems to me, or at the moment it appears to me, that it ought to be marked and entered.

Q. (The Chairman.) Senator, in my view—

Q. (Senator Loveless.) As an exhibit, that is.

Q. (The Chairman.) Thank you for that clarification, Senator. In my view, however, since as Mr. Hagsworth has said it is only Mr. Smith's views that he is seeking to get out, then the article itself is not evidence but merely an adjunct to questioning. Anyway, frankly, Senator, that's the way I see it. But I don't want to impose my will on the Committee. I hope you understand that, all of you.

Q. (Mr. Hagsworth.) Certainly, sir.

Q. (Senator Loveless.) Oh, none of us has any idea, or suspicion, Senator Schnell, that you have any such design, or purpose.

Q. (Senator Duffy.) Of course not.

Q. (Senator Fly.) No, not here . . .

Oh, time, time! I looked at the clock on the wall and time was going, I did not wish to be here when it started. Of course. Ten o'clock. Ten-thirty. Five minutes approaching eleven. Then this Mr. Pierce Truman's column at last was marked and entered and recorded after civil objection and polite concession from Senator Schnell and in thus wise made an immutable, permanent, indestructible part of the files of this mutable, transient, soon to be destroyed committee. Oh, comedy! But it would not be for laughing if I dawdled here too late.

Somehow, somehow, Mr. Hagsworth was entitled at last to read this column and it said as follows. Viz.

After yesterday's sensational revelations before the Schnell Committee, backstage Washington was offering bets that nothing could top the mysterious Mr. Smith's weird story of creatures from outer space. But the toppers may already be on hand. Here are two questions for you,

Senator Schnell. What were three Soviet U.N. military attaches doing at a special showing at the Hayden Planetarium last night? And what's the truth beyond the reports that are filtering into C.I.A. from sources in Bulgaria, concerning a special parade scheduled for Moscow's Red Square tomorrow to welcome "unusual and very special" V.I.P.'s, names unknown?

Exhausted from this effort, the committee declared a twenty-minute recess. I glowered at the clock, time, time!

Mr. Hagsworth had plenty of time, he thought, he was not worried. He cornered me in the cloakroom. "Smoke?" he said graciously, offering a package of cigarettes.

I said thank you, I do not smoke.

"Care for a drink?"

I do not drink, I told him.

"Or—?" he nodded toward the tiled room with the chromium pipes; I do not do that either, but I could not tell him so, only, I shook my head.

"Well, Mr. Smith," he said again, "you make a good witness. I'm sorry," he added, "to spring that column on you like that. But I couldn't help it."

"No matter," I said.

"You're a good sport, Smith. You see, one of the reporters handed it to me as we walked into the hearing room."

"All right," I said, wishing to be thought generous.

"Well, I had to get it into the record. What's it about, eh?"

I said painfully (time, time!), "Mr. Hagsworth, I have testified the Russians also wish the ship from Aldebaran. And it is coming close. Soon it will land."

"Good," he said, smiling and rubbing his hands, "very good! And you will bring them to us?"

"I will do," I said, "the best I can," ambiguously, but that was enough to satisfy him, and recess was over.

Q. (Mr. Hagsworth.) Mr. Smith, do I understand that you have some knowledge of the proposed movements of the voyagers from Aldebaran?

A. Yes.

Q. Can you tell us what you know?

A. I can. Certainly. Even now an Aldebaranian rocket ship is approaching the Earth. Through certain media of communication which I cannot discuss in open hearing, as you understand, certain proposals have been made to them on behalf of this country.

Q. And their reaction to these proposals, Mr. Smith?

A. They have agreed to land in the United States for discussions.

Oh, happy commotion, the idiots. The flash bulbs went like mad. Only the clock was going, going, and I commenced to worry, where was the ship? Was forty lousy million miles so much? But no, it was not so much; and when the messenger came racing in the door I knew it was time. One messenger, first. He ran wildly down among the seats, searching, then stopping at the seat on the aisle where Pierce Truman sat regarding me with an ophidian eye, stopped and whispered. Then a couple more, strangers, hatless and hair flying, also messengers, came hurrying in — and more — to the committee, to the newsmen — the word had got out.

"Mr. Chairman! Mr. Chairman!" It was Senator Loveless, he was shouting; some one person had whispered in his ear and he could not wait to tell his news. But everyone had that news, you see, it was no news to the chairman, he already had a slip of paper in his hand.

He stood up and stared blindly into the television cameras, without smile now, the gold tooth not flashing. He said: "Gentlemen, I—" And stopped for a moment to catch his breath and to shake his head. "Gentlemen," he said, "Gentlemen, I have here a report," staring incredulously at the scrawled slip of paper. In the room was quickly silence; even Senator Loveless, and Pierce Truman stopped at the door on his way out to listen. "This report," he said, "comes from the Arlington Naval Observatory—in, gentlemen, my own home state, the Old Dominion, Virginia—" He paused and shook himself, yes, and made himself look again at the paper. "From the Arlington Naval Observatory, where the radio telescope experts inform us that an object of unidentified origin and remarkable speed has entered the atmosphere of the Earth from outer space!"

Cries. Sighs. Shouts. But he stopped them, yes, with a hand. "But gentlemen, that is not all! Arlington has tracked this object and it has landed. Not in our country, gentlemen! Not even in Russia! But—" he shook the paper before him— "in Africa, gentlemen! In the desert of Algeria!"

Oh, much commotion then, but not joyous. "Double cross!" shouted someone, and I made an expression of astonishment. Adjourned, banged the gavel of the chairman, and only just in time; the clock said nearly twelve and my cosmetic bomb was set for one-fifteen. Oh, I had timed it close. But now was danger and I had to leave, which I did hardly. But I could not evade Mr. Hagsworth, who rode with me in taxi to hotel, chattering, chattering. I did not listen.

V

Now, this is how it was, an allegory or parable. Make a chemical preparation, you see? Take hydrogen and take oxygen—very pure in both cases—blend them and strike a spark. Nothing happens. They do not burn! It is true, though you may not believe me.

But with something added, yes, they burn. For instance let the spark be a common match, with, so tiny you can hardly detect it, a quarter-droplet of water bonded into its substance—Yes, with the water they will burn—more than burn—*kerblam,* the hydrogen and oxygen fiercely unite. Water, it is the catalyst which makes it go.

Similarly, I reflected (unhearing the chatter of Mr. Hagsworth), it is a catalyst which is needed on Earth, and this catalyst I have made, my cosmetic appliance, my bomb. The chemicals were stewing together nicely. There was a ferment of suspicion in Russia, of fear in America, of jealousy in France where I had made the ship land. Oh, they were jumpy now! I could feel forces building around me; even the driver of the cab, half watching the crowded streets, half listening to the hysterical cries of the little radio. To the Mayflower, hurrying. All the while the city was getting excited around us. That was the ferment, and by my watch the catalyst was quite near.

"Wait," said Mr. Hagsworth pleading, in the lobby, "come have a drink, Smith."

"I don't drink."

"I forgot," he apologized. "Well, would you like to sit for a moment in the bar with me? I'd like to talk to you. This is all happening too fast."

"Come along to my room," I said, not wanting him, no, but what harm could he do? And I did not want to be away from my purple armchair, not at all.

So up we go and there is still time, I am glad. Enough time. The elevator could have stuck, my door could have somehow been locked against me, by error I could have gone to the wrong floor—no, everything was right. We were there and there was time.

I excused myself a moment (though it could have been forever) and walked into the inner room of this suite. Yes, it was there, ready. It squatted purple, and no human would think to look at it that it was anything but an armchair, but it was much more and if I wished I could go to it,— z-z-z-z-*zit,* I would be gone.

A man spoke.

I turned, looking. Out of the door to the tiled room spoke to me a man, smiling, red-faced, in blue coveralls. Well.

For a moment I felt alarm. (I remembered, e.g., what I had left bound in the closet.) But on this man's face was only smile and he said with apology: "Oh, hello, sir. Sorry. But we had a complaint from the floor below, plumbing leak. I've got it nearly fixed."

Oh, all right. I shrugged for him and went back to Mr. Hagsworth. In my mind had been—well, I do not know what had been in my mind. Maybe z-z-z-z-z*it* to the George V and telephone Duplessin to make sure they would not allow Russians or Americans near the ship, no, not if the ambassadors made of his life a living hell. Maybe to Metropole to phone Tadjensevitch (not the Marshal, he would not speak on telephone to me) to urge him also on. Maybe farther, yes.

But I went back to Mr. Hagsworth. It was not needed, really it was not. It was only insurance, in the event that somehow my careful plans went wrong, I wished to be there until the very end. Or nearly. But I need not have done it.

But I did. Z-z-z-z-z*it* and I could have been away, but I stayed, very foolish, but I did.

Mr. Hagsworth was on telephone, his eyes bright and angry, I thought I knew what he was hearing. I listened to hear if there were, perhaps, muffled kickings, maybe groans, from a closet, but there were none; hard as it was, I had tied well, surely. And then Mr. Hagsworth looked up.

He said, bleak: "I have news, Smith. It's started."

"Started?"

"Oh," he said without patience, "you know what I'm talking about, Smith. The trouble's started. These Aldebaranians of yours, they've stirred up a hornet's nest, and now the stinging has begun. I just talked to the White House. There's a definite report of a nuclear explosion in the Mojave desert."

"No!"

"Yes," he said, nodding, "there is no doubt. It can't be anything but a Russian missile, though their aim is amazingly bad. Can it?"

"What else possibly?" I asked with logic. "How terrible! And I suppose you have retaliated, hey? Sent a flight of missiles to Moscow?"

"Of course. What else could we do?"

He had put his finger on it, yes, he was right, I had computed it myself. "Nothing," I said and wrung his hand, "and may the best country win."

"Or planet," he said, nodding.

"Planet?" I let go his hand. I looked. I waited. It was a time for astonishment, I did not speak.

Mr. Hagsworth said, speaking very slow, "Smith, or maybe I ought to say 'Plinglot,' that's what I wanted to talk to you about."

"Talk," I invited.

Outside there was sudden shouting. "They've heard about the bomb," conjectured Mr. Hagsworth, but he paid no more attention. He said: "In school, Plinglot, I knew a Fat Boy." He said: "He always got his way. Everybody was afraid of him. But he never fought, he only divided others, do you see, and got them to fight each other."

I stood tall—yes, and brave! I dare use that word 'brave,' it applies. One would think that it would be like a human to say he is brave before a blinded fluttering moth, 'brave' where there is no danger to be brave against; but though this was a human only, in that room I felt danger. Incredible, but it was so and I did not wish it.

I said, "What are you talking about, Mr. Hagsworth?"

"An idea I had," he said softly with a face like death. "About a murderer. Maybe he comes from another planet and, for reasons of his own, wants to destroy our planet. Maybe this isn't the first one—he might have stopped, for example, at Aldebaran."

"I do not want to hear this," I said, with true.

But he did not stop, he said: "We human beings have faults, Plinglot, and an outsider with brains and a lot of special knowledge—say, the kind of knowledge that could get a file folder into our records, in spite of all our security precautions—such an outsider might use our faults to destroy us. Senate Committee hearings—why, some of them have been a joke for years, and not a very funny one. Characters have been destroyed, policies have been wrecked —why shouldn't a war be started? Because politicians can be relied on to act in a certain way. And maybe this outsider, having watched and studied us, knew something about Russian weaknesses too, and played on them in the same way. Do you see how easy it would be?"

"Easy?" I cried, offended.

"For someone with very special talents and ability," he assured me. "For a Fat Boy. Especially for a Fat Boy who can go faster than any human can follow from here to Moscow, Moscow to Paris, Paris to the Mojave, Mojave to— where? Somewhere near Mars, let's say at a guess. For such a person, wouldn't it, Plinglot, be easy?"

I reeled, I reeled; but these monkey tricks, they could not matter. I had planned too carefully for that, only how did they know?

"Excuse me," I said softly, "one moment," and turned again to the room with the armchair, I felt I had made a mistake. But what mistake could matter, I thought, when there was the armchair and, of course, z-z-z-z-z*it*.

But that was a mistake also.

The man in blue coveralls, he stood in the door but not smiling, he held in his hand what I knew instantly was a gun.

The armchair was there, yes, but in it was of all strange unaccountable people this chambermaid, who should have been bounded in closet, and she too had a gun.

"Miss Gonzalez," introduced Hagsworth politely, "and Mr. Hechtmeyer. They are—well, G-men, though, as you can see, Miss Gonzalez is not a man. But she had something remarkable to tell us about you, Plinglot, when Mr. Hechtmeyer released her. She said that you seemed to have another shape when she saw you last. The shape of a sort of green-skinned octopus with bright red eyes; ridiculous, isn't it? Or is it, Plinglot?"

Ruses were past, it was a time for candid. I said—I said, *"Like this?"* terribly, and I went to natural form.

Oh, what white faces! Oh, what horror! It was remarkable, really, that they did not turn and run. For that is Secret Weapon No. 1, for us of Tau Ceti on sanitation work; for our working clothes we assume the shape of those about us, certainly, but in case of danger we have merely to resume our own. In all Galaxy (I do not know about Andromeda) there is no shape so fierce. Nine terrible arms. Fourteen piercing scarlet eyes. Teeth like Hessian bayonets; I ask you, would *you* not run?

But they did not. Outside a siren began to scream.

VI

I cried: "Air attack!" It was fearful, the siren warned of atomic warheads on their way and this human woman, this Gonzalez, sat in my chair with pointing gun. "Go away," I cried, "get out," and rushed upon her, but she did not move. *"Please!"* I said thickly among my long teeth, but what was the use, she would not do it!

They paled, they trembled, but they stayed; well, I would have paled and trembled myself if it had been a Tau Cetan trait, instead I merely went limp. Terror was not only on one side in that room, I confess it. "Please," I begged, "I must go, it is the end of life on this planet and I do not wish to be here!"

"You don't have a choice," said Mr. Hagsworth, his face like steel. "Gentlemen!" he called, "come in!" And through the door came several persons, some soldiers and some who were not. I looked with all my eyes; I could not have been more astonished. For there was—yes, Senator Schnell, gold tooth covered, face without smile; Senator Loveless, white hair waving; and—oh, there was more.

I could scarcely believe.

Feeble, slow humans! They had mere atmosphere craft mostly but here, eight thousand miles from where he had been eighteen hours before, yes, Comrade Tadjensevitch, the old man; and M. Duplessin, sadly meeting my eyes. It could not be, almost I forgot the screaming siren and the fear.

"These gentlemen," said Hagsworth with polite, "also would like to talk to you, Mr. Smith."

"Arakelian," grunted the old man.

"Monsieur Laplant," corrected Duplessin.

"Or," said Hagsworth, "should we all call you by your right name, Plinglot?"

Outside the siren screamed, I could not move.

Senator Schnell came to speak: "Mr. Smith," he said, "or, I should say, Plinglot, we would like an explanation. Or account."

"Please let me go!" I cried.

"Where?" demanded old Tadjensevitch. "To Mars, Hero of Soviet Labor? Or farther this time?"

"The bombs," I cried. "Let me go! What about Hero of Soviet Labor?"

The old man sighed: "The decoration Comrade Party Secretary gave you, it contains a microwave transmitter, very good. One of our *sputniki* now needs new parts."

"You *suspected* me?" I cried out of fear and astonishment.

"Of course the Russians suspected you, Plinglot," Hagsworth scolded mildly. "We all did, even we Americans— and we are not, you know, a suspicious race. "No," he added thoughtfully, as though there were no bombs to fall, "our national characteristics are . . . what? The conventional caricatures—the publicity hound, the pork barrel senator, the cutthroat businessman? Would you say that was a fair picture, Mr. Smith?"

"*I Plinglot!*"

"Yes, of course. Sorry. But that must be what you thought, because those are the stereotypes you acted on, and maybe they're true enough—most of the time. Too much of the time. But not *all* the time, Plinglot!"

I fell to the floor, perspiring a terrible smell, it is how we faint, so to speak. It was death, it was the end, and this man was bullying me without fear.

"The Fat Boy," said Mr. Hagsworth softly, "was strong. He could have whipped most of us. But in my last term he got licked. Guile and bluff—when at last the bluff was called he gave up. He was a coward."

"I give up, Mr. Hagsworth," I wailed, "only let me go away from the bombs!"

"I know you do," he nodded, "what else? And—what, the bombs? There are no bombs. Look out the window."

In seconds I pulled myself together, no one spoke. I went to window. Cruising up and down outside a white truck, red cross, painted with word *Ambulance*, siren going. Only that. No air raid warning. Only ambulance.

"Did you think," scolded Hagsworth with voice angry now, "that we would let *you* bluff *us*? There's an old maxim —'Give him enough rope'—we gave it to you; and we added a little. You see, we didn't *know* you came from a race of cowards."

"I Plinglot!" I sobbed through all my teeth. "I am not a coward. I even tied this human woman here, ask her! It was brave, even Mother could not have done more! Why, I sector warden of this whole quadrant of the very Galaxy, indeed, to keep the peace!"

"That much we know—and we know why," nodded Mr. Hagsworth, "because you're afraid; but we needed to know more. Well, now we do; and once M. Duplessin's associates get a better means of communication with the little Aldebaranians, I expect we'll know still more. It will be very helpful knowledge," he added in thought.

It was all, it was the end. I said sadly: "If only Great Mother could know Plinglot did his best! If only she could learn what strange people live here, who, I cannot understand."

"Oh," said Mr. Hagsworth, gentle, "we'll tell her for you, Plinglot," he said, "very soon, I think."